I0780248

The Fall of 69

William Peak Gaupp

*Dedicated to my wife, Patricia Ann Gaupp,
with love and joy.*

*Net royalties from this book
to be given to programs dedicated
to the eradication of homelessness and poverty.*

Sunday, August 17, 1969

Davey Crockett once told the people of Tennessee "You all can go to hell; I'm going to Texas." Michael Thornhill, age 17, driving through west Texas on a hot August day in 1969 decided Crockett had it wrong. He couldn't see much difference between hell and the dusty plains sapping the spirit from his young body. The open windows of his blue VW Beetle blew the hair off of his shoulders, but did little to cool his frustration. To make matters worse, Michael watched his fuel gage flirt with the empty line. He hadn't seen a gas station for miles and wondered if he would die of thirst or boredom should the gas tank run dry.

He finally pulled into a Texaco station in a tumbleweed town in the middle of nowhere. Two older mem wearing blue jeans and t-shirts that may have been white at one time were looking under the hood of an old Chevy truck parked nearby. They slammed the hood down and leaned against the side of the truck, observing Michael pumping gas.

"Young man," one of the men said, "If you're plannin to use that there surf board on top of your car around these parts, you're lost." Both men laughed. "And if you're plannin to use them ice skates you got on top of them boxes in your back seat, you're goin the wrong way."

"On my way to Stephenville," Michael explained. "You know how far it is from here?"

"Well now, I reckon you can make it before sundown if ya don't stop much and don't miss the turnoff in Sweetwater. You'll have a good chance to see plenty of God's country tween here and there."

Michael finished pumping his gas, paid the clerk and bought a cold bottle of Coca Cola from a vending machine. Leaving the gas station, he pointed his car southeast down Highway 84. Stephenville, Texas, population 7,800, was somewhere up ahead. East of Lubbock, the car's AM radio stopped picking up rock and roll stations, leaving a dreary menu of country music options. Farther east, the radio faded to static. No music of any kind and nothing to see but some short trees and a few cattle foraging under a blistering sun. "Shit!" he yelled at nobody, his emotions as sharp as the thorns on the mesquite trees that occasionally dotted the landscape.

Hundreds of miles behind his car's rear bumper was the Oregon home he had left three days earlier. Growing up in Oregon, he was one year from high school graduation. Now he was forced to give up the hockey team, orchestra, occasional weekends surfing at the beach and, worst of all, his friends. But the thing that bothered him the most was missing what could have been with Diane Streeter. He had known Diane for years, admired her spunk, sweet smile, long dark hair and vivacious personality.   A cheerleader with many friends, Diane always seemed to know what to say or do. She was the kind of girl he could never have but always dreamed of. The day before he left for Texas, he ran into Diane at a minor league baseball game. She said they needed to talk and walked with him to a spot behind the bleachers where few people would notice. It was there she stopped, gazed up at him with teary eyes, put her slender arms around his neck and gave him a kiss with more passion than he had ever known. "I'm going to miss you, hockey boy."

He pulled her closer, intoxicated by the full embrace. "I always wanted us to be together," he somehow managed to sputter with a stunned mixture of adolescent excitement, fear and a vague sense of despair.

"Me, too. You're special. Don't let those Texas girls change you, hockey boy." And with that, she kissed him again and walked away.

Thinking of Diane as he drove through the empty Texas landscape was like driving through the gates of paradise, going the wrong way. He made a vow to himself to get out of this dusty hellhole as soon as he could graduate and hit the road. Perhaps Diane Streeter would still be there when he escaped Texas. And even though his parents had told him to sell the surf board and the hockey skates, he had refused. His life would not be changed. This was just a two-semester interruption.

Five miles from Stephenville, Michael's melancholy was jolted by a gunshot. The car began to fishtail. Michael gripped the steering wheel with both hands and stomped hard on the brakes, which made the fishtailing worse. Tires skated across angry gravel as he struggled for control. For a moment, he thought he would demolish a barbed wire fence. Letting off the brake, he regained control of the car and was able to bring it to a merciful stop in a shallow ditch between the road and the barbed wire fence. Climbing out of the car, he discovered that what he thought was a gunshot was a blown tire. The tire was as deflated as his spirits. Even the VW was in protest of the dismal surroundings.

Michael knew he'd be OK if he could get to the spare, which was stored in the front trunk nestled with a mass of clothes that were crammed into the tight space. His frustration grew as he recalled leaving the car jack in a friend's garage in Oregon. Welcome to the hellhole.

About 50 yards from the road was a rather small, freshly painted white farm house with a front porch. The home was surrounded by a pasture that extended to a rusted barbed wire fence tacked to wooden fence posts of various sizes. A dirty white Chevy pickup came from behind the house, headed for the road and stopped when it reached Michael. From the pickup emerged what to Michael looked like a cowboy with boots, dirty jeans, Massey Ferguson Tractor baseball cap, Elvis Pressley sideburns and a warm smile. The cowboy walked slowly over to Michael, taking in the site of the surf board, hockey skates and busted tire. "You're not from around here are ya?" the cowboy said.

"No sir, just trying to get to Stephenville."

"I reckon that ain't gonna happen on that there tire."

Michael turned to the cowboy. "I have a spare, but no jack."

The cowboy offered a handshake. "Name's Buddy, but most folks call me Bud. I've got a jack in my truck. I'm thinkin my jack's likely big enough to turn that little car of yours just near plum over. How about we give it a try son? What's your name?"

Michael started to protest that he damn sure wasn't his son but thought better of it. "Michael, from Oregon."

"What brung ya here, Michael?"

"My dad lost his job at a university in Oregon. His boss was a jerk. He just started a new job teaching economics at Tarleton State. Mom's going to teach 2nd grade at Central Elementary. I'm starting my senior year at the high school."

"We don't get many Michaels around here and I ain't never seen a plate from Oregon. You got a middle name?"

"James."

The cowboy thought a moment. Slapping Michael on the back like they were old friends, Bud offered "Michael James, I spect we ought to get that there tire changed so you can get goin." Bud went to his truck, got a jack that stood about five feet tall and proceeded to jack up the car. A lot.

"That's high enough! Can we stop now?" Michael pleaded.

Bud stopped and smiled. "Nobody gonna harm your car. Where's the spare in this little fella?"

Michael opened the front trunk and proceeded to move clothes, including several hockey jerseys, to the front seat. He sorely regretted not putting his whitie tighties in a bag. In no time they had the tire changed and the car back on four wheels. Bud hadn't rolled the car with his monster car jack. Michael shook his hand, thanked Bud for his help and asked if there was something that he could do to return the favor. Bud looked at the boy and said "That's right nice of ya, but I figure you best get on to your parents' place. I spect they may be a bit worried havin a young'un like you drivin across the country. You be careful, Michael James, and get yourself a new spare, ya hear?"

"Yes sir. Thanks." Bud had gotten him out of a jam. The hellhole had at least one friendly cowboy.

As Michael was repacking his trunk with the whitey tighties and other clothes that were no longer folded, Bud drove his truck back towards the farmhouse, stopping briefly to speak with a girl about Michael's age who had emerged from the house. The girl continued on her way towards Michael. She carried herself with an air of confidence, her auburn hair shining as if the sun were in position just for her. Michael never imagined a girl dressed in bib overalls as if she had been working on a farm could look so desirable. She approached Michael, carrying a cold bottled soda.

"I told Daddy I was bringing you an RC, if you want it. I think you better take it. You look hotter than a dead armadillo on August blacktop."

Michael took the opened bottle. "Thanks. Umm, what's an RC?"

She laughed. "It's a cold drink. Here's the peanuts. Where are you from anyway?"

Michael took a drink of RC, which tasted a lot like Coca-Cola. With the refreshing drink in one hand and a small bag of salted peanuts in the other, he replied, "Oregon."

She got the giggles, which made Michael uncomfortable. He enjoyed making people laugh, but in this case, he was confused because nothing was the least bit funny. "What's so funny about Oregon?" he asked defensively as he opened the small bag of peanuts and ate a few.

She started laughing harder. "It's just what you did with the peanuts."

Michael shrugged. "I don't get it."

"You're supposed to put the peanuts in the RC."

"Why?"

"Because that's the way it's done. I don't know. You don't have peanuts in Oregon?"

"My first RC," Michael said as he dutifully poured peanuts into his drink without knowing why.   With peanuts treading water within the cold bottle as if they belonged there, Michael took another drink of liquid and peanuts. It tasted strange, but not bad. "Thanks for the drink. And the peanuts."

"I bet you're down here to start college. Got a name, college boy?" she inquired.

"Name's Michael. And no, I'm here for senior year of high school."

"I'm Kathleen, and you're definitely not going to my high school in Stephenville."

"My family just moved to town and I'm already enrolled."

"This will be fun. How long you think you'll last with that long hair of yours? First principal or coach to see you will show you the door until you get it cut. Hair past the collar isn't allowed."

"Why?"

"Because that's the rule."

Michael was incredulous. "It's a dumb ass rule! There're millions of people with hair like mine. In fact, your hair is even longer."

"It's different with girls."

"Why?"

Kathleen stared at him as if he were from another planet. "This will be interesting. See you in school."

As Kathleen turned to walk back towards the farmhouse, Michael finished repacking the car and pointed it towards Stephenville, past the cattle farms, pickup trucks, and vast fields sucking the spirit from his young body. Hellhole. Home. At least for a while.

§§§

Kathleen Wilcox sat on her front porch swing mildly amused as she watched her daddy lift up a VW Bug with his five-foot jack. Her daddy's hands were rough as the prairie, with a manner tough and stubborn at times but always there for Kathleen or a stranger in trouble. He had grown up in Stephenville, dropped out of high school to fight in Europe during World War II, returning home to work the farm and marry his high school sweetheart. He embodied the secure predictability that permeated the community. There was a cycle to life in Stephenville, as predictable as the autumn harvest and Friday night football. It grounded the community as if each person were the sequel to a novel and each novel had the same beginning and ending. It felt to Kathleen as if everyone in Stephenville wouldn't have it any other way. That is, everyone except her.

Kathleen was sure that the girl with shoulder length hair in the blue VW must be feeling the August heat. The Texas sun showed no mercy to anyone in late summer, as if the devil himself were trying to make Stephenville into hell's back yard. It was amusing to find that what looked to be a girl was a boy from out of state. It had been hard not to laugh too much when he didn't know about RC, much less what to do with peanuts. She pondered how it could be that in her almost 18 years of life, she had never spoken to anyone from Oregon and rarely met anyone from outside of the county. There had to be a world beyond Stephenville. But she had never crossed the state line and, with the exception of one trip to Abilene to help her daddy pick up some Hereford cattle, had never ventured more than 50 miles from home.

From all outward appearances, Kathleen knew that she was living the dream for any girl in Stephenville. Going into her senior year of high school, she starred on the Stingerettes high school dance team that was featured with the band at halftime shows during football and basketball seasons. She was crowned Rodeo Queen in her junior year and soon after began dating a popular and handsome football player. Making friends was as easy for her as helping her daddy deliver a calf or harvesting green beans from the garden. Everyone knew she was happy with her life. And everyone was wrong.

Kathleen's boyfriend for the past eight months was Rusty Dalton. Rusty stood 6 foot 3 with broad shoulders. His ability to outrun most of his peers was fact, shown by numerous track and field ribbons and medals that his mother insisted on displaying within a frame in her living room. With a muscular body honed by years of weight lifting, Rusty was a captain on the football team and a terror to opposing teams. He played defensive linebacker with grace and power. Nobody challenged Rusty, the hometown football hero, in any way. Add youthful good looks, and Rusty was the boy who could have most any girl he wanted.

Kathleen's mother came onto the porch to water the ivy growing from pots hung with perfect spacing between the white porch columns. Kathleen often wondered if she were seeing her future when she looked at her mother. Once a high school cheerleader and well-liked by her numerous friends, her mother had dreamed of becoming a nurse. But there was no money in her family for nursing school, so she married and settled into the life of a farmer's wife.

"Are we going to see Rusty today?" Mrs. Wilcox asked, clearly hoping he would visit. Everyone, including her mother, enjoyed seeing Rusty.

As if on que, Kathleen saw Rusty unlatching the barbed wire pasture gate blocking the packed dirt drive to the house. He drove a 1959 Ford truck that had been red at one time. Now it was hard to determine where the red paint stopped and the rust began. It was transportation and met his needs, even if cooling the cab only happened if the windows were rolled down. It had been his dad's truck at one time and Kathleen knew that Rusty was proud to have it.

Kathleen jumped off the porch to meet him as he turned off the engine in front of the house and opened the driver's side door. As he stepped out, she put her arms around his neck and tenderly kissed his lips. When he gazed down at her, now in his arms, they both smiled. "How about you and I go to the drive-in tonight? There's a movie that I'd like for us to see."

Kathleen pushed Rusty towards his truck and in her flirtatious way chided, "Well sir, you just want to get me alone in a dark truck. What kind of girl do you think I am? I bet it's one of those romantic movies, you trying to set the mood and all."

"Um, it's *Planet of the Apes*."

Kathleen rolled her eyes, laughed and said with sarcasm, "So that's the best you can do? You sure know how to sweep a girl off her feet." Rusty had a subtle concerned look on his face, so she gave him a wink. "OK, maybe we'll see what those apes do for fun."

"I'll pick you up at 7:30. Should give us plenty of time to get there before sundown." He leaned over, kissed her briefly, eased back into the truck and drove towards the road.

Kathleen felt safe with Rusty, safe enough to flirt and be suggestive without anything coming of it. There were times, actually frequent times, when she wished Rusty wasn't so safe. Some of her girlfriends in private moments would give hints that they were doing a lot more with their boyfriends than holding hands and kissing. Kathleen wasn't sure if she wanted to join the party, but she damn sure wanted the invitation.

§§§

Rusty Dalton examined the image in his bathroom mirror. Staring back at him was a pretender, an actor. He felt himself a fraud. His eyes searched the mirror image as his mind asked the one question haunting him, *Who are you, really?* Actors on a stage work their craft for a couple of hours, then return to being themselves. Rusty was on stage always, without intermission. He was a prisoner in his own mind, imprisoned by other people's expectations. He played the part well; fearful his act would be discovered and terrified that it never would.

Adults in general and his mother in particular viewed Rusty with admiration. Unlike the radical hippies in the news, he was respectful, hardworking and morally upstanding. He was by all appearances a hometown hero. Making friends came easy for him. Peers and adults enjoyed being in his company, as if the aura of admiration would somehow glow on them as well.

Rusty's father had grown up in Stephenville, married his high school sweetheart and soon after had their first and only child. They purchased a newly built white frame house with a well-manicured lawn in a friendly, quiet neighborhood. Kids of all ages played in the streets. There were bicycles in many front yards and basketball hoops attached above garage doors. Pickup trucks and station wagons occupied the driveways. If Norman Rockwell were to paint a picture of an American small-town neighborhood, this might be the place. Both of Rusty's parents worked for Farmers First National Bank; she as a teller, he as a loan officer. They were well known for their honesty in business dealings and community leadership.

Rusty's father had served in the Texas Army Reserve National Guard, determined to do his part to support his country's efforts to stop the spread of communism. Returning to his barracks following an all-night training exercise at Fort Hood, Texas in the winter of 1967, he smelled gas seeping from the building. Twenty soldiers were sleeping in the barracks. Running into the building, he yelled for everyone to get out. Some moved quickly, some not at all. He desperately tried to open windows, but most were painted shut in the old building. They didn't dare turn on the lights for fear of causing a spark from the building's antiquated wiring. Four soldiers were unresponsive. Rusty's father and three of his brothers in arms carried them through the darkness towards fresh air. Reaching the door, a quick head count revealed that one was missing. Without hesitation, Rusty's father ran back into the barracks and located the last soldier, unconscious in a dark far corner of the room. He grabbed the unconscious soldier and carried him towards the door, becoming dizzy from the fumes. They would have made it out safely if not for the engine misfire of an arriving ambulance, which set off a massive inferno. There were five soldiers with burns and two fatalities, Rusty's father being one of them. Nineteen men would live to serve another day, thanks to the quick thinking and bravery of Rusty's father, a modern-day hero much admired by all who had known him.

As the wife of the hero of Fort Hood, Rusty's mom accepted posthumously her husband's Commendation Medal. Rusty received a letter from the fort's Garrison Commander exuding admiration and appreciation for Rusty's father and the sacrifice that he had made for others. The commander ended the letter by telling Rusty how he could be proud of his father, as he knew that his father was proud of him. It was a wonderful letter, well written and heartfelt. But if the choice were Rusty's, he would rather have had his dad back. At the age of 15 years with a grieving mother and a deceased father, Rusty carried the burden of overwhelming responsibility. It felt as if everyone wanted him to be a junior version of his father. Over time, he found his father's voice, his persona. The better he became at playing the role, the more lost he felt. He carried the burden of other people's expectations with finesse and a deeply hidden fear of failure.

Most assumed Rusty's feelings were expressed on the football field, where he was a beast of a linebacker. But his real outlet was his drum set and his friends in his band Baked Cotton. His buddy Jake was a smooth guitarist. Jake and Rusty would get together Saturday mornings in Rusty's garage, where Rusty dripping in sweat would beat the drums while Jake played one riff after another. Eventually, they were joined by Tommy Wilson on bass and Tommy's sister Judy on keyboard. Though they focused on popular country music, they learned to mix in some songs by The Beatles and Bob Dylan to freshen the variety. When the band was playing well, Rusty was transformed into another world with no responsibility and no worries. He loved it. As Baked Cotton became better, they would land occasional gigs at birthday parties and anniversaries. Jake was the band's manager, though there wasn't much to manage as all of the musicians were in high school and had other activities. But Saturday morning practice was their time, never to be interrupted.

Rusty showered and got himself ready to pick up Kathleen to see *Planet of the Apes* at the drive-in. He enjoyed being seen with the well-liked, attractive Kathleen. Her laughter could melt Rusty's troubles down a river of forgotten tragedy, only to end like the crush of a waterfall when reality reemerged. Lately when they were alone his feelings had become more tense, or was it intense? For reasons he could not understand, Kathleen's subtle and sometimes not so subtle hints for more intimacy left him feeling uncomfortable. But no worries tonight. Several of the guys from the football team would be at the drive-in and he looked forward to the last night before the start of school.

As he headed out of the house, his mother stopped him to provide an inspection. Shorts, sleeveless t shirt and tennis shoes looked OK for the occasion. "I want you home by 11:00 tonight."

"Mom, it's the last day of summer!"

She smiled up at her almost grown son. "Yes, and you have school, football practice and your chores to get done tomorrow. Then it's homework and---"

"OK, OK," he interrupted, not wanting to start an argument that would make him late to pick up Kathleen.

"Have fun," she said as he made a hasty exit towards his truck.

§§§

Kathleen sat on the front porch swing watching the traffic pass, waiting for Rusty to arrive for their date. She had curled her hair and wore tight-fitting knee length blue denim shorts and sneakers. Her sleeveless cotton blouse with the top two buttons open accented her necklace of African multicolored trading beads. An evening with Rusty in his truck at the drive-in movie, his arms around her and the smell of popcorn would be the perfect end to the summer.

As the sun kissed the horizon, she saw Rusty open the barbed wire gate to the Wilcox family farm. His truck bounced along the short dirt road from the gate to the farm house. He killed the engine in front of Kathleen's front porch. Rusty opened the driver's side door and stood with his hand on top of the cab of the truck looking at Kathleen. "You ready?"

Kathleen didn't move from the porch swing. "Well, aren't you the romantic one, the way you drive up here to take a girl out."

She was amused at the bewildered look that he gave her. After a moment of indecision, he bowed low and said "Your chariot awaits my lady."

Kathleen laughed. "Damn chariot looks a lot like a truck to me." Walking across the porch, she called over her shoulder through the screen door "Bye y'all."

A parental voice from the house responded "You two be careful."

Kathleen walked up to Rusty, gave him a quick kiss and slid onto the truck's bench seat as he held the driver's side door for her. He joined her in the cab and turned the ignition. Using the lever on the steering wheel column, he eased the truck into first gear, let out the clutch and pointed the front bumper towards the drive-in movie theater.

The drive was short, just long enough for some small talk about the teachers that they would have for their senior year and prospects for the football team. When Jeannie C. Riley's song *Harper Valley PTA* came on the radio they sang with loud gusto. Kathleen laughed as Rusty tried, and failed, to sing in key. She was grateful that Baked Cotton never asked Rusty to do vocals.

As they reached the theater Kathleen put her head on Rusty's shoulder and her hand on his leg. Sometimes, she thought, a girl just needs to be held. She wasn't sure why, but tonight was one of those nights. Though there were numerous cars at the drive-in, the intimacy of the truck with the sun in decline made it feel as if they were alone. Rusty paid the $1.20 entrance fee and they drove slowly through the entrance. Before they found their parking spot for the movie, they heard shouts from the right side of the lot where the less desirable parking spaces were located. On this evening, those empty spaces hosted a pickup game of touch football.

Rusty parked the truck and jumped out, holding the driver's side door for Kathleen. "Come on, let's get in the game before it's too dark."

Kathleen rolled her eyes. It would be dark soon. There were eight friends playing, three of which were girls from the dance squad. If Rusty wanted to play, they would need another player to even the teams. May as well be her. She and Rusty soon found themselves welcomed with enthusiasm into the game.

The game went on for another 20 minutes, with each side taunting the other in a good-natured way. The boys were trying to impress the girls with their athleticism. Unfortunately for them, the girls found the effort more amusing than impressive.

Kathleen thought that everyone was having a good time. Everyone except Jake, who was the quarterback for his side. He was unusually quiet and appeared to throw each pass with anger. When one of his teammates dropped a pass, Jake yelled "What the hell's the matter with you! Catch the damn ball!"

Kathleen was taken aback by the angry affect in the middle of a friendly co-ed pickup game. She guessed that her friends thought the same, as the revelry of a moment earlier melted to silence. Rusty announced "Hey guys, it's getting too dark to see the ball. Let's knock off and get ready for the movie. Should be starting soon."

Jake's girlfriend Janice was hot and sweaty. Kathleen was also red faced and perspiring from the effort, her curled hair now mostly straight. As the group disbursed to their cars, Rusty turned to Jake and in a quiet voice said "Let's get the girls snow cones. They look like they could use it."

"Good idea."

Jake turned towards Kathleen and Janice as they started walking towards the concession stand. "Hey y'all, we'll be right back."

"It better be cold. I'm hotter than the hinges of hell out here," Janice replied.

"Two snow cones coming up," Jake said as the boys walked away from them.

Kathleen gave Janice a concerned look. "You and Jake have a fight?"

"No."

"So what's with the chip on his shoulder?"

"Don't tell him I told you, but I think he's really scared. His brother Clay dropped out of college. Gave up a music scholarship to North Texas State. Says he wants to play in his band."

"Maybe Clay will make it big. Happens sometimes. What's the problem?"

"Clay didn't tell his parents he dropped out. So, guess who got drafted? It's goodbye band, hello Vietnam. I don't think that was Clay's plan, but you remember how he is. Happy go lucky all the time. Says everything will be fine and maybe it will. They're not sure yet when he has to report. Jake and his parents are worried sick."

§§§

Jake and Rusty appeared disproportionate as they walked towards the concession stand. Though they were both seniors on the football team, Rusty was the larger of the two. Jake, of average size and ability, mostly watched games from the sidelines. Rusty turned to Jake. "You OK man?"

"Fine."

"What's bugging you?"

"Didn't I just say I was fine?"

They walked in silence, reached the concession stand and purchased snow cones for the girls. Strolling back to where their dates continued to stand talking, Jake suddenly stopped, looked directly at Rusty and said "Clay's going into the military."

"Why?"

"Don't you want to serve the country? Your dad's the military hero. Maybe now it's Clay's turn."

Rusty couldn't discern Jake's attitude. "Dad's dead, Jake. I wish he were here."

"Clay may end up just like your dad."

Rusty was unsure of how or why they were discussing his dad. "So, Clay signed up for the military. Which part?"

"Didn't sign up. He was drafted. Army infantry. Son of a bitch didn't have to do it. I mean, it's a good thing to serve, right? I should be proud of him. At least, I think I am. You know what chaps my ass? You see guys wearing dumb ass peace sign t-shirts while my brother's getting ready to go over to Vietnam to get shot at. People like that should get the hell out of our country."

16

Rusty searched for the right words to say, but nothing came to him. Janice and Kathleen walked up to them. Janice smiled. "Y'all trying to draw ants?"

The snow cones were quickly melting in the late summer heat. Melting ice and syrup covered the boy's hands and left two sugary puddles on the ground. Kathleen and Janice started to laugh. Rusty looked at them and said "We figured we'd let this age to perfection."

That brought more laughter from the girls. Kathleen said "Y'all better get rid of those and go wash your hands. Maybe get some drinks and popcorn. They won't melt on you."

§§§

Kathleen watched Rusty as he hurried into the restroom with Jake to clean up. The boys then parted, each with a tub of popcorn in one hand and a cold fountain drink in the other. Kathleen waited in the truck, leaving just enough space on the bench seat for Rusty to get in. He soon arrived and slid onto the seat next to Kathleen. Rusty closed the door, grabbed a silver speaker from a pole next to the truck and positioned it on the truck's door. He put his arm lightly around Kathleen and she leaned in closer, one hand on his leg. Most guys, Kathleen knew, would be pulling her close. But this wasn't most any guy. This was Rusty. He put the tub of popcorn on his lap and said something about the movie. She didn't respond, or care to. And there they sat in the dark watching a movie about apes that Kathleen cared nothing about.

Kathleen found it both amusing and frustrating that they were at the drive-in, watching all of the other couples make out. It was apparent to Kathleen that this was not going to be the romantic night she envisioned. It was as if she and Rusty were good friends, but pretending to be something more. They sat close, with his arm now over the seat of the truck. The arm that should have been around her shoulders.

17

The movie over, popcorn and cold drinks finished, Rusty started the truck and headed towards Kathleen's house. With headlights on the blacktop road, he rambled on about the songs that his band was practicing. She tried to seem interested, but found herself mildly troubled. When Rusty turned the truck off in front of her house, she turned to him. "Sometimes I don't know what you want. I don't know what you want us to be."

"Nothing's wrong with us." He put his arm lightly around her and kissed her.

"You never want to make out with me. What's wrong?"

"Nothing's wrong. You're great. We're great."

She didn't say anything, but searched his eyes for answers.

Rusty tried to explain. "I don't think we should go too far, not yet. Don't you listen in church? You need to be careful with what you do with guys."

She responded tenderly. "I'm not interested in guys. I'm interested in you. And just because a girl likes to be held once in a while doesn't mean she wants to go too far. Did you even notice how most of the couples were during the movie?"

Rusty was silent for a moment. "We can't sit any closer than we did at the movie. I like when we're together. It's nice." He kissed her softly.

She searched for meaning in his eyes but saw nothing. A wall, a barrier had formed between them that he didn't see. "Sometimes, I'm not sure you really know what you want. You're like a ship without a rudder, drifting along. But it doesn't have to be like that. You'll never get to whatever it is you're looking for if you don't know what it is you want. And there's no way I can be a part of that journey if I don't know what's going on in your head."

"Well, what do you want?"

"I want us to be happy together."

"Damn Kathleen, I am happy. We're fine! Just because we didn't make out at the movie doesn't mean anything. Up to now I had a good time tonight. I don't get it. Why are you being like this?"

Kathleen took a deep breath, trying to calm her growing frustration. "Sorry. Didn't mean to screw up our evening. You're right, we're fine," she said with sarcasm. Forcing a smile, she gave Rusty a quick kiss and slid across the bench seat to open the passenger door. "It's our senior year and I want to have some fun with it," she declared as she slammed the passenger door shut. The truck's lights were like a spotlight on Kathleen as she entered the house. She never looked back.

Monday, August 18, 1969

Michael's blue jeans and blue t-shirt were a suitable complement to the blue mood he felt getting dressed for the first day of the last year of high school in hell. He imagined his friends in Oregon, excited that they were finally seniors but trying hard not to show it. Michael couldn't help but wonder which of his friends he would see again, who would move away to college before he returned and if Diane Streeter would still be around when he finally returned to Oregon. The feeling of homesickness, of being isolated weighed on his soul, like a lingering virus that his body could not overcome.

Michael walked into the kitchen feeling glum. His mother had prepared his favorite breakfast of fried ham, eggs and an English muffin. She greeted him cheerfully. "Good morning, son!"

"What's good about it?" he mumbled as he sat at the breakfast table with his mom and dad. Picking up his fork, he added without enthusiasm "Thanks for fixing this, Mom."

His dad cleared his throat. "You know, this could be a good experience for you, living in a new part of the country, meeting new people. It's sort of a sabbatical from the familiar."

"Really? This place? It's in the middle of nowhere. Nothing is happening here and it's all a bunch of backwards cowboys who've probably never seen a beach, much less a hockey game." Michael never raised his voice, but the intensity of his feelings became more pronounced as he spoke. His parents remained silent. "It's just so damn isolated and small. Even the trees are mostly small and bent just like the people."

"This wasn't my first choice either. But it was the best choice for our family. Sometimes you have to bloom where you're planted," his father explained.

"You can't bloom in a wasteland."

"You seem to have learned a lot about this place in the short time that you've been here. How many people did you say you've met?" his dad asked.

"Two, a cowboy and his daughter."

"And these backwards people as you call them must have treated you horribly," his mother added with annoying sarcasm.

Michael looked down at his breakfast. "They were fine. Did you know they put vegetables in their sodas here?"

Both parents laughed. "And you know this how?" his mom asked.

Michael chuckled. "Well, the girl I met, Kathleen, said I should put peanuts in the soda so I did."

"If she had asked you to put mashed potatoes in the soda, would you have done that, too?" Michael's dad asked with a grin.

Michael rolled his eyes and chuckled a little in spite of himself. "Glad that didn't happen."

"So basically, you met two people," Michael's dad said in a professorial voice as if he were concluding one of his economics lectures. "They were both friendly and helpful and you learned something about peanuts. What we have here is a sample size of two, both of which were positive experiences, and based on that sample size we have come to the conclusion that the entire town is, how did you say it, full of backwards cowboys."

"You're trying to tell me I need a bigger sample size," Michael replied with resignation.

"Clearly," his dad said. "And a less biased approach."

"OK, then I'm off to school," Michael mumbled as he finished his breakfast, his mood only slightly improved.

Michael drove into the school parking lot. Looking around, it was clear that he had the only VW on the lot, or perhaps in the entire town. What he saw were pickup trucks and a few sedans, mostly AMCs, Chevrolets and Fords.

Michael's mom had enrolled him in school several weeks earlier. The school office had provided her with his schedule, allowing Michael to report directly to class. The first class was orchestra. Michael had sent an audio tape of his solo performance of Boccherini's *Menuetto* to the orchestra conductor. No doubt the tape would land him an assignment in the first section of violinists, populated by the strongest players. Perhaps he would even be Concertmaster, the first violin in the first section. After all, in Oregon he had been in the second section, which certainly merited Concertmaster here. To his surprise, he found himself in the second section, just as he had been in the school orchestra in Oregon. He concluded that living in a wasteland must have warped the conductor's understanding of what music talent sounds like.

The conductor began the rehearsal by asking the Concertmaster to play the introduction to *The Four Seasons* by Vivaldi. A skinny, effeminate boy with a starched plaid shirt stood nervously. The boy moved his bow across the strings beautifully, his technique a model to behold and his body showing more confidence as he played. His fingers moved across the neck of the violin as if he were exerting no effort. What he lacked in physical presence he gained in musical prowess. Michael was impressed, if not vaguely intimidated by the distance between his skill level and that of the Concertmaster. They would never believe this back in Oregon.

First period orchestra class passed quickly. Michael packed his violin away in the instrument storage room as the bell rang for second period. Making his way into an unfamiliar hallway, it felt as if everyone but he had someone to talk with. At last, he could see the room number for his second period English class. Just before he entered the classroom Michael felt a sudden, almost jarring hand on his shoulder. Startled, he turned to see a middle-aged man with a starched white short sleeved shirt, thin black necktie and flat top haircut. The man looked similar to pictures that Michael had seen in *Life* magazine of NASA engineers. "Who are you?" the man asked.

"Whoooo," several nearby students said in unison.

"It's your funeral, man," another student said.

Michael noticed that about a dozen students had slowed their walk to observe whatever was about to happen. "Who are you?" Michael asked, feeling suddenly defiant.

The man paused without taking his arm off of Michael's shoulder. "I'm Mr. Jamison, your principal. Let's go to my office for a talk." Michael understood that declining the invitation for an office visit was not an option. So off they went to the office, students parting in the hallway to look at Michael as if he were going to the gallows for some terrible crime. Some seemed entertained by the scene while others looked more concerned. There was no doubt that Michael had gotten more attention than he expected during his short tenure at the school.

They walked through the school office waiting area, past the waist high counter, past the secretaries' desks and finally into an office. Mr. Jamison motioned for Michael to sit in a wooden chair with no upholstery across from his desk. The principal closed the door behind him and sat at his desk in an impressive leather chair. He had a gruff, no-nonsense appearance. Michael noticed a photo hung on the wall of a younger version of Mr. Jamison in the army, dirty and unshaven with a rifle in his hand, standing next to the city limit sign for a town in Germany. He wasn't smiling in the photo and he wasn't smiling now. Mr. Jamison sat back in his leather chair like a courtroom judge. "You never told me your name."

"Michael Thornhill."

"Oh yes, your mom came by a few weeks ago to get you enrolled. I believe she's a teacher and your dad is in economics at the university," Mr. Jamison said with a slightly more friendly tone.

"Right."

"And you're from Washington State?"

"Oregon."

"That's right, now I remember. OK, Michael, you need to know that we have a Student Handbook," he said as he slid the booklet across the desk towards Michael. "On page 11, it states that no hair is allowed below the collar. You need to get a haircut." His tone was blunt and to the point, not unfriendly but not warm either. All business.

Michael took the booklet but made no effort to open it, "OK, so my hair's fine as it is. Thanks for the booklet."

Mr. Jamison sternly responded, "No, your hair is clearly too long."

"Can't be. There's no collar on this shirt so by definition my hair can't be below the collar."

Whatever small element of friendly rapport that had developed moments before vanished. Leaning forward and pointing a finger at Michael he said "Young man, around here you say yes sir. You will not be allowed to disrupt this school with blatant disregard for the Student Handbook. I expect you to get your hair cut above the collar like every other student." Then sitting back in his chair, "Now, we can be your friends or we can be your enemies. You decide. But either way, the hair is getting cut. Until that happens, you're suspended."

Michael started to argue, but Mr. Jamison put up his hand to cut him off. "No further discussion. Get it cut and then get back to your classes."

With great effort Michael controlled his anger towards this backwards principal in this backwards town. He was determined to look calm, not giving Jamison the pleasure of seeing an angry, emotional response. Mr. Jamison's phone rang and it was clear that the discussion was over.

Walking out of the principal's office, Michael saw Kathleen and another girl standing in the waiting area, apparently expecting to speak with someone. Michael walked up to them from the secretaries' side of the counter. Looking very serious, Michael placed his hands on the counter, striking an authoritative pose. "I'm sorry girls, but you've been suspended."

Kathleen put her hand in front of her mouth like she was pretending to look surprised. "Oh, no. My mom's going to kill me," she said with a serious voice but a noticeable mischievous twinkle in her eyes.

"What did we do?" asked the other girl, looking nervous and confused.

"I was just informed that hair below the collar is grounds for suspension. You both have hair that's way too long. Read your Student Handbook. Get out and don't come back until---"

"Stop!" Jamison barked at Michael from his office door. Then, pointing towards the door, "Out!"

Michael turned towards Mr. Jamison. "Yes, sir." Turning quickly towards the hallway door, he noticed Kathleen biting her lip as if she were trying not to laugh. Michael managed to give her a wink as he stepped into an empty hallway.

§§§

Michael drove away from the high school feeling a volatile mixture of anger and frustration. *These idiots think I'll learn better with a haircut*, he thought. "Bullshit!" he yelled. Not sure what else to do, he drove towards home. On the way, two choices occurred to him. He could fight the stupid hair rule, a fight that his gut told him he would probably lose and could delay his graduation from this hellhole. Or, get the haircut and get back to class, which was a demoralizing but reasonable way forward. He turned the car towards a small strip shopping center not far from his home and shortly thereafter walked into Floyd's Barber Shop.

From the wall of Floyd's Barber Shop hung three large dead deer heads with glass eyes. Under the watchful eyes of the dead deer were four barber chairs, only one of which was occupied. On the front of the counter with the cash register was a bumper sticker with a peace sign and the words "Footprint of the American Chicken." An issue of Guns and Ammo magazine was on one of the waiting area chairs. Michael's feet stopped as soon as the glass door closed behind him. He had obviously interrupted a conversation between the middle-aged barber and his older customer, as they both became quiet and took in the spectacle of this long-haired kid standing in the doorway.

"What can I do you for?" the barber asked with a thinly disguised smirk.

The customer getting a crew cut chuckled and said to the barber, "That boy sure could use a haircut."

The barber smiled and opened and closed his scissors several times in the air, as if he were looking forward to what he assumed would be his next customer.

Michael felt as if he had stumbled into enemy territory. Getting a haircut was bad enough, but this was too much. Without saying a word, he turned and walked out the door. There was laughter from the two men as the door closed behind him.

A few doors down in the strip shopping center was Jolene's Beauty Shop and Supplies. Lacking any other options, Michael reluctantly entered. His anger was transformed into apprehension as he surveyed the shop. No dead animal heads here. Instead, his eyes were assaulted by pink, lots of pink. Pink walls, chairs with pink flowers and four pink hair dryers, two of which had middle aged women in curlers sitting below them with magazines. The air between the pink walls was thick with the smell of hair perm chemicals. Behind the counter stood a thin middle-aged woman wearing an apron with pink flower designs. She gave him a friendly smile. "Welcome, stranger. Can we help you?"

"Do you do haircuts? I mean, for guys?"

"Sure do. Have a seat. I'll be free in about 5 minutes, as soon as I finish up with one of my ladies."

Michael sat in a pink waiting room chair. The *Brownwood Bulletin* newspaper was on the empty seat next to his. Browsing the contents, he found an article on page seven titled *Beautiful People Conclude Peaceful Stay at Festival*. Michael had heard about the Woodstock Music and Art Fair on the radio. Though it was billed as a music and art event, Michael knew that bringing an end to the unjust war in Vietnam was an underlying theme. The paper reported that youth in the hundreds of thousands had gathered peacefully for the event. To Michael's surprise, the article was mostly positive, an unexpected finding from a small-town Texas newspaper. Reading the article, Michael felt a longing to join the peace movement that would hopefully one day force an end to the war in Vietnam. For now, he was miserably stuck in a pink chair alone in the middle of nowhere.

"OK, lets see what we can do for you," the woman with the pink apron announced. "You must be one of our college students."

Michael sighed. "No. Still in high school."

"Oh. Now, uh," she hesitated and became more serious. "Well, I'm just going to say this. The high school doesn't allow hair below the collar for boys. But I can sure fix that. I'm Jolene." The smile returned. "Come on in and let's see what we can do."

Michael reluctantly walked towards Jolene. "It's a stupid rule. I only want enough cut so that I can get back to school," he said as Jolene pointed towards a hair wash sink that was, of course, pink. Michael put his head on the edge of the sink as Jolene gave him a shampoo. The scalp massage and warm water rinse did little to relieve the tension in his neck and shoulders.

"You look worried. Relax sweetie, it's going to be OK. I think you'll like the look when I'm done with you."

Jolene's voice had a reassuring quality and Michael tried to relax and think more positively. She wrapped a towel over his head and led him to one of the pink chairs in front of a large mirror, as if she had done the same for high school boys a million times. Jolene unwrapped the towel, combed his hair and pulled a pair of scissors from a drawer. "Just enough to get you back into school, right?"

"Right," Michael replied as she started cutting. "Just enough to get me past that jerk off Jamison."

"You mean Harold Jamison? The principal?"

Michael noticed that Jolene's smile had evaporated and for some reason she was frowning. He wasn't sure how to interpret her reaction. "You know him?" As he asked, it occurred to him that it was probably a stupid question. A grown-up who cuts hair in a small town probably knows everybody.

Jolene stopped cutting Michael's hair and leaned over his shoulder to whisper in his ear as if there was a secret only he should know. In a soft, low voice, she said "I'm sleeping with Harold." Then, after a moment's hesitation she whispered "A lot." Jolene then resumed the hair cut with her scissors and a mischievous grin.

Michael was speechless. His instinct was to leave, but Jolene was half finished with the haircut. "Sorry."

With a twinkle in her eyes and a repressed smile, she asked "Sorry for the jerk off remark or sorry that I'm sleeping with him?" Michael squirmed in his chair without answering. Leaning over as if she were telling him another secret, Jolene said "He's my husband."

As Jolene finished the haircut, she asked "You know, those sideburns going to the bottom of your ears, what are we going to do with those?"

"Hopefully nothing."

With a smile she said, "Harold hates sideburns, but he can't do anything because several school board members also sport long sideburns." She winked at him in the mirror. "I think you should leave yours just as they are."

Michael examined his image in the mirror. He liked the look with longer hair better. But Jolene was right, this wasn't as bad as he feared. The result was hair long enough to partially cover his ears but stopping just above where his collar would be if his shirt had one. He was grateful that Jolene had cut his hair and not Floyd. "It looks good. Nice work. Thanks."

As Michael paid for the haircut, Jolene said in a friendly manner "I hope you have a wonderful school year, sweetie. Come back to see us any time."

After having lunch alone at home with his thoughts, Michael found himself walking back into the school, hoping for less drama during what was left of the day.

Autumn, 1965

Kathleen loved to spend time with her grandmother Emma. As a little girl, she would crawl onto her lap and talk of her hopes, fears and dreams. Grandma Emma would hold Kathleen with boundless love, offering words of reassurance and wisdom drawn from her many years of living.

Emma lived in a small wood framed farmhouse, painted blue with white trim. The home on two acres was within easy walking distance of the Wilcox farm. A dozen chickens in the front yard pecked the ground and sometimes each other. In back of the house was a large garden and a chicken coop where the flock spent their evenings. Kathleen's grandma had purchased the home soon after her husband died, wanting to be close to her family. Hibiscus were planted around the house. An old gray cat slept on the front porch and kept the snakes away. To Kathleen, it felt like the house where love lived.

When Kathleen was 13-years-old, Grandma was hospitalized with a foot infection that was slow to heal. She had long ago been diagnosed with diabetes, which was well managed through diet and twice daily insulin injections. When Kathleen visited her grandma in the hospital, she learned that the diabetes was making it difficult for the intravenous antibiotics to work as they should.

Kathleen couldn't remember ever having been in a hospital. It was a fascinating, bewildering new world. Each time a nurse entered the room, Kathleen was ready with yet another question about how a piece of equipment worked and what they were doing for her grandmother. A nurse allowed Kathleen to listen to Emma's heart with a stethoscope. When the physician came in the room to remove the bandages and inspect the wound, he asked Kathleen to leave. Emma firmly informed the physician of her desire to have Kathleen remain in the room. Kathleen stayed. Rather than becoming sickened by the sight of decayed foot tissue as the physician had warned, Kathleen peppered the physician with question after question about what they were seeing.

As the antibiotics finally began producing favorable results, Emma was discharged to a nursing home to complete the intravenous treatment. Kathleen visited daily. It wasn't long before she started to meet other nursing home residents. With her parent's approval, she became a nursing home volunteer. Her task was to bring ice water to residents, listen to their stories and sometimes read to them. She loved it. Kathleen also enjoyed being with the nurses, listening to them discuss their patients' unique medical needs. Although she did not understand much of what they were saying, she had a strong desire to learn more about this new world.

In the course of Emma's treatment, it became clear that the diabetes had taken a toll on her vision. This created an obstacle to discharge, as she could no longer accurately fill an insulin syringe for the twice daily self-injections into her abdomen. The lettering on the bottle and the markings on the syringe were too small for her to see, even with a magnifying glass. If she were to go home, someone would have to give her the insulin injections. Kathleen volunteered. The medical staff scoffed at a 13-year-old taking this responsibility. Kathleen would not be dissuaded. She had given injections to cattle with needles a lot bigger than the tiny insulin syringes the nursing home was using. And cattle were often trying to move. At least Emma would not be a moving target. Word of Kathleen's proposal spread through the nursing home and before long other residents were telling the medical staff how helpful Kathleen had been to them.

So, on a Saturday afternoon, under the watchful eye of a nurse, Kathleen pinched the skin of her grandmother's belly and gave her first human injection. "Sweetie, are you sure you're OK with this?" the nurse asked as Kathleen put the used syringe in a sharps container.

"That was easy," Kathleen replied. "We have cattle over a thousand pounds that I've given injections to. That's a lot harder than what I just did."

The nurse smiled. "Well then, the doctor says that if you're ready to do this, your grandma can go home. If you have any questions, you be sure to let us know."

Emma smiled at the nurse. "She'll be fine. Now that my foot is healed, I'm not worried."

Kathleen could easily walk to Emma's home twice daily for the insulin injections. The visits gave them time to talk, with Kathleen trying to learn all she could from her grandmother. When Kathleen complained about her inability to do some of the chores on the farm, Emma told her "Don't say can't, just say it's hard." When she lamented the difficulties involved with maintaining her stellar grades, Emma would say "It's not the can do, it's the want to." Her grandma had a loving sternness about her, always supportive of Kathleen but never accepting anything but her best.

Not long after discharge from the nursing home, Kathleen told Emma about trouble in the Palmer family. Mr. Palmer labored in the lumber yard. His son confided to Kathleen that somehow his father's foot had been run over by a careless forklift driver. For three months, he would be unable to work as the foot healed. Long term, the doctors said he would be fine. But with no short-term income, the proud family's savings were rapidly depleting.

"It's not fair the Palmers are in trouble. It's not their fault Mr. Palmer's foot was run over," Kathleen told her grandmother with considerable frustration. "I saw their boy Jake in school and he looked miserable."

"What do you want?"

Kathleen was taken aback by her grandmother's question. "It's just not fair."

"What do you think the Palmers need, a thirteen-year-old complaining about their situation or a young girl doing something about it?"

"I don't have any money. There's nothing I can do."

"The fact is, the Palmers are a proud family that wouldn't accept your help even if you had the money to give them. The loss of pride would be too big a burden to carry," Emma explained.

"So we watch them suffer?"

"I don't think that's what Jesus would do." Emma reached into her dress pocket and gave Kathleen a $10.00 bill. "Ask your mother to take you to the store. Tell her that I asked for 5 pounds of hamburger, a sack of flour, a bag of dried beans and four tubes of toothpaste. She'll ask what we're up to. You can tell her that it's a surprise. When you get back, take a dozen fresh eggs from my refrigerator and as many green beans and tomatoes as you can get from my garden. If we have time, you and I will make some cookies for good measure."

Kathleen was puzzled. "We're going to give this food to the Palmers, right? You said they're too proud for that."

"They'll never know where it came from. The Palmers always go to Wednesday Bible study at 7:00 in the evening. Tell your mother that you have a delivery to make and take it to their house while they're gone. Trust me, your mother will understand."

"But they'll never know. They won't even be able to thank us. That doesn't seem right."

Emma softly said, "Sweet girl, are you looking for recognition or are you looking to help a family in need?"

Kathleen did exactly as her grandmother had asked and never said a word to anyone about the scheme. It was Kathleen's first effort at clandestine service. It wouldn't be her last.

Three weeks later, Kathleen's father found Emma dead on her front porch. The doctors said that she probably died of a massive heart attack or stroke. Kathleen cried every day for two weeks. One evening she and her dad were sitting together on the front porch swing. She mournfully told her dad, "It's not fair. I wish she didn't have to die. I wish there was something left of her. She did more good than anyone will ever know."

Kathleen's dad put his arm around her shoulders and pulled her close. "Darlin, ya know how them relay runners, they run the best they can and then hand the baton to the next runner. Well, life's kinda like that. Your grandma done lots of good things, and when she died, it was like she handed the baton off to the next runner, someone to carry on all the good things she done."

Kathleen gave her dad a teary look. "So, who's the next runner?"

"It's you."

Monday, September 15, 1969

Rusty greeted his Monday in a foul mood. The third game of the football season had not gone well for the Stephenville High School Yellowjackets, losing to Duncanville High School 13 to 28. Rusty had managed his linebacker position well, twice knocking the breath out of ball carriers with bruising, violent tackles. In both cases, his teammates swarmed him with adulation while the hapless ball carrier laid on the ground gasping for air. The "nice hit" screams from the coaches failed to block out the look of fear in his opponents' eyes as they fought for breath, a breath that would eventually come after several moments of uncertain terror.

Rusty knew that scouts from the hometown Tarleton College Texans football team were in the stands watching, evaluating. Although a couple of their players had made it to the NFL during the 1960s, the college team's overall record was lackluster. They saw Rusty as a piece of the puzzle to turn the losing record of the 1960s into a winning team for the 1970s. The scholarship they offered would pay for most of the cost of his education, thus freeing his mother from a responsibility she was not well equipped to handle. Football was his ticket to the life he aspired to, or at least the one his mother wanted him to aspire to.

Rusty's release, the one thing that put his mind at ease and helped him through his conflicted teenage emotions, was Saturday morning garage band practice with Baked Cotton. After the football team's tough loss on Friday night, he was eager to practice the drums with his friends on Saturday morning. It never happened, as Jake cancelled the practice to go dove hunting with his father. Rusty would have done the same, if only he had a dad. He recalled a winter hunting trip when he bagged a white tail deer. The look of pride on his father's face as the deer fell would be forever in his memory as one of the greatest days of father/son comradery. Jake's opportunity to hunt was a reminder to Rusty of all he once had. Fathers are not supposed to die, at least not while their children are still in school.

Rusty walked towards his locker with a feeling of pissed off melancholy. Conflicting emotions that he didn't fully understand and wasn't sure how to deal with. To make matters worse, Ian Freestone, the wimpy, skinny effeminate kid from orchestra with the locker next to his was in the way. Ian had his locker door open, blocking Rusty's access and displaying a peace sign on the inside of the door. For reasons Rusty could not understand or explain, the presence of this kid around his locker had left him feeling uncomfortable since the first day of class. "Move it," he growled.

"Wait a minute," Ian replied as he pulled a book from the locker.

Rusty had seen enough. He slammed Ian's locker door closed, narrowly missing the boy's fingers. As Ian reached to reopen his locker, Rusty gave him a shove, soft enough not to hurt but hard enough to make an impressive sound as his chest landed on the lockers. Ian stepped aside with a look of fear and intimidation as Rusty dialed his locker combination and gained access to his books. Several students in the hallway stopped to observe the drama. Rusty slammed his locker door shut, secured the combination lock and walked to his next class.

A few hours later, Rusty found himself sitting across from Jake at the lunch table as Jake elaborated on the success of the dove hunting trip with his dad. Rusty let him talk and tried to feign being friendly as he listened to Jake's father/son exploits with growing envy. Finally, thankfully, Jake changed the subject. "Hey, I got us a gig!"

Baked Cotton hadn't played in public for several months, so this was indeed good news. His mood brightened. "Paid?"

"No such luck, but it'll be fun. We're playing at the school's sock hop on Saturday night. We're supposed to start at 7:00 and end at 9:00. Maybe we can do something with the girls afterwards."

Rusty had seen fliers posted on several bulletin boards around school for the sock hop. The dance would be held in the gym. No shoes would be allowed on the gym floor and students must leave by 9:00. "I thought Jamison wanted to use a jukebox."

"He did, but I convinced him otherwise. Told him it would be a better turnout with a band. Gave him some bullshit about how it would increase school spirit. He bought it, so we're in!"

Rusty's mood improved as they discussed the upcoming sock hop. "What did the others say?"

"Everyone in the band is good to go. What's wrong man?"

"Why was I the last to know?"

Jake rolled his eyes, mildly annoying Rusty. Leaning forward he said "I know I usually tell you first, but I had class with the others this morning. They're excited about the gig. What's wrong with you?"

Rusty was suddenly aware that his sour mood had been misinterpreted as a lack of enthusiasm for the gig. He managed a laugh. "Sorry man, having a rough morning. The gig sounds great. It'll be fun. But we better practice Saturday morning."

"You got it."

The boys finished their lunch and Rusty went to afternoon classes with a better spirit. His last class was football practice, which on Monday started with film review from Friday night. The coaches were yelling so loudly about lack of focus and missed opportunities that the only thing Rusty heard was their anger, not their message. When the tirade finally ended, the team took to the field for hitting drills, most of which involved two players trying to push each other onto their backs. The harder the hits, the more painful the experience for the players, the more the coaches seemed to enjoy the drill. Inevitably, some players became angry with each other and minor fights broke out. While Rusty was certainly adept at the drill and knew it well, the coaches' joy at seeing boys inflicting pain was troubling. This wasn't about skill training. This was about revenge. Revenge for losing on Friday night.

Coach Childress was responsible for the defense. He was older than the other coaches by at least a couple of decades. Rusty knew Childress had been a star on his college football team and may have turned pro if he hadn't injured his knee during his junior year. Following college graduation, Childress embarked on a coaching career that was by most accounts mediocre. After years of being an assistant coach, he finally got an opportunity to be a head coach at a small town somewhere west of Stephenville. He demonstrated considerable consistency as a head coach, leading his team to three consecutive losing seasons. The result was a head coaching career that was even shorter than his four failed marriages. Now nearing retirement, he came across to Rusty as an embittered, hostile son of a bitch who never regained the glory of his high school and college days. The only time Rusty could recall seeing Childress smile was when someone on the field was hurt.   And yet, Coach Childress and Rusty needed each other. Rusty needed to play ball to get his scholarship and Childress needed his star linebacker to help salvage whatever was left of his pathetic career.

Coach Childress and the offensive coach organized an Oklahoma Drill whereby two offensive players would face one defensive player in a small area. The offensive player would attempt to block the defender while the second offensive player tried to run the ball past the defender. They would typically put a large offensive lineman opposite a defensive lineman or linebacker. Blocking ability and strength were keys to the exercise. To Rusty's surprise, Coach Childress matched him with a rather small offensive player and a quick but smaller running back. The same running back who had fumbled on Friday night as they were driving for a touchdown. The whistle blew and Rusty easily shoved the offensive player aside and wrapped the ball carrier in a bear hug.

Coach Childress blew his whistle and turned with a scowl towards Rusty. "What was that? When you get to the ball carrier, I want you to hit him and hit him hard! Got it? Now do it again."

The boys lined up; Coach Childress blew his whistle. Once again, Rusty easily pushed the offensive blocker aside, this time tackling the ball carrier effectively but almost apologetically. Rusty helped the ball carrier to his feet.

"Rusty!" Coach Childress yelled, his face red with anger. He grabbed Rusty's face mask and glared at him. Rusty fought the temptation to shove the angry coach to the ground. "I told you to hit him hard! Make him feel it!"

Rusty recognized Coach Childress' intent. He wanted Rusty to injure the ball carrier. To inflict a punishing blow in retaliation for the boy's fumble on Friday night. The coach told the boys to line up for a third try at the drill. Rusty's teammates became quiet. He guessed that they also recognized what was happening. Rusty didn't move.

"I said line up!" Coach Childress screamed.

"No."

Coach Childress marched straight to Rusty and grabbed his face mask. "I said line up! Put his ass in the grass!"

Rusty looked at his coach with defiance and a vague sense of fear. He tried to keep his voice even. "Sometimes you have to man up and do the right thing. Coach, we don't need an injured player."

Coach Childress put his finger on Rusty's chest. "Get lined up or you and every one of your teammates will have to do a mile run!"

To Rusty's surprise, most of the team turned towards the track that circled the field and started to jog. Rusty could not hide the smirk from his face as he followed them, leaving Coach Childress seething. Jogging with his teammates, Rusty became aware that he was not alone in his lack of respect for the hostile coach. He had never liked Coach Childress. This incident would not make things any easier.

Adjacent to the field, Kathleen's dance team was learning a new routine. They finished practicing a few minutes before the football coaches tired from their merciless anger towards the boys. Kathleen and some of the girls stayed near the sidelines, probably wondering why the boys were running laps on the track. When the practice finally ended, Rusty, dripping with sweat and dirt, walked over to say hello before heading to the showers. "Hey."

"You stink."

"Well, it's good to see you, too!"

Kathleen laughed. "Are you OK?"

"Well, apparently I smell like a pile of manure, but otherwise I guess I'm OK." Rusty noticed Kathleen's skeptical look. "Guess what? Baked Cotton's playing at the sock hop on Saturday in the gym. Jake and I were hoping you and Janice would want to do something afterwards."

"Definitely," she smiled as they started walking towards the team's locker room. After a few moments of silence, she softly began, "I heard you had a problem with Ian this morning."

"The twerp wouldn't get out of the way, so I gave him a little shove. Didn't hurt him. Not even bruised. No big deal."

"I heard you scared the bejesus out of him."

"Maybe he'll get the hell out of the way next time. I could have been late to class just because he moves too damn slow." As Kathleen gave him a dubious look, he braced himself for an argument that he had no interest in pursuing. "Aren't you excited about our gig?"

"Definitely. I haven't heard Baked Cotton in public for months. It'll be fun!"

He smiled, gave her a quick kiss, and went into the locker room to clean up.

Rusty was pensive as he showered and dressed among his teammates. He was well liked, a football hero with a scholarship, a girlfriend most people enjoyed being around and a bright future. So why didn't he feel more content? And why had he picked on a skinny kid like Ian? His life was like a jigsaw puzzle with a couple of pieces lost somewhere in the couch. He'd give anything to find those pieces.

Tuesday, September 16, 1969

Michael struggled to contain his frustration as he sat through a mandatory after school rehearsal of all violins. After a long day of school, he would have preferred to go home and learn the music on his own. Ian sat in front of Michael in the first section in a plaid button shirt stretched over his slumped shoulders. He had gotten to know Ian, though not well. In Michael's eyes, the kid was a bit unusual, but a masterful musician. As the rehearsal ended and the students packed their instruments, Ian sat quietly staring at the floor.

Michael found an empty chair next to Ian. "Hey man, you OK?" he asked, trying to sound friendly.

"Fine." There was no eye contact and even less enthusiasm.

"Your technique is amazing. I'm impressed."

Ian shook his head and starred at the floor. "I could have lost it all yesterday. Everything."

"What happened?"

"I came within half an inch of breaking my fingers. Jerk named Rusty slammed my locker door and nearly got me."

"But he missed, so you're good, right?"

"You're not from around here, you don't get it. You wouldn't understand."

"Try me."

"The violin is my ticket out of here. I have a scholarship. Juilliard. If my fingers get smashed, there's no scholarship. Then I'm stuck here forever. I have to leave. There's no other way."

"You have a scholarship to Juilliard? That's amazing!"

"It won't be if Rusty finds a way to break my fingers. It's a long time until the end of school. His locker is next to mine. He'll have a lot more opportunities," Ian explained with a strange mixture of fear, depression and resignation.

"Well, then use my locker. We'll switch."

"Can't. It's in the Student Handbook, can't switch lockers."

"I'm pretty sure nobody cares. Who reads the stupid Handbook anyway?"

"I did."

Michael took a few moments to scheme how best to help Ian and simultaneously screw the damn handbook. "I bet you and I take most of the same classes, just different periods."

"So?"

"So, we don't trade lockers. I'll loan you my books and you loan me yours. If anyone asks, they'll see your books are in your locker where they're supposed to be. I'll need your locker combination and you'll need mine."

Ian looked at Michael for the first time. "Why do you want to do this? You could get in trouble."

"Look, I want out of this hellhole too, though probably for different reasons."

Ian finally smiled. The boys exchanged locker combinations and verified that they had the same textbooks. Michael was pleased to be able to help a musician into Juilliard and simultaneously find a way to screw the system.

Feeling accomplished in his small victory, Michael gathered his violin and books and walked towards the mostly empty parking lot. As he opened the door to the VW, he heard a girl yell "Hey!" from a few parking slots behind him.

Michael turned and saw Kathleen, the girl with the cowboy dad, standing next to an Oldsmobile. He smiled. "Hey. What are you doing here?"

"Just finished dance practice. You coming to the sock hop on Saturday?"

"Wasn't planning on it. I don't really know many people around here."

"Come on. It'll be fun. It's a good way to meet people. Good music. Good times. What's not to like?"

Michael found Kathleen's smile and friendly nature appealing in spite of himself. "Will they have peanuts? You know I've never had an RC Cola without peanuts. I think it's a law around here."

Kathleen laughed. "Count on it, Oregon. I'll see you there. Don't disappoint me."

Something about Kathleen's smile brightened his mood. It was the first time anyone had reached out to Michael when it wasn't regarding music or academics. For a moment, he allowed himself to feel good. On the drive home, he wondered if it were possible to have a good day in hell.

Wednesday, September 17, 1969

The next morning, Michael opened Ian's locker and was relieved, but not surprised, to find the textbooks arranged in neat order and in good condition. As he closed the locker, someone beside him asked "What are you doing?" The voice wasn't unfriendly, but had a matter-of-fact quality. Michael turned to see a tall, muscular student with a very short haircut studying him with curiosity. If this was the guy who scared Ian, it was easy to see why he was intimidated. Michael was several inches shorter and, though somewhat muscular from playing hockey, he was certainly smaller than the guy standing next to him.

The kid kept staring at Michael. "Not your locker."

"No shit, Sherlock," Michael replied and turned to walk away.

"Who the hell are you?" the big kid sneered.

Unfortunately, Mr. Jamison walked by in time to hear the profanity. "Stop right there, both of you." Then, turning to the big guy, asked in a stern voice, "Rusty, what have we said about profanity on this campus?"

Rusty looked directly at Mr. Jamison. "Sorry, sir. I'm sure this guy had every reason to be in Ian's locker."

Michael rolled his eyes. "I have to get to class."

"Not yet," Jamison said. "Were you in Ian's locker?"

"Yes, sir."

"Did you trade lockers with Ian?" Jamison inquired.

"No."

"But you were in his locker?"

"Yes."

"Getting your books?"

"No."

"Probably stealing them," Rusty interrupted.

Mr. Jamison pointed a finger at Rusty and in a firm voice ordered, "You get to class, now. And watch your mouth."

Mr. Jamison turned back to Michael. "Let's have a talk. You know the way."

Michael walked into Mr. Jamison's office and sat in the familiar wooden chair. Mr. Jamison took his spot in the leather chair. Déjà vu.

Mr. Jamison began, "Looks like you and I are having regular meetings. You want to tell me what's going on with the locker?"

Michael felt like he had received the opening salvo in a hostile interrogation. Not responding was not an option. "I borrowed Ian's books."

"Where are your books and how is Ian supposed to study without his?" Mr. Jamison asked with exasperation.

"My books are in my locker, where they belong, except that Ian's borrowing them."

Mr. Jamison looked at Michael with a penetrating gaze. "You need to be aware that the Student Handbook that I know you have a copy of expressly forbids the trading of lockers," he growled.

"We didn't trade. His books are in his locker. We're just borrowing." Michael found himself feeling provoked by the questioning. "What's the harm?"

"I'm asking the questions here!" Mr. Jamison barked. "What are you and Ian up to?"

"Ian has a scholarship and---"

"I know he has a scholarship. Juilliard. I wrote one of his reference letters!"

Michael was surprised by Mr. Jamison's knowledge and support of Ian's scholarship. "Well, some asshole," Michael caught himself escalating what was becoming a confrontation. "Excuse me. Sorry, sir. Some big guy almost broke Ian's fingers by slamming his locker door shut yesterday."

"Let me get this straight. You and Ian are using each other's lockers so that Ian doesn't have to risk getting his fingers broken? Because we both know that no fingers, no scholarship. But you haven't traded lockers, just borrowed each other's books?"

Michael was unsure of how to respond. There was probably a Student Handbook policy about borrowed textbooks. Maybe someday he would actually read the damn handbook. For now, he remained silent.

Mr. Jamison looked sternly at Michael. "So, you concocted this little scheme to protect a fellow student and a gifted musician." There was direct eye contact between Mr. Jamison and Michael. He had the impression that Mr. Jamison had interrogated enough students to know, even without their answering, where the truth lay. It was as if he could dissect the teenage brain and find the truth, the very truth that the student was trying to conceal. Michael had the uncomfortable feeling that whatever the principal was considering, it was not going to be good. Mr. Jamison sat back in his chair, relaxed his shoulders, and appeared to be pondering his next move. Finally, he smiled and said, "Well done, son. Get to class."

Mr. Jamison and Michael stood up together and walked towards the hallway door. Just before they stepped into the hallway, Mr. Jamison put his hand firmly on Michael's shoulder. Michael found the contact to be uncomfortable. He turned to face Mr. Jamison directly, ready for the next confrontation.

"One more thing, Michael." Mr. Jamison paused for a moment and looked piercingly at his student. Then, with a slight smile, he continued. "Your hair dresser says nice sideburns."

What happened next surprised Michael. They laughed, together.

Saturday, September 21, 1969

Friday night football left Rusty and his teammates in high spirits. It was a decisive victory over nearby Nolan High School which proved to be an elixir for the team. A few victories would erase the lingering frustration from the prior year record of four wins and six losses. The locker-room celebration had an intoxicating quality and Rusty savored their accomplishment on the field, though he successfully hid misgivings he neither understood nor wished to share. When he thought about it later that evening, he realized the feeling grew from one play in which the coach had him blitz. The opposing linemen were too slow to respond and the quarterback never saw him coming. Rusty hit the quarterback, hard, in a collision that drove his opponent into the solid turf. His teammates swarmed him with congratulatory head slaps while the opposing quarterback slowly, unsteadily, regained his footing. The quarterback's night was over as he staggered to his team's bench like a drunken sailor, confused about where he should go or how to get there. During a time out, Rusty saw the quarterback on the bench, bent over and heaving vomit. A student trainer helped the quarterback to the locker room, after which Rusty never again saw the young man. Another opponent injured. As Rusty went to bed for the night, he felt as if he possessed two souls, one basking in the glory of the team's victory and the other shamed by the quarterback's injury.

Baked Cotton started practice in Rusty's garage promptly at 10:00 AM Saturday morning. At Rusty's suggestion they learned Merle Haggard's *I Take a Lot of Pride in What I Am*. It was an easy tune and the band quickly had it mastered.

Several weeks prior to the rehearsal, Jake had talked the band into adding to their repertoire a new rock and roll song from Steppenwolf, *Born to be Wild*. Rusty didn't see why they were doing hippie music, though it was clear that Jake was having fun playing the lead guitar.

Jake had tried to explain. "Come on man, it's fun. We need variety in our act. Besides, we should have at least one song for the weirdo freaks in our school."

"You mean both of them?"

Jake laughed. "No, there's only one I know of. New kid you're locker buddies with."

Rusty rolled his eyes. "Whatever." Over the next few days, he learned the drum patterns and was ready for practice the Saturday morning before the sock hop.

§§§

Rusty arrived early at the Saturday evening sock hop. Jake helped him unload the drum set from the back of his truck. As the boys were setting up their equipment on the carpeted platforms under the basketball goal, Rusty could hear multiple voices from the nearby hallway. He knew that the Parent Teachers' Association would be trying to sell various sodas while acting as unofficial chaperones. Rusty guessed that sales would be slow, as food and drinks were prohibited on the well-polished gym floor.

Mr. Jamison's voice boomed over the excited hallway conversations. "Remember, leave your shoes in the bleachers. Unless you are a faculty member, parent or a member of Baked Cotton, shoes on the gym floor are prohibited."

Rusty gazed over the empty gym as the band took their places on the platform stage. "This is going to be great!" Rusty said to nobody in particular, making no effort to hide his excitement.

"Let's hope so," Jake replied. "The acoustics in here are going to suck, but there's nothing we can do about it. Let's rock this place!"

Rusty didn't care about the acoustics. He relished the opportunity to play his drums in front of his classmates.

At 7:00 P.M., Mr. Jamison unlocked the door from the hallway to the gym. Rusty saw a sudden surge of students through the door, some with their shoes already off. Baked Cotton began their set as students crowded in front of the platform stage. Rusty felt a tingle up his spine as he savored the joy of playing in the band.

§§§

Michael arrived at the sock hop fifteen minutes late. He removed his shoes and stepped onto the gym floor with great ambivalence. Although the sock hop promised to be a socially awkward waste of time, it might be better than spending another Saturday evening at home with his parents. It was clear that most students knew each other and, in his view, had little interest in an out of towner like him. Surveying the scene, he saw numerous groups laughing or standing in front of the stage listening to the music. Michael recognized many faces but knew few names. He felt like an island, conspicuous only to himself in his aloneness. His first inclination was to return home but he willed himself to join those standing in front of the band.

Michael noticed a few shoeless couples dancing to country and western music, their feet gliding across the floor as if they were ice skating in each other's arms. The dancing style was unfamiliar and of little interest. There was something mildly nauseating in seeing students his age dancing and enjoying redneck music when, thousands of miles away, young men only a few years older were dying in what Michael saw as a senseless, immoral war in Vietnam. Would these students ever rebel, or were they content to blindly follow the instructions from Washington politicians out of some misplaced patriotic obligation?

Standing near the band with the speakers louder than they needed to be, the students around Michael had little opportunity to converse. To his surprise, Michael heard a voice behind him loud enough to be heard over the band. "Hey, Oregon."

Michael turned to see Kathleen, wearing tight fitting denim blue jeans, white socks and a sleeveless red blouse with a scoop neck. The outfit was casual, but in Michael's eyes, had a sexy, appealing quality. Her sudden appearance caused a momentary disorientation as he struggled to make a swift transition from critical thoughts towards his fellow students to something more friendly. Feeling mentally disoriented, all he could offer was a smile and "Hi."

Kathleen responded with a sarcastic frown. Placing her hands on her hips, she asked "So, Oregon, I want to know why you've been here all this time and you haven't asked me to dance?"

Michael quickly regained his composure. "Well, not asking you to dance until now is the most dumb ass thing I've ever done. Would you like to dance?"

Kathleen smiled. "Sure."

He turned suddenly serious. "OK, but first there's something you need to know."

Kathleen looked into his eyes as if she were expecting him to reveal some grave secret. As he paused, she suddenly looked uncomfortable. "What?"

"I don't know how to dance. At least, not this kind of dancing."

After a brief moment, Kathleen laughed. "You're a musician, right?"

"Violin."

"Fiddle."

"OK, fiddle, but I still don't know how to dance."

Kathleen giggled and took his hand, leading him to the dance floor. She turned and put her left arm on his shoulder and her right hand in his left in a classic ballroom dancing pose. "It's called the two step. You're going to take one slow step towards me with your left foot, then one slow step towards me with the right foot, then a quick step with the left and a quick step with the right. It's to the beat of the music, slow slow fast fast." She looked into his eyes and smiled. "You can do this."

And he could. Michael quickly mastered the two step and, in spite of himself, was enjoying the experience. The song ended much too soon. "That was fun. How about one more?"

Kathleen made a quick glance at the band. For a moment, Michael feared that she might walk away. As the band started playing *I Take A lot of Pride in What I Am*, Kathleen suddenly looked more relaxed. She smiled and looked into Michael's eyes. "Sure. I'd love to dance another one." As they two stepped around the gym floor, her left arm relaxed and they found themselves dancing more closely. She laughed as Michael twice twirled her as he had seen other boys do with their girlfriends. "I'm impressed. You learn quick. Be careful though. You might accidentally have a good time," she teased.

Holding Kathleen in his arms as they danced was enticing to Michael. He wasn't sure where this was going, but he sure was interested in finding out. At minimum, he hoped to have gained what he hadn't had since Oregon. A friend. At best, perhaps they would be more than friends. Time would tell.

As the song ended, Kathleen gave Michael a brief hug and stepped back. "Hey, Oregon, you're a really good dancer. Got to head to the restroom. See you later."

Michael watched her walk away as the band began playing *Born to be Wild. Finally*, Michael thought. *A song I can dance to*. Feeling more confident as he walked back towards the band, he passed a girl walking alone in the same direction. "Want to dance?" he asked.

"Not to this music," she said with clear disdain for rock and roll.

A few minutes later, he saw Kathleen returning to the gym, walking with two girlfriends, laughing and talking as if Michael didn't exist. He suddenly felt back on his socially isolated island, alone and once again invisible to those around him. Having seen enough, Michael made his way to the second row of the bleachers where he found his shoes. As he was putting them on, he heard Kathleen's voice from the gym floor.

"Hey, Oregon," Kathleen said. "I'm glad you came tonight."

Michael smiled and paused for a moment. "Me, too. Thanks."

§§§

Kathleen was disappointed to see Mr. Jamison walk towards the band platform at precisely 9:00 PM. Turning to Janice, she asked "Ever wonder how time goes so fast when you're really having fun?"

"I was just thinking the same thing," Janice responded. "Jake looks like he could play guitar all night."

"Let's give a hand for Baked Cotton! Nice job they've done for us tonight, don't you think?" Mr. Jamison asked after Jake reluctantly surrendered the microphone. The crowd clapped and hollered in appreciation for the band. "It's 9:00, so please make your way out so our janitors can dry mop the gym. Get your homework done and we'll see you on Monday."

Kathleen was sure that not one student in the gym had any intention of doing homework on a Saturday night. Some would probably go home, others would sit in the parking lot talking with friends and a few, like she and Janice, would drive together to the Dairy Queen for a bite to eat. The girls found their shoes in the bleachers and lingered a bit as Baked Cotton put their instruments and equipment away.

At the Dairy Queen, Kathleen and Janice slid onto a bright red bench in a booth. They sat together facing the door, amused by the comings and goings of their classmates while waiting for the boys. Some of the girls from school stopped at their table to gossip about various couples they had seen at the dance. Spirits were high when Rusty and Jake came through the door and walked towards their booth. Kathleen grinned as the boys carried themselves in a triumphant manner, clearly pleased with their performance at the sock hop. *And well they should be*, she thought. It was a success by any measure, except for the fact that they had played for free.

"These seats reserved?" Jake inquired of the girls with a smile as he pointed at the empty red bench seat.

Janice feigned a serious look. "Well yes, as a matter of fact they are reserved. Seems they are being held for two country boys with musical talent and small butts."

Other students at the Dairy Queen started to laugh. Rusty looked at Jake "I think she means us."

Kathleen laughed. "Well then slide your ass in here and order us some ice cream."

Jake slid onto the bench seat across from the girls. Rusty took the seat next to Jake and announced, "It's going to take more than ice cream for me. I'm hungrier than a tic on a truck. I've gotta have a cheeseburger and fries. You just want ice cream?"

"Yes sir" the girls said mockingly in unison.

"Should I ask the Mexican girl behind the counter to put chocolate dip on the ice creams?" Jake asked.

"Mexican girl?" Kathleen frowned. "She has a name, you know. My God Jake, you've been going to school with her forever."

"You won't believe this," Jake said. "I know two guys who have asked her out and she turned them both down flat. Isn't that weird? She never goes to school functions, doesn't seem to have friends. All she ever does is go to school and work at Dairy Queen. We should call her the dairy queen of the wetbacks."

Janice laughed. "Her name's Anna. You better stick with that."

Kathleen was uncomfortable with Jake's attitude towards Anna. "Would you guys just order the damn food?"

Rusty responded. "Yes ma'am, we're on it." Turning to Jake he added "Come on man, let's let Anna know what we want."

§§§

Rusty walked with Jake towards the counter of the Dairy Queen to order their food. Anna de la Rosa stood in front of the counter, wiping off the remnants of ketchup, sticky soda and dirty handprints. As she was cleaning, Rusty saw a drunk college student stumble into the Dairy Queen. Although Anna was wearing a red smock over her blue jeans and blouse, Rusty saw the student staring at her. As she bent over to pick up a dirty napkin from the floor, her back to the door, the drunk student grabbed her ass. Anna jumped and turned with fury towards him. "Damn you!" she shouted, eyes glaring and index finger pointing at the drunk student's nose.

Jake stepped between Anna and the drunk college student as Rusty grasped the student by the back of his collar and slammed his chest onto the counter. Grabbing the drunk's left arm, Rusty flipped him onto his back. As Rusty gripped the neck of the drunk's shirt and one arm, Jake caught the other arm as the drunk started to swing his fist towards Rusty. The drunk had his head in the air on one side of the counter top and his legs dangling off the other. Suddenly seeming more sober, he yelled "Get your hands off, son of a bitch!" His legs pumped like he was doing an air bicycle but stopped when he heard the room erupt in laughter.

Jake glared at the drunk. "You owe this lady an apology, asshole."

"Fuck you!"

Rusty twisted the shirt collar more tightly. "Wrong answer."

"OK. Sorry! Let me go!" he winced and tried briefly to resume his air bicycle routine, generating additional laughter.

Rusty looked at Anna and back at the drunk student, his pulse racing with adrenaline and anger. "How did you get here?"

The drunk glared at Rusty the best he could with his head hanging off the edge of the counter. "You don't know who you're messing with! I'm the sophomore running back for Tarleton State. You hurt me and you're in big trouble."

Rusty glared. "Well then, I'm your worst nightmare. Next year I'll be a Tarleton State linebacker and I can't wait to put your ass in the grass. But you didn't answer the question." With a menacing glare Rusty asked again "How did you get here?"

"In my damn truck! How do you think?"

"Where are your keys?"

"What? Why?"

Anna put her dirty rag on the drunk's now exposed belly, reached into his pocket and pulled out a key ring with two keys, one to a Ford truck and another presumably to a dorm room. She turned to Rusty with a smile. "You mean these keys?" She put the keys in Rusty's shirt pocket, picked up a half full cup of soda without ice from the counter and slowly poured the drink on the drunk's crotch, being careful not to spill any onto the floor. The drunk started to air bicycle again, but this time with what looked to be piss in his pants. Everyone minus the drunk laughed at his expense.

The Dairy Queen manager emerged from the store's walk-in refrigerator and quickly surveyed the scene. "Y'all take it outside. Now."

Jake and Rusty jerked the drunk student off of the counter and pushed him towards the door. Anna followed them out as did most of the other high schoolers. Once outside, the drunk turned as if he were ready to fight Rusty, then thought better of it. "You can't have my truck! Give me my damn keys!"

Rusty grinned and threw the keys onto the flat Dairy Queen roof. "Oops."

"Son of a bitch!" the drunk yelled as a cop car drove into the parking lot to investigate the commotion. "You're in trouble now asshole," he sneered.

Everyone became quiet. Two stern looking officers walked towards the boys. Rusty figured that the officers had much better things to do than deal with a group of unruly teenagers.

The younger of the two asked, "Someone want to tell us what's going on here?"

The drunk looked at the officers and pointed at Rusty. "He stole my truck!"

The officer watched the drunk sway a little as he spoke. "What kind of truck?"

"Ford. It's right there!" As he pointed, the kids again erupted in laughter. "Well, OK, he didn't steal my truck exactly, but he stole my keys."

Turning to Rusty, the offices asked "Do you have his keys?"

"No sir. They're on the roof and he's too drunk to be driving."

The second officer looked at the drunk. "You must be one of them college boys."

The drunk nodded.

"You live on campus?"

"Yes sir," the drunk student answered. "Tarleton State running back," he added, as if it were somehow germane to the conversation.

"The dorm isn't far. You can start walking to campus or we'll take you to jail. It's up to you. Either way, you'll need to get your truck tomorrow morning. I know the manager here and he'll loan you a ladder to get your keys when it's light out and you're sober. Don't wait too long tomorrow or we'll have your truck towed. Understood?" Then turning to the students, he ordered "I want all of you to disperse. Either get back inside or go home, it's up to you."

The drunk student, now looking defeated, started walking towards the college. Most of the crowd ambled back into the Dairy Queen. Rusty turned to face Anna. She looked directly into his eyes with an intensity that made him feel as if she could see into his soul. "Thank you," she said.

Rusty felt an instant bond that he could neither understand nor explain. "No problem," he stammered and then followed her back into the Dairy Queen, now feeling even more hungry.

As Anna took her place behind the counter, the manager gave her a smile. "You OK?"

"Sure. I'm fine."

The manager then looked at Jake and Rusty as they waited to place their orders. "Whatever those boys want, it's on the house."

§§§

Kathleen watched Jake and Janice walk out of the Dairy Queen, arms around each other. She and Rusty would have left sooner, but they were interrupted by several students slapping Rusty on the back and telling him what a fine thing he and Jake had done in dealing with the drunk college boy. She knew that Rusty was already held in high regard at school. Tonight's Dairy Queen incident would only enhance his reputation.

Kathleen slid onto the bench seat of Rusty's truck, allowing him just enough room to drive and shift gears, but no more. In the light of the truck's dashboard as he drove her home, Kathleen could see that he was deep in thought. About what, she wasn't sure. They were both silent for a few minutes. Finally, Kathleen said, "You did a good thing tonight, taking that drunk dumbass out of the Dairy Queen."

Rusty smiled. "You know, sometimes, like in football, when I hurt someone, it feels like crap. But tonight felt good. Didn't really hurt the guy, but I might have if the cops hadn't showed up. I don't think it would have bothered me at all." He shrugged his shoulder. "It's weird."

Kathleen studied his profile for a moment. "You remember the movie Camelot? The musical?"

"Oh God. What does that have to do with anything?"

"Remember, King Arthur said he would use might for right? Well, maybe that's what you did tonight. Used might for right."

"So, you're saying football isn't right?"

"Football is your ticket to college, a good deal in my book."

"So, it's OK to hurt guys on the football field because it gets me into college."

Kathleen wasn't sure if Rusty were making a statement or asking a question. The conversation was taking an unexpected turn. Something about Rusty sounded pensive, perhaps confused. As he stopped at the fence to her family's farm, Kathleen left the cab of the truck to open the gate. The brief halt to the conversation gave her a moment to collect her thoughts. Neither spoke as Rusty drove them down the dark dirt road through the pasture towards Kathleen's home. Her parents had left the front porch light on, an annoying habit that made the area seem less private. As Rusty killed the engine, she turned to him and smiled. "I don't think you try to hurt guys when you're playing football. Getting hurt is just part of the game."

Rusty put his arm lightly around her and looked out the truck's window. His gaze focused on some far-off object, his thoughts a mystery to Kathleen. "Most times I don't," he said, as much to the stars as to Kathleen. "Sometimes I do." He suddenly looked uncomfortable, vulnerable, as if she had entered the private realm of his feelings uninvited. "Sometimes it's like my life is a scripted adventure where I'm a robot trying to do what's right. People expect a lot and I can't let them down. When I do good, like when I put some guy on his ass in football, everyone's happy. Even the adults. Don't get me wrong, it's nice when people say I'm doing great. What they're really saying is that I've met or done better than what they expected."

"What's wrong?"

He continued searching for something in the stars, avoiding eye contact. "Nothing."

"Sometimes I'm not sure of what you want. From school, from football." She paused and voiced what had been concerning her for weeks. "Or even from me."

"Maybe I'm not so sure either!" he loudly replied.

The anger she felt from Rusty was startling. She starred at him in disbelief as he continued to study the night sky. The silence between them made her uncomfortable. She took a deep breath and whispered "Rusty Dalton, I'm not sure what you want or where you're going. But if you can figure it out, the world sure as hell will stand aside and let you get there. You can be whatever you want to be, and that's a special gift."

She kissed his cheek. He finally turned towards her and lightly kissed her lips. Kathleen felt no passion from him, as if the kiss was made in an obligatory thank you sort of way. "Good night," he said.

"What's wrong?"

"Why do you keep asking questions I don't have answers for? Why do you think something's wrong?"

She stared at his face for a moment, then gazed out the windshield looking at nothing. There was a gulf between them, as if she had peeled back Rusty's inner emotions as far as he would let her and she could go no further. Kathleen felt that she and Rusty knew each other well, but not well enough. Neither of them had ever said I love you, and probably never would. Kathleen wasn't sure what she wanted in a boyfriend, but this wasn't it. And yet, she enjoyed being with him. They had fun together and she did care about him. Her tangled emotions were confusing, the future uncertain.

Suddenly the front porch light was turned off and on several times, a signal from Kathleen's parents that it was time for her to come into the house, alone. Kathleen rolled her eyes. "I have to go" she said as she gave Rusty a quick kiss, slid across the bench seat and opened the truck door.

§§§

Rusty watched Kathleen walk across the front porch and into the house. Starting the truck, he wondered what the hell had just happened.

Driving home, he worried that Kathleen's questions would expose him as shallow and superficial. He couldn't, wouldn't, let her or anyone else see that side of him. It was too confusing and undefined. Although they had been dating for a while, their conversations were seldom of any emotional depth. He liked it that way. Rusty willed himself to control his emotions, to return to the scripted adventure. True, it was an act, but it's all he knew to do.

Of all the events of an eventful night, the one he thought most about was the look in Anna's eyes as she thanked him for defending her. It was as if they had connected at a deeper level than any words that were spoken. It was a strange feeling. Parking his truck at home, he concluded that the feeling was probably an illusion to be ignored.

Thursday, September 25, 1969

Having completed almost five weeks at Stephenville High School, Michael had settled into a routine of sorts. Still feeling socially isolated and culturally disconnected, he resolved to live on his lonely island of social invisibility until graduation. He would then leave this little scrapheap of hell, never to return, a bad dream, a mere hiccup in life's journey. His so-called peers were neither friendly nor hostile. He had gotten to know a few students on a superficial basis and quickly learned that he had little in common with them. He was new, an outsider, and always would be.

A strong person can live for a time on hope. Hope for a brighter future if only the current time can be endured. Hope for better days to come. Hope crushed when Diane Streeter wrote him a letter from Oregon, casually mentioning that she was dating one of Michael's friends. As he pondered the letter, it occurred to Michael how unreasonable it would be for Diane to sacrifice her social life waiting for him to return. That was his fantasy, not hers. She had made no promises when she kissed him under the bleachers at the minor league baseball game. Michael knew he would meet other girls. Diane Streeter would be no more than a pleasant memory. But today, as he read the letter for a third time, it was painful.

As evening fell over Stephenville like the emotional cloud falling on his spirits, he told his parents he was going for a ride. He needed to drive. He wasn't sure where he was going, but he couldn't stay in the house. Maybe the movement of pavement beneath his tires would provide reassurance that he could, and would, eventually be able to leave. After a few minutes of aimless travel, he passed through the campus of Tarleton State University. Depressingly, the few people he saw walking around looked like slightly older versions of students from his high school. It disgusted him. With the Vietnam War raging and the youth of America dying daily, these students seemed uninterested in doing anything to stop the misadventure. In fact, he guessed that they probably supported the effort.

At the next stop sign, he noticed the Dairy Queen. Night captured the city streets as he parked his car in the store's empty lot. An attractive girl behind the counter welcomed him with "Evening," and a smile as he ambled through the door.

Michael approached the counter and ordered a vanilla ice cream cone with a chocolate dip.

"Good choice," the girl behind the counter said as she took his money. "Nothing like ice cream to cool off on a hot night."

"Hot night in hell if you ask me," Michael mumbled.

She made a fake pout as she handed him his vanilla ice cream cone dipped in chocolate. "Rough day?"

Other than what looked to be a college couple sitting in a far corner oblivious to everything but themselves, the restaurant was empty. "Girlfriend trouble. I'll get over it." He turned towards a table, but decided to keep conversing with the attractive girl behind the counter. It wasn't like she was overly busy. "Have you worked here long?"

She looked him in the eye and smiled. "About a year. Why?"

"Just asking. Don't mean to keep you from your work."

She laughed. "Well, you know, I can hardly keep up with the crush of customers we have here. This sweatshop's kicking my ass tonight. You have a name?"

Michael chuckled at her sarcasm in spite of himself. "Michael."

She reached across the counter to shake his hand. "Anna."

Michael wiped vanilla ice cream drippings onto his pants before shaking her hand.

She glanced over her shoulder at an older guy scrubbing a grill in the kitchen. "Don't think I've seen you around here before."

"I'm new. Moved down from Oregon a few weeks ago."

Anna grinned. "You're fast! Just got here and already have girlfriend trouble. Most guys probably wouldn't even have had a date after only a few weeks. You some sort of Casanova?"

Michael blushed a little in spite of himself. "No, she's back in Oregon, apparently now dating one of my friends. Meanwhile, I'm stuck here. It sucks."

"You don't like our town?"

"Sorry. I'm sure it's fine if you grew up here. It's not me. I just don't fit in here. Kind of like the courthouse clock on Belknap Street."

"Hijole! You don't even like the courthouse clock?"

Michael tried to explain. "There're four clocks on the courthouse tower, right?"

"Yes."

"Well, three give the correct time. The one facing Belknap Street has a four where the five should be."

Anna looked puzzled. "I've never even noticed the courthouse clock."

"Check it out. The numbers are out of place and so am I. Are you from Stephenville?"

"Born and raised." Anna looked at him with growing recognition. "Wait a minute. You're the guy they almost kicked out of school on the first day because of your hair, right?"

"Guilty."

"Well, Mr. Michael, you don't sound too impressed with our town. Give it a little time. It'll grow on you. We're not all what you may think we are."

"I guess you're happy here?"

"Me? Hell no. I'm working on a plan to get out, see the world, further my education. But that doesn't mean it's a bad town. It's my home, at least for now."

"Mine too, at least for now."

"See ya," Anna said as Michael finished his ice cream and threw his napkin into the trash.

As he drove home in the darkness, he pondered how to make his prison sentence in Stephenville a better experience.

Perhaps Anna was right, he needed to give it some time.   If only he knew how to do so without first dying of frustration or loneliness.

Walking through the front door of his home feeling better than when he left, he found a letter addressed to him from Oregon State University.   It contained his admissions application. Although it was getting late in the evening, Michael began completing the paperwork. Technically, it was only an application, but to Michael it felt like a ticket home. A get out of jail opportunity if only he could do his time. The effort of assembling the application lifted his spirits in spite of the late hour.

Thursday, October 2, 1969

"Kathleen, supper time," her mother called from the kitchen.

Kathleen had taken to using the front porch swing for her studies, the fresh air and the familiar smell of the country somehow put her mind at ease and helped her focus. Grateful for a break, Kathleen replied "OK, Mom. Be right there." Supper came at a good time, as she was becoming increasingly frustrated with trying to translate Shakespeare into English. If Shakespeare's writing was so great, why the hell was it so hard to understand? It reminded her of reading the King James version of the Bible. Lots of pretty sounding words but difficult to comprehend without considerable effort.

The wonderful smell of fresh baked dinner rolls enveloped Kathleen as she came to the kitchen table. Her mother served the meal, the dinner was blessed, and the family passed around bowls of fresh bread, black eyed peas, okra and fried chicken. Usually, their dinners featured nonstop conversation. Tonight, both of her parents were uncharacteristically quiet. Her dad's face looked particularly troubled. "What's wrong?" she asked, not sure if she really wanted to hear the answer.

"You wanna tell us about this?" her father asked, sliding three envelopes across the table.

Three envelopes, each with a return address of Admissions Office, but each from a different school. No doubt, each envelope contained an application for admission. The first was from Tarleton State. No surprise there. Every senior with college interest applied to Tarleton. It was the only school many students could afford, saving considerable money by living at home. As an added bonus, there would be no pressure to meet new people since numerous high school friends would be attending. It would be easy, safe and affordable, which to Kathleen sounded predictable and boring. To make matters worse, there were no nursing classes at Tarleton State and Kathleen had set her sights on nursing since she was a little girl visiting her grandmother in the nursing home. "Well," she began, "You knew I was planning to apply to Tarleton."

Her mother spooned some black-eyed peas onto her plate and said, "We sure enough did."

"I want to be a nurse!"

"Darlin, nobody's ever sayin you shouldn't be a nurse," her father said with an attitude both reassuring and concerned.

"OK, well, that's why I'm applying to St. Joseph's School of Nursing in Fort Worth It's only an hour away and I can live at the school if I can get in."

Her mother looked concerned. "It's a Catholic school. Might be different than what you expect."

Kathleen hadn't known many Catholics and wasn't sure what her mother was implying by the question. "I don't know."

Her father tried to explain. "They're a bit more strict than you're used to. Some of them folks like the structure, some don't."

"Well, I can be finished in three years. It's not like I have to stay there forever. I figure I can do anything for three years, then I'll be a nurse. Besides, it's close enough I can come back home whenever I want. Trailways has bus service between Fort Worth and Stephenville regular."

"What about the money part of it? Tuition, housing, books and all?" her mother asked.

The truth was, Kathleen had thought a lot about the money, which was precisely why she didn't tell her parents to which schools she was planning to apply. Her dream was to go to school in another town, another county, a new adventure with the opportunity to meet new people and learn about how they lived. She longed to escape the conformity embraced by most everyone she knew. Perhaps she would one day come back to Stephenville. Perhaps she wouldn't. But she had a yearning to travel, to explore, to take chances. She also had a desire not to disappoint her parents. Though annoying at times, they had supported her, loved her and cared for her through almost eighteen years. She couldn't bring herself to ask them for the extra expense that an out-of-town school would require. They had sacrificed enough for her. She wasn't sure how to make it happen, but she would try to find a way to finance the extra cost of living elsewhere. Or perhaps it was all a dream and she would resign herself to being a Tarleton State student. The thought was depressing. She wasn't sure if she could be successful in pursuing her dreams, but she was determined to try. "I'm not sure about the money. I got a $200 scholarship for being Rodeo Queen last year, but it's not near enough. Maybe I'll get a part-time job. Lots of students have jobs. Besides, I haven't even applied anywhere yet, much less gotten accepted. You know, if going to college means you have to like Shakespeare, maybe I'll end up working at the feed lot. At least I know something about cattle," she offered with a sarcastic smile.

Her mother chuckled. Her father didn't. They were both looking at the third envelope, the one from the University of Texas at Austin. Her dream school. Home to the State Capital, Longhorn football and thousands of students from all over Texas and some from other parts of the country or perhaps other parts of the world. Kathleen had never been to Austin, but she had seen pictures in books and watched athletic events on TV. It was bigger than life, about as far away from Stephenville as she could possibly dream of going. And, they had recently started a school of nursing. The application for admission was a reflection of her dream, not her reality. A seeking of confirmation that she was capable of something big. The reality of attending was another matter. "I just want to apply to Texas. Probably not smart enough to get in, and if I do I doubt if I could figure out a way to go."

The room became quiet as they ate their dinner. Finally, her father looked her in the eye and with the calm, nurturing voice Kathleen loved said "Your mother and me, we're mighty proud of you."

Kathleen felt a lump in her throat and her eyes became misty as she fought back tears. "I'm sorry I didn't tell you about the schools. I didn't want you to worry. It's my responsibility. My problem."

Kathleen's mother smiled. "Sweet girl, we've been on your side since the day you were born. We've learned a few things in this life." She put her hand on Kathleen's. "We're on your side and we want your dreams to come true. But we can't be helpful if we don't know what's going on."

Kathleen looked down, avoiding eye contact. "Sorry."

Her mother stood and fetched some fruit salad from the refrigerator. "What does Rusty have to say about all this?"

"He doesn't know. Well, he sort of knows. Everyone knows I'll be going to Tarleton State like all the rest. Haven't told them any different. Besides, they're probably right."

Her father broke a brief silence. "Well, I've got one question." Looking scornfully at Kathleen he asked "Who in the hell said ya wasn't good enough for UT Austin? That's crazy talk!"

Kathleen smiled and brushed a tear from her cheek. "We'll see."

Tuesday, October 7, 1969

The following Tuesday evening Rusty was alone in his garage, learning the drum cadence from The Statler Brothers modestly popular tune *You Can't Have Your Kate and Edith Too*. Baked Cotton would be practicing the tune on Saturday, if they could find the time to learn their individual parts before then. On top of a tool chest was sheet music for the tune Jake had carelessly forgotten to take home the previous Saturday. Although Jake was a skilled guitarist and vocalist, even he needed to practice the new tune before Saturday. That clearly wasn't going to happen if he didn't have his music.

Rusty stopped playing his drums as his mother came into the garage. She moved the music aside and opened the tool box. "What are you working on?" he asked.

"That silly part on the blender came loose again. I need a screwdriver to tighten it."

"That's Jake's music," he explained, though she hadn't asked and didn't seem particularly interested. "Mind if I drive it over to him? He'll need it to practice."

"It's almost 10:00. Can't you give it to him at school tomorrow?"

"I'm done practicing, done with homework and done with chores."

"OK, but I want you home by 11:00. Understood?"

"Thanks, Mom. Good luck with the blender."

"Your clock's ticking young man."

Rusty laughed, got up from his drums, grabbed Jake's music and hurried towards his truck parked in the driveway. The drive, though short, was an excuse to get out of the house. He didn't need an excuse, but his mom sounded more agreeable if he had a reason. Driving home from Jake's house after dropping off the music at just after 10:00 PM, Rusty saw Anna crossing the street in front of the Dairy Queen. She looked vulnerable, alone under the late evening street lights. Rusty stopped the truck near the curb a few feet in front of Anna's direction. He leaned over and rolled down the passenger side window as she walked towards the truck.

"Evening," he said, trying to sound friendly.

Anna gave the truck and its occupant a dubious look. After a moment, she smiled. "Hi there."

"Where you headed?"

"Home."

"You live around here?"

"About a mile or so down the road. It's not far."

"Hop in. I'll give you a ride."

Anna wore a tired, weary look as she hesitated to respond. Without a word, she opened the passenger door and climbed onto the bench seat.

Rusty couldn't imagine why someone would want to walk home alone after 10:00 PM. "Car trouble?"

"What?" she scornfully asked.

Rusty was suddenly unsure of himself. She had responded as if he had asked an absurd question. He was only trying to be friendly. "Your car in the shop?"

Anna smirked. "I wish. Don't have a car."

"So how do you get home from work?"

Anna gave him an incredulous look which he interpreted as having asked a dumb question. "In three blocks, you'll make a right."

"You always get off around 10:00?"

"Why do you care about my hours? What difference does it make when I work?" Then, after a brief awkward silence, she added "Weekdays. Weekends I work till 11:00 or later, depending. Turn left at the stop sign."

Rusty drove into a part of town he had been to on occasion but never stopped. Small but neat frame houses were nestled among a few homes that were not so neat. Some looked barely habitable. Interspersed with the houses were trailer homes, some of which were well kept and others clearly needing repair. Cars and trucks were parked in several of the front yards. Battered metal trash cans, some with lids, most without, were placed near the street. A stray dog ran briefly along the side of the truck, as if chasing Rusty out of the neighborhood. "How long you been working at the Dairy Queen?"

"About a year. It's an OK job. Pays the bills."

Rusty considered this for a moment. Pays the bills? They're in high school, she doesn't have a car. What bills? He started to ask but thought better of it. "Which house is yours?"

"It's up a ways. On the right with the yellow porch light on." As she was talking, Anna removed her shoes and socks. "Sorry, been standing for five hours straight. Toes needed some air."

Rusty stopped the truck in front of Anna's home and was surprised by its modest appearance. Other than the porch light, the house was dark. "You worked five hours at the Dairy Queen tonight?" Rusty found the prospect of so many hours working on a school night incomprehensible.

"Hijole. You ask a lot of questions. I helped my mom clean a customer's house for an hour, then I worked four hours at the Dairy Queen." Changing the subject, she turned towards Rusty and gave a tired smile. "You sure took care of the drunk dumb ass from the college. I don't think we'll see him in there again."

They laughed. Anna with shoes in hand exited the truck, closed the door and gazed at Rusty through the open passenger side window. "Appreciate the ride," she said and headed toward her house. After taking a few steps, to Rusty's surprise she turned and marched back to him with a look of determination. Placing her hands on the open passenger window, she sternly asked "Why did you do it?"

Rusty was taken aback by her confrontational attitude. Was she angry with him for some reason? Once again, he was dumbfounded by a girl. Would he ever unravel the mystery of the opposite sex? He hesitated, then replied, "Well, I thought you might want a ride."

"Not that. The drunk. Why did you get involved? It wasn't your problem."

"Are you saying I should have ignored what he did to you?"

Anna rolled her eyes and smiled. "No. What you did was sweet, even honorable. I just don't know why you did it."

"Well, I figured it was the right thing to do at the time. He needed to be put in his place." He paused as he gazed at Anna, not sure what was happening. Her dark eyes held his, searching for something in him. "Did I do the wrong thing?"

"No. I appreciate what you did," she softly replied. "It was just unexpected."

She paused, and Rusty sensed that she wanted to say more but wasn't sure if she should. He remained quiet.

"Actually, it was really sweet," she explained. "I'm usually on my own when things happen. A lot of kids at school, probably some of your friends, see me as a dirty Mexican. They call me names when they think I don't hear, then say they were only joking when I get in their face. But it's no joke. At least, I'm sure as hell not laughing. I work harder than any of them. Anyway, it was nice to have someone in my corner."

"It was a team effort. You pouring the Coke onto his crotch was hilarious!" They both laughed. "Did you see him doing the air bicycle thing? What a dumbass."

Anna's smile was warm, her beauty intoxicating. A light breeze blew her long dark hair from a face that glowed in the yellow hue from the porch light. "Gracias," she said warmly as she turned towards her home.

As Anna reached her porch, Rusty said, "Hey."

"What?" she asked as she turned from the first step of the wooden porch.

"I don't know how you work so much and go to school. I'm impressed."

She smiled. "Good night, Rusty."

Rusty watched her walk to the front door, shoes in hand, and try her keys in the lock. He wondered how anyone could look so beautiful after working so many hours. The door squeaked as she opened it. Too quickly, she was gone. Driving towards his home, he reflected on his life, his home, his everything. He had just glimpsed another world and realized how much of what he had was taken for granted, as if he deserved it all. But Anna was no less deserving. Perhaps more deserving. She certainly worked harder than anyone he knew. She was different. A woman. A girl. Tough and resilient. He wondered if he would get to know her better and if he did, where it might lead. It was as if she were a mystery Rusty wanted to solve, but wasn't sure if he could, or should.

Saturday, October 11, 1969

Michael never knew what to expect from Ian. The strange kid didn't ask much of his orchestra classmates. He was mostly quiet and kept to himself, engrossed in music and little else. He and Michael were on friendly terms, but did not know each other well. They hadn't had a significant conversation since the sharing of lockers drama at the beginning of the school year. Michael was surprised when Ian sat in a chair next to him a few days ago following orchestra rehearsal. "What's up?" Michael had inquired.

"My grandmother's in the nursing home," Ian began. "I think they'll really like it if we provide them with a concert. I already have the sheet music. Easy stuff. Mix of classical and some turn of the century popular tunes. There's three of us playing, but we could use another violin. I was hoping, if you're not too busy maybe you would join us on Saturday."

Michael couldn't help but smile. The idea of being too busy for anything in this speck of a town was laughable. "Sure, I can do that," he replied.

The next Saturday morning Michael rolled out of bed and, for the first time in his life, walked into a nursing home, violin in hand.

Michael wasn't sure what to expect at the nursing home. The first thing he noticed was the smell. Not really a bad smell, just unusual. Sort of a mixture of hospital smell and cleaning products. The second thing he noticed were the smiles. As he walked into the dining room where the concert was to be held, an elderly woman grabbed his arm, looked directly at him, and with a grin said, "We're so happy to see you."

"Thanks. I'm glad to be here."

Another older woman's voice from the side of the room chided, "Now Ruth, quit flirting and come sit down. He has to get ready."

Ruth let go of Michael's arm and rolled her eyes. "Gotta go. Sheriff's after me." She winked at Michael and turned to join her friend.

Michael expected to see a lot of elderly people. He expected to see wheelchairs. He expected to see nurses. What he did not expect to see was Kathleen. Across the room she was carefully applying makeup to a woman who was clearly enjoying the experience. The woman sat in a wheelchair, apparently with limited ability to speak or even move without assistance. And yet, there was Kathleen somehow communicating, making the old woman laugh.

The other three members of the quartet had found their seats and were waiting for Michael, who was mesmerized by Kathleen's interactions with the old woman. Finally, Ian said, "You know Michael, in my experience the violin is much easier to play if you actually take it out of the case."

Michael laughed. "Sorry." He found his seat and proceeded to tune his violin with the other members of the quartet. Kathleen hadn't seen him yet, but he couldn't help but steal a glace her way as the quartet prepared for the concert. There was something warm and nurturing in the way she interacted with the old woman. She was clearly at ease. Michael guessed she had been to the nursing home before, perhaps many times.

The last tune was a piece by Bach that Ian clearly enjoyed but Michael and most everyone else in the room found boring. A few residents had fallen asleep while others started shuffling out of the room. As they were putting their instruments away, several residents walked or wheeled by to let them know how enjoyable the concert had been. Michael felt good about the experience and found himself in no hurry to leave. Kathleen was helping residents to their rooms, apparently to prepare for lunch. A janitor was beginning to set up folding tables for lunch, converting the room back to its intended purpose. Michael finished putting his violin away and approached the janitor. "Need some help?"

The janitor, who was not much younger than many of the residents, smiled. "Is a pig's butt pork?" When Michael didn't respond, he laughed and added, "Darn tooten I'd like some help. I'll arrange the tables where they sposed to be and you tote them chairs."

Michael was placing the last of the chairs into position when Kathleen entered the room. He looked at her, then turned towards the janitor. "We finished, boss?"

"We sure enough is. Thank ya, son."

Kathleen picked up her purse as Michael walked her way. "Look at you being all helpful," she chided.

"You finished here?"

"Yes."

Michael picked up his violin. "Come on, I'll walk out with you. I hear this place can be dangerous."

Kathleen laughed as they turned towards the front entrance. "Good concert. The residents had a fun time. Especially the old tunes they actually knew."

"Thanks. I saw you helping with that woman's makeup. She loved it. You're good at this stuff. You work here?"

"No, just volunteer some. It's fun. I love these people, all of them."

They reached Kathleen's mother's Oldsmobile far too quickly. As Kathleen was opening the driver's door, Michael took a deep breath to gather some confidence. "I'm starving. How about you and me get some lunch? I'll buy."

"What did you have in mind?"

"Dairy Queen?"

Kathleen chuckled. "You certainly have an eye for the fancy places." She smiled and added, "Actually, it's a great idea. I'll meet you there."

§§§

Driving to the Dairy Queen, Kathleen felt an anxious tension. She had been happy to see Michael in the string quartet, though she didn't know why. Since the sock hop they had often seen each other in the hallway and were friendly in a casual sort of way. And yet, as she watched him play his violin, she had to admit to herself that there was something intriguing and rebellious about Michael. He was certainly different than anyone she had known. In her world, girls were not supposed to be attracted to hippie boys, which Michael seemed to be. And boys certainly would never challenge authority, as Michael had with Mr. Jamison. While she and her friends were concerned about what others thought of them, Michael appeared to go his own way with an air of confidence. Watching him perform, Kathleen could not deny her desire to know him better. She just wasn't sure how.

Kathleen arrived at the Dairy Queen three minutes before Michael. The wait felt like an hour. *Settle down*, she told herself as she found a table. *It's only a burger then you'll be on your way.* Fortunately, she didn't recognize anyone in the restaurant, just a few students from the college and nobody she knew working the kitchen.

Michael walked in and slid into the opposite bench. "You always keep the girls waiting?" she asked.

"There were three red lights! How did you get here so fast? Were you burning rubber in an Oldsmobile?"

"No, my mom would kill me." She smiled, "I know my way around."

"What are you hungry for?"

Kathleen didn't feel as hungry as she was a few minutes earlier. "Just a ham and cheese sandwich with a small Coke."

Michael ordered Kathleen's sandwich, two Cokes and a cheeseburger at the front counter. Returning to the table, he handed Kathleen her drink. Kathleen took a sip and smiled. "Tell me something I don't know about Oregon."

"OK, what do you know about it?"

"Nothing really."

Michael tried to look serious. "Well, it's a state in the northwest," he answered as their food was delivered.

Kathleen took a piece of crust from her sandwich and playfully threw it at Michael.

"Oregon is great," he began. "Trees that touch the sky. The Cascade Mountains are amazing. Then out east there's a lot of farm land. It's a different world from Stephenville."

"You miss it, don't you?"

"Yes. A lot."

"Do you miss it because of what it is, or because it's where you grew up and you know people?"

Michael pondered her question for a moment. "I don't know. Probably both. You know how it is when you're away from home."

"No, I don't" she replied with intensity while looking Michael directly in the eyes. "Never been outside of Texas. Never been far from home. Never seen a damn thing."

"I figured you liked it here."

"Didn't say I don't. But that doesn't mean I might like somewhere else too. I bet lots of people move from wherever they're from and find other places to like just as much or more than where they came from. You never know until you try," she shrugged. "It's like, you're probably not happy here. But who knows, maybe Stephenville will grow on you."

Michael shook his head. "Not likely. I don't exactly fit in around here. Wrong accent, wrong car, wrong everything in most people's eyes. Don't get me wrong. The nursing home gig was fun. But it's obvious that I don't have much in common with most anyone around here. I'll head back to Oregon this summer and be done with this place."

"Sounds lonely. Give it some time."

Michael changed the subject. "What are you looking for? Are you applying to college?"

Kathleen told him about her dream of being a nurse, of exploring new parts of Texas or even areas out of state. She also told him about Rusty, mostly the good, a little of her frustrations. Thirty minutes passed. She found Michael easy to talk with, as if her private thoughts were safe with him. He was a good listener. Another thirty minutes passed. Michael began sharing his frustrations with being forced to leave his friends in Oregon, his feeling of isolation in Stephenville and his adamant objection to the war in Vietnam.   Another thirty minutes passed.

Kathleen glanced at her watch. "Oh, no. I have to get going. I was supposed to be home over an hour ago. My mom's going to wring my neck," she explained, quickly grabbing her purse and sliding off of the bench seat.

Michael slid off of his bench seat and walked out with her towards the Oldsmobile. As they reached the car, Michael said "You know, the concert and lunch with you have made this a good day. Didn't know that could ever happen in Stephenville."

Kathleen quickly turned to face him with a look of mocking concern. "So, you didn't like the sock hop?"

"No, I did. It was fun," he stammered.

Kathleen smiled and gave him a quick kiss on the cheek. "Thanks for lunch, Oregon," she said as she slid into the car and got it started.

§§§

Kathleen was gone, leaving Michael alone in the Dairy Queen parking lot. He smiled as he turned towards his VW Beetle. What just happened here? Did he actually have a good time with someone from Stephenville? Do girls here often kiss guys on the cheek, or did it mean something else? He drove home feeling confused. Feeling happy.

Monday, October 13, 1969

Michael rushed to his seat for after school orchestra practice. In the first row Ian sat, shoulders slumped with a heavily bruised face. As the students were preparing their instruments for rehearsal, the director looked at Ian with concern. "Are you OK? What happened?"

"Accident. I'm OK to play."

From Michael's seat in the second row, he could clearly see Ian's facial bruises. *Whatever it was*, he thought, *it was no accident*. Ian's face reminded Michael of some of his hockey injuries.

When the rehearsal ended Michael moved to the seat that had been vacated next to Ian. As Ian gathered his sheet music, Michael asked, "Who did that to you?"

"Nobody."

"Well, Nobody sure landed a hard punch. What happened?"

"Apparently, your history book cover with the peace sign gets some people pissed off."

Michael suddenly felt guilty and indignant. "Oh crap. I'm so sorry. Who did it?"

Ian hesitated. "Jake. But if you tell anybody it will only make things worse. It's not the first time, you know."

"Jake the guitar player?"

Ian nodded.

"Did you report it? Who saw it?"

"We were in the restroom. Nobody else was there. I went to the school secretary and asked for an excused absence from class for a couple of hours. My eyes were swollen so much I could barely see. Did she ask why? Nope. Ask what happened? Nope. Just said OK like she didn't want to know and told me my absence would be excused. This place doesn't give a rat's ass about me."

"Not true. What about Mr. Jamison and our orchestra director? I bet they'd help."

Ian turned towards Michael and hesitated, as if he were uncertain of what to say next. "It won't happen again," he said as he crossed his legs just enough to reveal a switchblade knife protruding from his sock and secured with a rubber band around his ankle.

Michael was speechless for a moment. "Do you know what you're doing?"

"Actually, I do." Ian stood up and walked out of the building, leaving Michael sitting stunned in an almost empty rehearsal room.

Driving home, Michael considered his options. If he talked with Mr. Jamison, Ian would almost certainly be expelled. The cruel reality was that word would get out and Ian would no doubt be beat up, likely worse than occurred today. Further, he would have violated Ian's trust. However, not reporting could result in serious injury. Something needed to be done, quickly. Maybe he could talk Ian into leaving the switchblade at home. Maybe he couldn't.

Tuesday, October 14, 1969

Rusty drove his truck into the school parking lot a few minutes before the first period bell. As he gathered his books from the bench seat, he saw Jake drive into the lot in his AMC Rambler. Rusty decided to wait for his friend as Jake locked his car and started walking towards Rusty's truck and the school. Jake looked tense, perhaps troubled. Baked Cotton's practice the prior Saturday morning had gone well enough, but Jake had been all business. None of the usual kidding around between songs. Something was not right.

As Jake approached the truck, Rusty gave a cheerful "Hey, man. How's the best guitarist in Stephenville?"

Rather than continue walking past the truck towards school as Rusty expected, Jake stopped and stared at him. Tension lined his face. "Clay's starting basic training. He'll be shipping out to Vietnam when they're done. It sucks."

Though the news had been anticipated, Rusty was still surprised. "Your brother's doing a good thing for the country."

"Mom and Dad are worried as hell. So am I. He didn't have to get drafted. He was in school with a scholarship. Who the hell does that?" Jake's emotions escalated. "Then I turn on the TV and the damn hippies are raising hell. They call it *The Days of Rage*. I saw one guy on TV with a sign *Politicians Lie, GIs Die*. Like we need to be reminded that thousands of our guys have already been killed in Vietnam. Then I see that pussy Ian with a peace sign on his history book. I may lose a family member fighting for the very people who don't have the balls to support their country. I like the bumper sticker; *America, Love it or Leave It*. Ian and the damn hippies need to get out of here."

"Where would they go?" Jake's look made it clear to Rusty his question wasn't relevant.

"Straight to hell."

"Clay's a strong guy. He'll do well. The Commies will never know what hit them. And you know what, I'm proud to know Clay. He's a hero, doing what's right even if a bunch of fools say he's wrong. Your brother's a good man."

Jake looked away as his eyes misted. He took a deep breath and said more calmly "It chaps my ass when people don't support the military."

"Me, too. I'm on your side buddy. Let's get to class."

The boys walked into the school building and went their separate ways. After second period classes, Rusty noticed Ian walking the hallway towards him with Jake close behind. Ian had replaced his book cover, this time with a larger, bolder peace sign. Jake knocked the book from Ian's hand, the book with peace sign sliding across the hallway floor towards Rusty. Somebody laughed. Rusty kicked the book soccer style back towards Ian, but Jake intercepted and again kicked it. Ian turned to Jake with fear and anger. "Stop it!"

More laughter. Rusty kicked the book back towards Ian. When Ian leaned over to pick up his book, Jake shoved him against the lockers, making a loud noise as Ian landed against the metal doors and slid to the floor in pain. A small cut near his eye started to bleed. Students slowed to watch the drama. Some laughed. Jake stood over Ian. "Pussy."

Ian reached towards his ankle for his switchblade. Seemingly from nowhere Michael ran towards Jake and knocked him to the ground. Jake looked startled for a moment, but got to his feet quickly. Jake took a step towards Michael and received a fist to the side of his head. Trying to protect his friend, Rusty grabbed Michael from behind. As he did, Jake landed two hard fists to Michael's face. Michael violently elbowed Rusty's gut, taking his breath away for a moment. Ian disappeared into the crowd of students gathering to watch the fight. Determined not to let the elbow to his gut go unanswered, Rusty shoved Michael's chest into the metal lockers. As Michael turned towards Rusty with a clenched fist, Rusty punched hard, determined to end this fiasco. Michael ducked, and Rusty hit a locker with his fist. Rusty felt searing pain in his hand and for a moment was afraid that it might be broken. As he stepped back to inspect his hand, Jake lunged towards Michael. Defending himself, Michael took a swing at Jake. To Rusty's surprise, Michael's arm was stopped cold in mid swing by a strong grip.

Red faced and frowning, Mr. Jamison took quick control. "You three boys in my office. Now! The rest of you, get to class. We will not have fighting in this school!" The crowd dispersed as Mr. Jamison escorted the three boys to the principal's office.

Michael took one of the wooden chairs in front of the desk while Jake took the other. Rusty stood with his bruised and bleeding hand concealed in the pocket of his pants.

Mr. Jamison stared at the boys in disbelief and frustration. "I expected better from the three of you."

Jake looked incensed, sitting on the edge of his seat. "He started it!" Jake yelled as he pointed to Michael. "Came at me for no reason."

Rusty became worried where this would go. As long as he could keep his hand in his pocket he appeared unscathed. Michael clearly was injured by the bruises on his face. The side of Jake's face was swollen and he was almost out of control with anger. The normal punishment for fighting was two to three days suspension. If they got three days, he and Jake would be ineligible to play in Friday's football game. Mr. Jamison would be unpopular with the coaches as well as folks from the community who enjoyed the games. Worse, Rusty would have to explain to his mother why he was not allowed in school. Her disappointment in him would be heartbreaking. Mr. Jamison was tough. This could go either way.

Mr. Jamison looked at Michael. "Do you have anything to say?"

"They were kicking Ian's book around in the hall. Jake pushed Ian into the lockers. Could have hurt him. It wouldn't have been the first time."

Jake shot a look of hate towards Michael. "Liar!"

Michael ignored Jake and continued. "Have you seen the bruises on Ian's face? Teachers don't care." He turned towards Rusty and Jake. "Don't you guys get tired of hurting people?"

Rusty was confused. He had helped a friend in trouble. He had no regrets. He had also helped humiliate a weaker student. Michael's question left him remorseful and agitated. He decided to stay quiet.

Jake looked at Mr. Jamison and, in an effort to sound reasonable, said "We were just having some fun. Rusty shouldn't even be in here. It's between me and Michael."

"And Ian," Mr. Jamison added. He sat for a moment, obviously collecting his thoughts regarding what to do next. The boys were silent before him. Finally, in a voice of resignation, he said with quiet authority "I'm disappointed in all of you. I expected better from you. The school has a policy of mandatory suspension for fighting. Jake, Michael, you are suspended for the balance of today and the next two days."

Rusty felt a surge of relief. "Can I go?"

Mr. Jamison looked carefully at Rusty. "No. We're not finished here." Then looking at Jake, he said "You boys did a good job at the sock hop. I bet you'd like to play in front of your friends again, right"?

Jake sat back in his chair, "Yes, sir."

"Not going to happen. Ever. You've lost the privilege with your behavior today. We're planning another sock hop in November. We'll find another band or use a DJ, unless of course you can make some changes."

Jake looked confused. "Changes?"

"Two conditions. One, if I see or hear of anybody hurting Ian in any way, Baked Cotton will be history at this school."

Jake turned to Rusty. "Can he do that?"

Rusty was impressed with Mr. Jamison's thought process. Once word got out, Ian would be safe. Rusty smiled a little in spite of himself. "I think he just did."

"Second," Mr. Jamison continued. "Next sock hop, Ian has to play at least two songs with you."

Michael snorted. "This I've got to see."

Mr. Jamison leaned forward and sternly said to Michael, "You're not to say a word about this to anyone. This is Rusty and Jake's issue. Don't interfere or there will be consequences, understood?"

"Yes, sir," Michael responded with what to Rusty sounded like an air of sarcasm.

Rusty looked at Mr. Jamison. "I don't think after today Ian will want to be around us."

"Two songs. And you'll have to find a way to convince him."

Rusty marveled at how Mr. Jamison had enforced the rules, protected Ian and forced Jake to try to make amends with a boy he disliked. Brilliant. Annoying, but brilliant.

Mr. Jamison shook his head. "I don't ever want to see this behavior from you boys again. Understood? You're better than this. Jake, Michael, you need to leave the campus now. Rusty, get to class."

§§§

Michael made his way to his car and sat in the driver's seat, considering what to do next. He had to get to Ian. Had to get him to give up the knife. However, Michael was banned from campus. Perhaps he could somehow sneak into the school through a back door. As he pondered his options, the lunch period bell rang. Soon after he saw Ian, sitting alone under the flag pole, eating his sandwich. Michael was struck by how lonely and vulnerable he looked. Getting out of the car he yelled "Hey, Ian."

Ian looked up and, recognizing Michael, walked across the street to the parking lot. Face bruised, shoulders slumped and eyes looking down, he appeared dejected as he approached Michael's car. He finally looked up when the boys were face to face. "You didn't have to do that," Ian mumbled.

"Give me the knife."

"No. I need it. It's the only one I have."

"I just got suspended from school because of you." Michael's voice was measured as he tried not to let his frustration escalate. "I want the knife."

"They're coming after me. You know that, don't you?"

Michael laughed. "Give me the knife. Nobody's going to hurt you, except maybe me if you try to walk back into school with a weapon. I'm serious. Give it to me or I'll take it from you."

Ian looked skeptical. He reluctantly pulled his pants leg up, retrieving the knife from his sock and handed it to Michael.

"Any other weapons at home or anywhere else?"

"No."

Michael gave him a hard look. "I saw you reaching for your knife. Lucky for you, nobody else seemed to notice. You could have gone to jail today. Don't be stupid."

"I'm tired of getting beat up! Tired of being made fun of."

Michael smiled and put a reassuring hand on Ian's shoulder as he placed the switchblade knife in his pocket. "You're going to be fine. Better than ever. Trust me on this one." Michael could tell that Ian wanted to believe him. "Be cool."

Ian shrugged. "OK," and turned back towards the school.

Michael drove home with a jumble of emotions. Relief at having kept Ian out of trouble and getting the knife from him. Frustration that he was suspended for doing the right thing. And more than ever, feeling like an outsider, homesick for Oregon. He suffered a deep loneliness, knowing he had no friends in school and didn't fit in socially with his classmates or, for that matter, the town. He wondered if this nightmare would ever end.

Arriving home, he slumped in a recliner in the den and took out the switchblade knife. Pushing the button, he was startled at how quickly the blade extracted itself from the handle. He carefully returned the blade to the handle and pushed the button again. The shiny silver blade with a sharp tip again sprang from its handle. Picking up a piece of newspaper, he made a cut that felt more like a razor blade than a knife. It would have taken little effort for Ian to inflict a serious injury with a blade so sharp, so lethal. He closed the knife into the handle, wrapped it in newspaper, found an empty cardboard milk carton and deposited the wrapped knife into the carton. Making sure the top of the milk carton was closed, he felt some relief as he placed the package in the trash.

Eating his lunch alone at home, Michael began to worry about the implications of his suspension. Staying home from school for a couple of days was no burden. But he had no books, no assignments. If his grades took a dive, his chances of getting into Oregon State could be in jeopardy. Thus far, his grades were good enough, but not so much that he could afford to fall behind. He couldn't stand the thought of getting stuck in this hellhole of a town.

§§§

Kathleen heard about the fight while sitting with Janice and several other students during lunch. The rumor mill generated different versions of events. But there was one constant. Jake and Rusty had harassed Ian, and Michael had come to Ian's rescue. Students around the lunch table laughed when they described how Ian slumped to the floor. The consensus feeling was that Ian probably got what he deserved and Jake's suspension was somehow unfair. Few students seemed to know Michael's name. They wouldn't miss Michael, or even give him much thought. He was a new kid, an outsider, different and not like the others. A misfit.

The lunch period over, Janice and Kathleen walked the hall to their next class. Kathleen finally asked Janice, "Why do you think Jake and Rusty were picking on Ian?"

Janice hesitated long enough for Kathleen to suspect that Janice knew more than she was willing to discuss. "Jake's having a hard time with some things. He'll be OK."

"What things?"

"Nothing. He's fine," she replied with a hint of irritation. "Ian probably deserved what he got."

Kathleen didn't think so. She and Janice had been friends for a long time. She gave Janice a skeptical look. As Janice rolled her eyes, Kathleen asked, "You think I should let it go?"

"Definitely."

But Kathleen couldn't let it go. Something about the fight made her uncomfortable. Kathleen felt unsettled and wasn't sure why. She had trouble showing enthusiasm at the Stingerettes after school dance practice. As usual, the dance team practice ended a few minutes before the football team's workout. She decided to watch the football boys and wait for Rusty. She didn't have to wait long.

The autumn air made the outdoors more tolerable for everyone. Rusty noticed Kathleen in the stands and approached as soon as the coach dismissed the team. With helmet in hand, he smiled and said "Hey, good lookin," as he approached.

"How was the workout?"

"Good. I think we'll kick ass on Friday."

Kathleen eyed the dried scabs on Rusty's knuckles. "What did you do to your hand?"

"Long story."

"I've got time."

"I've got to shower."

"Mom's making oatmeal cookies tonight. Want to come over after dinner?"

"The ones with coconut and raisins?"

"Absolutely."

He blew her a kiss. "See you this evening."

She watched him stride towards the locker room. Something didn't feel quite right. She walked towards the parking lot determined to talk with Rusty about it that evening, if only he would talk.

§§§

Rusty could smell the fresh out of the oven oatmeal cookies as soon as he walked onto Kathleen's front porch. They were his favorite, and nobody made them quite like Kathleen's mom. He knocked on the front door and heard Kathleen holler from the kitchen for him to come in, which he did. Kathleen's hands were covered with suds as she washed mixing bowls. Her mom removed a cookie sheet from the oven. The entire kitchen smelled wonderful. He smiled and faked a concerned look. "Now, Mrs. Wilcox, I'm not sure those cookies are good enough for your family. You should probably let me try one while they're hot to make sure they meet standards. Your family should only get the best."

He saw Kathleen roll her eyes. She dried her hands as her mother offered Rusty a fresh baked cookie. He marveled at how cookies always tasted great hot out of the oven. "Well now, I'm not sure these are good enough for your family. I think I'll try another so we can be sure," he said as he reached for another from the pan. After finishing the second sample, he smiled. "Actually, that's the best I ever had."

Mrs. Wilcox smiled. "Oh, you always say that. You just want another one!"

Kathleen interrupted Rusty's efforts to be charming towards her mother. "Why don't we take a few cookies on the porch with some iced tea?"

Mrs. Wilcox winked at her daughter. "Oh, I don't think so. I'll be watching *The Glen Campbell Goodtime Hour* on TV."

Kathleen smiled. "You and Daddy have fun with your show," she said as she poured two glasses of iced tea and Rusty grabbed more cookies.

The autumn air was crisp but not too cold. Kathleen wore a light sweater. Rusty was in short sleeves, enjoying the cool country breeze. The autumn grass was turning the color of straw. Leaves blew through the yard. A billion stars were only partially obscured by the front porch light. They sat close on the porch swing. Kathleen picked up Rusty's injured right hand and frowned. "That looks painful."

"Looks worse than it feels. I'm all right."

"What happened?"

"Damn hippie jumped Jake in the hall. Ducked when I swung at him and I hit the locker."

"You mean Michael? Why would he want to fight you?"

"Got me. We didn't do nothin to him. Weirdo," Rusty replied with agitation. "He should mind his own damn business."

They were quiet for a moment. Then Kathleen said tentatively "I heard that Jake shoved Ian."

"So? We were just having some fun, playing a little soccer with Ian's book in the hall. No big deal."

"How much fun was Ian having?"

"Hell, I don't know. We were just goofing around. It was no big deal until Michael got pissed. He and Jake both got suspended. What a dickhead." Kathleen moved slightly away from him on the porch swing.

"I don't get why y'all would pick on someone like Ian who can't defend himself. What did he do to you?"

"Jake started it," Rusty responded defensively.

Kathleen gave Rusty an angry piercing look and firmly said "Then why didn't you end it, the way you did with Anna at the Dairy Queen? How come you didn't defend Ian? If you had done that, Jake and Michael wouldn't have been suspended. How do you think Ian felt?" There was a tense silence between them. "Don't you get tired of hurting people?"

The question stung. It was the same question Michael had asked in Mr. Jamison's office. Rusty hadn't meant to hurt anybody, except perhaps Michael for attacking his friend. Kathleen's questions left him feeling embarrassed and angry with himself for his part in harassing Ian. He stared across the porch at nothing and was silent for a moment to consider his options as Kathleen glared at him, waiting for answers he could not give. His resentment building, he felt a distance growing between them. For the last few weeks it felt as if they were pretending to be boyfriend and girlfriend when they were really just friends. At the moment it didn't feel particularly friendly. He stood and walked toward the porch rail. The television could be heard faintly from the house. Turning to Kathleen he tried to change the subject. "I bet Ian and Michael are both queer," he said, trying to better justify his actions.

Kathleen laughed. "I'm pretty sure that's not true." Then in a prosecutorial voice she added "And even if it were true, what difference would it make?"

Rusty didn't have a response, so he tried another tact. "My dad died in the military. I bet he would have hated Michael and Ian with their peace signs on books and all. They're just a couple of freaks. And Michael, he's the biggest damn hypocrite of all. Puts peace signs on his book covers and then attacks my best friend! What a dumbass." He shook his head. "Maybe the beating he got will teach him a lesson."

They were quiet for a moment. As Rusty grabbed another oatmeal cookie, Kathleen said, "I'm pretty sure Michael was trying to protect Ian the same way you were trying to protect Jake. I just don't get why you and Jake need to pick on Ian. He hasn't done anything to you. How can you defend an employee at the Dairy Queen but not Ian? Or does your sense of justice only apply to hot girls?"

Rusty felt himself becoming increasingly annoyed with Kathleen. Although her voice was calm, he felt she was being accusatory. To make matters worse, her accusations had merit, at least where Ian was concerned. He expected support and understanding from Kathleen, not this. It felt as if the distance between them was growing, adding to his frustration. In exasperation, he raised his voice. "You're supposed to be on my side! What's wrong with you?"

"I am on your side," she responded with unfiltered frustration. "But this time, you were the bully! My God Rusty, you're more than twice as big as Ian!"

Rusty's anger escalated. He pointed at Kathleen. "Don't you judge me! You don't know everything!"

"I know you and I know Jake. And I know you're better than this!"

"You don't know what the hell you're talking about!" he responded louder and angrier than he intended. "I don't need this crap from you." Rusty's outburst had clearly surprised Kathleen. The distance between them was now growing quickly. Then in a more measured tone he added "You have no right to lecture me on what's right and wrong. You don't even know what you're talking about. Back off."

Kathleen stared penetratingly, her face with a look of determination, her hands tightly gripping the seat of the porch swing. "You want me to back off? OK, how far?"

Rusty knew that they had reached a breaking point. He found that he had neither the energy nor the desire to continue. This was no longer about the fight at school, this was about he and Kathleen. He stared at her for a moment then looked down. In a quiet voice he asked, "Are you happy? I mean, with us?" Kathleen looked at Rusty with a blank expression. It wasn't a trick question, but one he had wanted to ask for several weeks but never had the courage. She remained silent. As he leaned against a porch post looking at his boots he said with a soft, sad voice. "I don't know. This isn't working." He shook his head and with a sad voice added, "I'm done." Kathleen said nothing as he walked towards his truck. He started the pickup and put it in gear. Kathleen never moved from the porch swing, never made a sound. As the headlights found her face, he saw a tear fall across her still blank expression. He drove away.

§§§

Kathleen dried her tears. Both of her parents were on the couch watching TV, her mother snuggled close to her dad. They looked at her with concern as she walked into the house. Her mother asked, "What was that yelling all about?"

"Rusty and I had a fight. I think we just broke up."

Mrs. Wilcox shook her head. "I doubt it. Couples have fights from time to time. He'll cool down. Then he'll be back."

"But Mom, I don't know if I want him back. It doesn't feel right any more," she explained as her eyes became misty.

After a brief silence interrupted by a TV commercial, Kathleen's father said, "Ya know darlin girl, there's lots a fishes in the ocean. There's a million guys out there that would love to have ya."

Kathleen managed a smile. "Well, it would be nice to find just one. I don't need a million."

Her mother gave a reassuring smile, stood up and hugged her daughter. "We love you and we think you're wonderful. You'll be at the university in Austin before you know it. I'm sure you'll meet lots of boys there."

Her father added "Ya don't havta rush sweet girl. I mean, if he's a goodun, he's worth waitin for. If he's a badun, you end up spendin too much time with him anyways."

Kathleen marveled at her daddy's wisdom. "Well, before I get to meet all those boys in Austin, I still have to find a way to pay for it."

"We'll figure somethin out," her father said as Kathleen sank into a recliner.

Her mother sat back on the couch and looked at her daughter with concern. "Kathleen Wilcox. Did you leave my ice tea glasses on the front porch?"

Kathleen smiled. "Guilty," she replied as she went back to the porch to retrieve the glasses before retreating to her bedroom for the evening. Something within her sensed that there was unfinished business. What that business was, she could not yet identify. Perhaps it would be more clear in the morning.

Wednesday, October 15, 1969

Michael's parents left him at home to brood over his misfortune. Never had he felt so isolated and miserable. And for what? He had done the right thing. Even his parents, never the ones to support getting suspended from school, had told him how proud they were of him. He had told them the story, unedited, including the part about Ian's switchblade and how he had disposed of it. They had wanted to appeal his suspension and expose the reason for the fight. However, Michael had assured them that, thanks in large measure to Mr. Jamison, future violence was unlikely. Though skeptical, they agreed to wait on talking with anyone at the school, at least for now.

Michael spent the morning looking through college catalogs, trying to consider where to apply as a backup plan to Oregon State. Until he could leave for college, he would be alone, with more bruises on his face than he had friends.

Michael considered himself an antiwar pacifist. He could get rough in the hockey ring, having no misgivings about hitting his opponent with a hard body check. It was part of the game. He was trying to stop his opponent. But he never wished to inflict injury on another player, even when the game became intense. The fact that he had found himself in a fight at school and that it was the right thing to do was confusing.

Though he harbored some anger at his misfortune, he mostly felt isolated and mistreated. Senior year of high school was supposed to be a happy time. Michael was anything but happy. He had to get out of this hellhole. The sooner the better.

§§§

Kathleen's alarm clock awoke her as usual. She showered and turned on her transistor radio as she dressed for school. Moving the dial from the normal country station to rock and roll, the tune *Here Comes the Sun* from The Beatles' new *Abbey Road* album played. As the band sang the chorus, it felt as if the music was

94

directed to her.   She found a colorful blouse with a determination to overcome whatever obstacles the world had waiting. While putting on her makeup, her spirits were further lifted as The Lovin Spoonful sang their hit *Do You Believe in Magic*.   Turning off the radio, she considered herself in the mirror and liked what she saw. Speaking to her reflection, Kathleen asserted, "OK world. You can knock me around, but you can't knock me down."

Kathleen drove her mom's Oldsmobile to school. With a few minutes before class, she went directly to Mr. Jamison's office. She was greeted by his secretary. "Good morning, Kathleen. Can I help you?"

"I think so. What happens to a student's assignments when they're suspended? Do they get to make up the work?"

"Kind of depends on the teacher. You'd have to ask them. If you're worried about Jake, Janice told me she was going to get his assignments from his teachers, so I think he'll be fine," she said reassuringly.

"What about Michael?"

"Who?" The secretary frowned, "Oh, yes. Well, I don't know about him."

Kathleen said, "Thanks," and left.

Since the long lunch at Dairy Queen with Michael, she knew that getting into Oregon State was important to him. She could relate. She also knew that three of their six classes were the same, though at different class periods.

She found Ian in the hall after fifth period. He had a small scratch on his forehead and he looked as if he were trying not to be noticed as students moved through the crowded hallway. Kathleen caught up to Ian and tapped him on the shoulder. "Hey," she said with a friendly smile.

Ian held his books tight to his chest and looked at the floor as they walked the hall. For a moment, Kathleen felt that she was being ignored. Finally, Ian said, "What do you want?"

"I'm sorry you got pushed around yesterday."

"Me too."

"Here's the deal. Michael was suspended. I've been talking with his teachers and the only two classes with assignments due while he's out are Pre-Cal and Latin. I don't take those classes, but I bet you do."

"Yes. So what?"

"I want you to loan him your books."

"Why?"

"So he doesn't fall behind. Come on, it's the least you can do after what he did for you. Be cool."

"What if I don't get the books back?"

"Really? I can't believe you're even asking that question. It's for Michael. You know you'll get your books back." The bell for 6th period rang, startling them both. "Come on!"

Ian reluctantly handed the books to Kathleen. "You're a sweetie. Thank you."

Kathleen should have been in sixth period dance with the Stingerettes. She found the dance teacher. "I have to go. Cramps are killing me," she lied.

"I understand. Hope you're better tomorrow," the teacher said, then quickly turned her attention to other matters.

Kathleen returned to Mr. Jamison's office. A student helper who Kathleen had known for some time, though not well, was filing documents. No doubt, she was part of a vocational education program. Kathleen smiled. "Hey Deb, how are ya?"

"Busy. What's up?"

"I need a favor. Can you look up Michael Thornhill's address?"

"Who's he?"

"He had to miss school today. I'm taking him his homework so he doesn't fall behind."

"Well, we're not really supposed to give out addresses."

"Correct. But you're also not supposed to stop a student from being successful. I'm sure Mr. Jamison would be OK with it." Kathleen wasn't sure if it was true, but didn't have much else to offer.

"What would I approve of?" Mr. Jamison asked, startling both girls as he came out of his office.

Kathleen started to smile, then remembered she was supposed to not be feeling well. "I have Michael Thornhill's assignments. I'm not feeling too well. Thought I'd drop his assignments off to him on the way home."

Mr. Jamison looked skeptical. "What's wrong with you?"

Kathleen blushed. Somehow using cramps as an excuse in front of Mr. Jamison felt embarrassing.

As if he could read her thoughts, he said "Never mind." Mr. Jamison and Kathleen had known each other for several years. There was a level of trust between them. "Deb, let's make an exception this time and give Kathleen the address."

Deb opened a grey metal cabinet and found Michael's file. She wrote Michael's address on the back of a discarded envelope and handed it to Kathleen.

"North Lydia Avenue," Kathleen read aloud. "No idea where that is."

Deb responded, "It's in the new area near the college. You know, where they've been building those brick homes for the professors."

"Got it. Thanks, Deb," Kathleen smiled and turned towards the door.

Five minutes later Kathleen was on her way to Michael's house, feeling anxious and not knowing why.

Michael's home was in one of the nicer parts of town. Not affluent, but comfortably middle class. There were no cars parked in front yards, dogs were kept behind fences and all of the lawns were well kept. Though there were some pickups in the driveways, most people here apparently preferred sedans. It wasn't hard to find the right house. The blue VW Beetle parked next to a Dodge Dart in the driveway stood out, even in this neighborhood. Kathleen parked at the curb in front of the house as a middle-aged woman came out of the front door. The woman paused as Katheen gathered Michael's books and got out of her car.   Walking up the driveway towards the house, Kathleen smiled at the woman and said "Hi."

The woman looked at her quizzically. "Can I help you?"

"Yes ma'am. I was hoping to find Michael at home. Are you his mom?"

"I am."

The women shared a friendly handshake. "I'm Kathleen. A friend of Michael's. Sorry about what happened to him at school. I was able to get a couple of assignments for him. Thought I'd drop them off so he doesn't fall behind."

Michael's mom paused. "Wait a minute. Are you the girl with the RC Cola and peanuts?"

"Yes ma'am."

Mrs. Thornhill laughed. "Door's open. Go on in. See if you can cheer him up a bit. He told us what happened with him trying to protect that Jake kid. It's a shame."

Kathleen started to explain that it was Ian who Michael was protecting, not Jake. However, she decided it didn't matter. Mrs. Thornhill probably got the story confused. "Pleased to meet you ma'am." They shook hands again and Kathleen walked towards the front door as Mrs. Thornhill got into the Dodge Dart.

Entering the house, Kathleen heard a Bob Dylan record playing loudly.   She was reasonably sure Michael's parents would not approve of the volume. Parents are like that. She walked into the den and found Michael, sitting on the floor in baggy sweat pants and a white t shirt with his back against a couch. In front of him was *Life* magazine. Michael seemed focused on an article about Martin Luther King. The late minister was sometimes referred to by locals as a communist or a radical. It occurred to Kathleen that the views seemed racist, though they were not often challenged.

Michael obviously hadn't heard her come into the house. She watched him for a brief moment, then with a voice that was markedly louder than the record player said "Hi, there!"

Michael jumped, clearly startled by the intrusion. As Kathleen laughed, he looked at her, momentarily speechless in his surprise. He finally offered a tentative "Hi. Um, what's going on?"

His face still showed a bruise on his left cheek and a black eye on the right, noticeable but not as bad as Kathleen expected. The rumor mill at school made it sound as if Michael had been beaten badly by Jake. He looked to Kathleen to have taken some hits, but certainly not badly beaten. "Your mom told me I could come in. You look better than I expected."

"That's good, I think. Come on in. Have a seat."

As Michael stood up to turn the record player off, Kathleen sat cross legged on the floor, back to the couch near where Michael had been sitting. "I heard about how you tried to defend Ian. I'm impressed. Ian doesn't deserve to be treated like crap. He's kind of a weird kid, but Jake needs to quit picking on him."

Michael sat cross legged in front of Kathleen, their knees almost touching. "I thought Jake was a friend of yours."

"He is. Known him since elementary school. I like Jake, but picking on Ian isn't right."

"Jake's an asshole! Damn bully."

Michael's black eye couldn't hide a look of despair. Kathleen changed the subject. "I'm not sure what's gotten into Jake lately. Anyway, you have assignments due in Pre-Cal and Latin while you're suspended. Ian loaned me the books. Teachers said if you turn in your assignments the day you get back, they'll grade as if you were in class." She looked at him and smiled as his attitude softened before her eyes.

"Why?"

"Well, school policy says---"

"No. I mean, why are you doing this?"

"You told me when we had lunch about how you want to go to Oregon State. Figured you'd want to keep up while you're suspended."

"Thanks. I didn't think anybody cared what I did around here."

"I do," she said, looking into his eyes as if searching for something.

Michael's bruised face relaxed. He changed his position, sitting next to Kathleen with his back to the couch. "I'm glad you're here, but surprised as hell. I mean, it was your boyfriend who held me so Jake could take his cheap shot punches."

She paused, then softly asked "What boyfriend?"

Michael chuckled. "Is there more than one?"

Kathleen was quiet for a moment. Although word of the breakup had gotten around school, the acknowledgement saddened her. She felt mixed emotions. Hopeful anticipation that she was finally free to find someone who would make her happy, and melancholy resignation that it wouldn't be Rusty. "There's less than one."

Michael looked at Kathleen with surprise. "I'm sorry."

"Don't be. It's a good thing, I think. Sort of inevitable. May as well get it over with."

"Maybe you and Rusty will find a way to get back together."

Kathleen looked down and shook her head. "I don't think so. He's a good guy. We've known each other forever and maybe we'll stay friends. I just don't know. What I do know is I'm done dating him. He feels the same. We've been good friends and a lousy couple. It's weird. Time to move on." She suddenly had an urge to talk, and talk she did. For the next few minutes, she expressed her sadness that Rusty didn't seem happy with her as more than a good friend. How she felt a failure in her efforts to be more. Kathleen explained how her frustration with being Rusty's girlfriend had grown over time. She was sure that he felt the same.

Kathleen appreciated that Michael was a patient listener, allowing her to drone on about Rusty without interruption. It felt good to verbalize what she had been feeling. Finally, she said, "It's time to move on. I'll be OK."

"OK? Are you kidding me? You're amazing! I bet there are guys all over town who would love to take you out. You're smart, a nice person, fun to be with and you're the best-looking girl in the whole damn high school!"

Kathleen smiled. She knew she was well liked. But she didn't want guys all over town. She didn't know if Michael was the guy for her, but she wanted to find out. He was certainly different from anyone she knew, and different might be a good thing. They didn't know each other well and perhaps nothing would come of it. He was an adventure she was anxious to take, if only he would make the invitation. She turned to look at him. "Well, Rusty says--"

"Can we talk about something else?"

Kathleen realized that Rusty was her history. Michael was, maybe, her future. She felt better for having unloaded her feelings about Rusty on Michael. There was nothing more to be said. Time to move on. "Does your eye hurt?"

Michael ignored the question and suddenly looked a little nervous. "Um, I'd sure like to have your phone number."

Kathleen took a pen from her purse and wrote her number on the cover of Michael's *Life* magazine, near the picture of Coretta Scott King. Handing the magazine to Michael she asked "How's your eye? Does it hurt?"

Michael smiled. "Never felt better."

Kathleen rolled her eyes. "Macho boys." Standing up she said "I'm supposed to be home sick, so I'd better get going." She gathered her purse and they walked towards the front door. Pausing before leaving the house she turned towards Michael with a warm smile. "Well Oregon, I'm glad you're OK."

Michael smiled. "I'm fine." He gave her a quick hug, then added "Hey, thanks for bringing my assignments."

"No problem." The hug, though brief, was just what she needed. To her surprise, the pain of her breakup with Rusty was already starting to recede. She turned to smile and wave as she noticed him watching her walk towards the Oldsmobile. As she started the car, she marveled at how a week that had started so poorly could maybe end up good after all. Maybe.

§§§

Rusty sat on the floor of his bedroom, trying with minimal success to focus on his English homework. It felt as if his world was churning in slow motion and all he could think of was Kathleen. If walking away from her was the right move, why did he feel so alone? It felt like a sucker punch to the gut. As the crescent moon rose, he might have gone to her house to apologize if Janice hadn't told him Kathleen wasn't feeling well. To make matters worse, if he apologized, what exactly would he apologize for? Except for kicking Ian's books across the hall in school and scaring the kid, he had done nothing wrong. And if they were together again, would he be happy? Most days he enjoyed her company. The mystery of girls was why they, or rather Kathleen, couldn't just enjoy the friendship, the comradery.

At 9:45, Rusty could no longer tolerate the lonely confines of his room. Vowing to finish the English homework later in the evening, he wondered into the kitchen. His mother was on the kitchen phone, immersed in what sounded like a long and pointless conversation about a colleague at the bank. "Mom," he interrupted.

She covered the phone speaker. "I'm on the phone. Don't interrupt."

"I'm going out for an ice cream."

"OK, son. Don't stay out too late. School night." She then continued her phone conversation as if Rusty had never entered the room.

Rusty parked the truck in the Dairy Queen parking lot shortly before 10:00. He could see Anna in the store cleaning up. Her hair captured within a net, she worked with quiet efficiency and determination. Finishing her work, she playfully threw a rag at her manager who pretended to throw it back at her before laughing and waving goodbye. As she walked out of the store, she removed her hair net and shook out her long black hair. Rusty was awestruck. There were other hard-working people in school. There were other smart, attractive girls in school. But none of them could compare with Anna. She walked briskly across the parking lot. Rusty rolled down the truck window to get her attention. "Hey, Anna, how about you pull back your reins a bit."

She walked towards the truck. "What are you doing here?"

"Thought I'd come by and give you a ride home."

"Why?"

"I don't know. Just like your company, I guess. Do I have to have a reason?"

"There's a reason for everything. You may not know what it is, but there's a reason." She walked around the truck and settled into the bench seat.

Rather than starting the truck, Rusty turned to Anna. "Looks like you're in a good mood. What happened?"

"Everything. Made an A on the Pre-Cal test."

"Nobody makes an A in Pre-Cal."

"Well then you can call me Nobody, because I sure did. Plus, my papa got a big fencing job on a farm in Bluff Dale. Should keep him busy for the next three weeks. Good money and close to home.   And to make it even better, I don't have any homework tonight. Are you going to start this truck or are we going to try to talk it into taking me home?"

Rusty managed his first smile of the day as the ignition came to life. The churning feeling in his gut eased a bit. Anna watched him for a moment while they drove in silence. "Why the long face? Rough day?"

"You have no idea. I don't want to bring you down with my troubles."

"Look here, gringo, I made an A in Pre-Cal today. There's nothing you can say that would bring me down. And by the way, you just missed my street."

Rusty made a U-turn. "I guess you heard about the fight."

"What fight?"

"The one with Ian Freestone."

"The skinny kid Ian? Dios Mio. Why would anyone want to fight him?"

Rusty found her question to be more curiosity than judgmental. As they stopped in front of her home, he said "If I tell you about it, you'll think I'm really an asshole and I can't take that right now."

"Mira. First, I would never think of you as an asshole. Your ass is kind of cute really. Second, I could tell you sad stories that would make yours look like Disneyland. Third, I don't have homework, so I have some time for once. And by the way, thanks for the ride."

Something about Anna was different. Very different. Never one with the gift of gab, the idea of talking with Anna felt strangely safe. She clearly wasn't one to gossip. In fact, she didn't seem to have many friends, or the time for them. Rusty rested his head on the steering wheel. "I broke up with my girlfriend."

"I'm sorry," she softly said, and Rusty was sure she meant it.

Rusty sat back in the bench seat and stared out the windshield. "It was going to happen sooner or later. We'd been together for almost a year. She's a lot of fun, but it no longer felt right. It's my fault."

"So, you beat up Ian because you broke up with your girlfriend?"

"Nobody beat up Ian. He's fine." Rusty told her of the fight, how he had hit the locker with his fist and how Michael and Jake had been suspended.

"You were as involved as Jake, but you get to stay in school. What's that like for you?"

"Maybe a little guilty. That's stupid huh?"

"No."

"What the hell. There's nothing I can do about it anyway."

"Wrong, mi amigo. In the Catholic church, we say confession is good for the soul. You're a good person. I bet you know the right thing to do."

"You think I should tell Mr. Jamison what happened? That's nuts. I could be suspended."

"You want to do the right thing or the easy thing?"

What was it about this girl? It was as if she had a window to his soul. How did she do that? She didn't seem impressed with his football prowess or his popularity. Somehow, she saw beyond all that in a way that others did not. He felt vulnerable and yet safe with her. Her brown eyes had a soft, nurturing quality as she waited for his response. "You ask tough questions."

"I bet they're the same questions you've already asked yourself."

"You want to go out some time?"

"You don't want to take me out. I work all the time. Only day off is Sunday afternoon. Besides, what would your friends say if you went out with a Mexican girl?"

Rusty looked directly at Anna. "To tell you the truth, I don't give a damn what they'd say. I only care about what you'd say."

She opened the passenger door and turned with a smile. In a somewhat seductive voice she said "Well, you know where to find me." She closed the door and looked through the open window. "I know you'll do the right thing."

Rusty watched her walk towards the front porch. Her long black hair blew in the breeze. Anna turned to wave as she walked through the front door. Then she was gone, leaving Rusty alone in his truck wishing she was still with him.

Thursday, October 16, 1969

Rusty awoke feeling apprehensive about his day. He recalled the time he refused to obey Coach Childress in football practice. How it felt like the right thing to do, but wasn't much fun. What he had to do today would be a similar experience.

Before first period class, Rusty stopped by the principal's office. The secretary smiled. "Well good morning, Rusty. How's your mom doing?"

"She's fine. Thanks for asking."

"What can we do for you this morning?"

"I'd like to talk with Mr. Jamison if he's available."

"Sorry, he's meeting with one of the faculty. Let's see," she said as she looked at an appointment book. "He could see you at third period. Would that work for you?"

"Sounds good."

"I'll put it in the book, give you a hall pass and see you back here at the beginning of third period. Can I tell him what this is about?"

"I need his advice on a couple of issues."

She handed Rusty the hall pass. "OK. I'll let him know."

After his second period class, Rusty made his way to the principal's office. He had never known anyone to visit the principal voluntarily. This would be a new experience. He was determined but nervous. Mr. Jamison was speaking with the secretary as Rusty walked through the door from the hallway.

"Hello, Rusty. I heard you were coming by today. Come on in."

Rusty sat in the wooden chair across from Mr. Jamison's desk. "Thanks for seeing me."

Mr. Jamison closed the door and settled into his leather chair. "No problem. What can I do for you?"

"Well, I need to let you know what really happened yesterday and also need your advice on a couple of things." He swallowed, cleared his throat and fought the nervous feeling that was tying his guts in a knot. "The fight with Jake and Michael, I was in it. Jake and I were playing a little soccer with Ian's book. Didn't mean anything by it. Jake shoved Ian. Didn't hurt him. Then Michael came out of nowhere and attacked Jake. I grabbed Michael and Jake landed a couple of punches before Michael elbowed me in the gut, hard. I took a swing at Michael but he moved and I hit the locker." Rusty held up his hand showing abrasions across his knuckles. "Basically, I was as involved as they were."

Mr. Jamison sat back in his chair and gave Rusty a curious look. "Why are you telling me this?"

"I don't know, it seemed like the right thing to do."

"You know son, they say confession is good for the soul."

"Are you Catholic?"

"Heavens no. Why?"

"You remind me of something a Catholic friend told me."

"So why would you and Jake pick on Ian? What did he do to you?"

Rusty looked at the floor, feeling ashamed. "Nothing."

"I could suspend you for this, though I'm not sure there's anything to gain by doing so." Mr. Jamison leaned forward with his elbows on the desk. "If I don't suspend you, will you give me your word that you will never pick on Ian again?"

"Deal."

Mr. Jamison relaxed his shoulders and leaned back in his chair. "You said you needed some advice. What kind of advice?"

Rusty felt relieved that the worse part of the discussion was over. "Two things really. How are we supposed to get Ian to play in our band if he's scared of us?"

"Well, if it were me, I'd start with a sincere apology. You'll have to find a way to convince Ian you mean it. He probably doesn't trust Jake. I think they have a history. I imagine it will have to start with you. It can be done, but it won't be easy. You'll need to find some way to be helpful to Ian, to build his trust."

"You're right. It won't be easy."

"You said there were two things you wanted advice on."

"Your making Jake and me defenders of Ian was brilliant. How did you learn to do things like that?" Rusty asked, proud of himself for recognizing Mr. Jamison's intentions.

"Before D-day, I was stationed in England. We had a lot of young, scared and restless GIs. Commander assigned me to the MPs, Military Police. We needed all the men we could get for the invasion, so I figured locking them up wouldn't help us any. I had to find ways of keeping the peace among the troops."

"I've been thinking. Maybe I want to go into law enforcement. You know, be a policeman. How would I do that?"

"Well, military experience is helpful. That plus a couple of years of college would probably get you a job. It's not an easy life, Rusty. Police work a lot of nights and weekends and have to deal with difficult and often dangerous situations. It's an important job. I think you'd be good at it."

"I think it's what I'd like to do."

"You're also a gifted football talent. You have options."

Rusty was suddenly nervous, afraid to reveal his private thoughts. He took a deep breath and in a low voice mumbled, "Don't like football."

Mr. Jamison looked surprised. "Most people do best when they follow the thing they have a passion for. Discover your passion and you can do anything."

The confidence Mr. Jamison showed towards Rusty left him feeling hopeful for the future. A future of his own making, not the preconceived assumptions of others. He stood and shook Mr. Jamison's hand. "Thank you, sir. That's really helpful."

"Glad to help, son. Follow your passion and you'll do well."

§§§

Michael looked through the *Stephenville Empire-Tribune* newspaper. While the war in Vietnam dominated most TV broadcasts and print media, the local newspaper reported that the hours of operations had changed for the Stephenville City Dump. Michael's more immediate problem was trying to determine where to take a date. The newspaper offered few options. He knew of a bowling alley. The movie theater was showing a western called *100 Rifles*. Not the kind of title Michael wanted for a first date. The drive-in movie was showing *Funny Girl*. After that the only option was dinner at Dairy Queen. He shook his head at the limited offerings. The drive-in was the only reasonable choice.

Michael sat alone in front of the yellow rotary phone in his parent's study feeling nervous. Beside the phone lay the magazine with Kathleen's phone number. He'd asked out a few girls in Oregon. Most said yes, a few said no. But this was different. Kathleen was the only possible friend he had in Stephenville. It was her or nothing. His entire social life, limited as it was, could be crushed by one phone call. Without picking up the receiver, he dialed her number, hoping it would give him courage. The exercise didn't help. Taking a deep breath, he picked up the receiver and dialed the number.

"Hello."

"Hey. It's Michael. How's it going?"

"Well, Michael, it's going fine."

Something sounded slightly formal in her voice. Not a good sign. He gathered his courage. *"Funny Girl* is playing at the drive in. I was hoping you'd want to go on Saturday."

"Well, Michael, that sounds lovely. I've heard it's a good film. But wouldn't you rather go with my daughter?"

"Excuse me. Who..."

Michael heard a voice holler, "Kathleen, some boy wants to take me to the movies. That's sweet, but I think he'd rather go with you."

"Mom!"

Michael heard laughter as he felt enough heat in his face to burn the sun. His hands were wet with perspiration against the phone receiver. He closed his eyes for a moment to collect himself.

"Hello."

"Hi. Um, who is this?"

"It's me, Kathleen."

"Hi. It's Michael."

"Did you just ask out my mother?"

"I think so, but I got the impression she turned me down. Since she's not available, I was hoping you'd want to go see *Funny Girl* at the drive in Saturday evening."

"I'd love to. You know where our farm is, right?"

"I'll never forget it. The movie starts at 7:30. How about I pick you up at 7:00?"

Kathleen laughed. "Sounds good. Since my mom turned you down it's the least I could do. I've been wanting to see that movie."

Michael relaxed. The phone call had not gone as planned, but the end result was excellent. "Hey, thanks again for bringing my homework by."

"No problem. You're a good listener. I promise not to say a word about Rusty on Saturday."

"You know, this is going to be the best date I've ever had in Stephenville."

Kathleen giggled. "Let me guess. Your first date in Stephenville. See you Saturday, Oregon."

"Bye."

"See ya."

§§§

Rusty waited outside the Dairy Queen just before 10:00 PM. As before, Anna took off her hair net as she left work, shaking her long black hair in the breeze. Rusty wondered if he would ever tire of looking at her. She had a beautiful, exotic quality. Anna recognized the truck and walked his way, opened the passenger door and settled onto the seat.

"What are you doing?" he asked.

"You're here to take me home, aren't you?"

Rusty smiled. "Well, since you're already in the truck, I suppose I could." As they drove, Rusty told her about the meeting with Mr. Jamison. "You were right. Confession is good for the soul. But it wasn't much fun." Stopping the truck in front of Anna's home, he noticed that she seemed distracted. "What's wrong?"

"Papa hurt his back setting fence posts. It's happened a couple of times before. Aspirin and a heating pad should make him OK, but he can't work for a couple of days."

"Bummer. But you told me he's a strong guy. I bet he'll be OK. He'll probably need a little time to recover. What did the doctor say?"

Anna looked at Rusty with a pained expression that told him there was no doctor. "He needs to finish the job in Bluff Dale. Contract says he gets a bonus if it's done on time. I'm not sure he'll make it. The bonus money would have meant a lot."

"I've never known anyone who had to worry about taking care of their family the way you do."

"You rich white folks don't understand."

Rusty laughed. "Do you see the truck I drive? I'm not exactly rolling in the dough."

"But you have a vehicle. Health insurance. And I bet you don't have to eat beans and rice for lunch when business is bad. You probably even buy all your clothes new."

Rusty stared at Anna for a moment, unsure of how she felt about him. As impressive as Anna was, her distrustful nature left him uneasy. It felt as if she were exposing him to a new world, expecting him at any moment to run back to his secure way of living. Anna's world was different. It was less secure and more brutal than anything he had ever experienced. He was humbled and somewhat troubled by the recognition. Anna's strength in navigating her world left him in wonder. "How far along is he with the fence?"

"The corner posts and H braces are set, but he hasn't put in the t posts." She looked at Rusty and shook her head. "You have no idea what I'm talking about do you?"

"I'm guessing he runs a five-wire fence with the t posts 10 feet apart, but I could be wrong."

Anna smiled. "Well Señor Fence Builder, I'll have to ask Papa about that."

"You told me you're off on Sunday afternoon. How about you and I run over to Bluff Dale to work on those t posts?"

"Can't."

"Why not?"

"Rusty, it's a sweet offer. I'm sure there are lots of things you'd rather do on Sunday afternoon. And besides, we can't pay you for the work."

"I've helped put up several fences. And for the record, I don't give a damn about getting paid. Anna it's just that," he paused, unsure of how much he could, or should, reveal of himself. Anna was intriguing and a little intimidating. "If building a fence with you makes things easier for your family then it seems worthwhile. Come on, let me help out." He gazed at Anna, waiting for a reply. For the first time, she looked vulnerable and uncertain.

"Why are you doing this? Fencing is hard work."

"If I have to build a fence to help out and spend an afternoon with you, then it doesn't seem so bad. I wish you wouldn't look at me like you don't trust me. How am I supposed to change that?" Rusty wasn't accustomed to expressing his feelings to a girl. This was new territory. "Maybe it's time for me to quit doing what's easy and start doing what's right."

Anna scooted closer to Rusty on the bench seat and squeezed his arm. She rested her hand on his shoulder. "I still don't understand why."

"Maybe it's time you quit asking why and start asking why not." He put his hand lightly on her cheek, leaned over and kissed her softly.

"Que bueno," she whispered.

Rusty wasn't sure what that meant, but he sensed it was a good thing. "I'll be here at 1:00 on Sunday. We'll drive out to Bluff Dale and make a day of it."

Anna looked at Rusty with bewilderment. It was clear she had little trust in anyone outside of her family. He hoped to change that. "OK, but if you change your mind I'll understand."

"Anna, I'm going to be here come hell or high water."

"We'll see," she said as she slid across the seat, opened the passenger door and got out. "Sunday."

"Sunday." He watched her walk towards the house. The home appeared normal though modest on the outside. From the little that Anna had told him, he guessed that it was anything but normal on the inside. And he had only scratched the surface.

Friday, October 17, 1969

Rusty and his teammates didn't talk much as they dressed for the game. They were facing Brownwood High School, their toughest opponent of the season and a likely contender for the State championship. Well coached with an intimidating roster, Brownwood was seldom beaten. Their coaching staff and players moved with a confident swagger as if they were telling the world, or at least parts of west Texas, that they were very good, and knew it.

The Stephenville Yellowjacket locker room was tense with a cocktail of adrenaline and a vague sense of fear. Stephenville's head coach came into the locker room looking grim. He was followed by Coach Childress and the other assistants. The room was quiet. All eyes were on the head coach. "Boys, Brownwood has a fine football team. They think they're better than you. But they don't have Stephenville Yellowjacket pride." His voice started to rise until he was shouting. "They don't have your desire. They don't have your character and they sure don't have your talent. Let's show em how it's done! Our game. Our night. Right here. Right now!"

Rusty cheered with his teammates as his mind focused on the challenge before them. While the band played the fight song, the Stephenville quarterback ran through a big paper banner that proclaimed *Yellowjackets Burn B'wood!* Rusty and his teammates followed, the cool autumn air a welcome relief from the stale locker room.

Rusty was one of four team captains who met the officials and opposing captains at mid field. A coin was tossed and Stephenville won, electing to receive the opening kickoff. Rusty jogged off the field and stood on the sidelines, helmet in hand, ready to meet the challenge before him. The near capacity crowd whooped and hollered in anticipation of the drama about to unfold. Marching bands and cheerleaders from both schools were doing their part to keep the fans excited, though the crowd didn't seem to need much encouragement. Rusty didn't stand on the sidelines long. After the kickoff, Stephenville's offense ran three plays with minimal gain. Following a punt, Rusty was in the game.

Brownwood ran three offensive plays, one of which Rusty ended with a tackle for no gain. The night would be a slugfest. At halftime, the game was tied three to three.

Stephenville kicked off to start the second half. Brownwood's kick returner ran the ball to near mid field, where the ball was ripped from his arms and went airborne. The ball sailed towards Jake in what felt to Rusty like slow motion. Jake easily caught the ball and sprinted untouched towards the goal line. Rusty couldn't remember Jake ever touching the ball during a game. He cheered loudly for his friend, happy that Jake would finally experience a moment of high school football glory. As Jake approached the goal line, he slowed and extended his arms to the side as if he were imitating an airplane. "No!" Rusty yelled just before a Brownwood player knocked the ball from Jake's hand and recovered on the two-yard line. Rusty jogged onto the field as the coaches screamed at Jake. Rusty knew that Jake would spend the rest of the game on the bench, alone and dejected, head down.

On the first play from scrimmage, Brownwood ran for a one yard gain up the middle. Coach Childress called for Rusty to blitz from his linebacker position on second down. It was a good call. Rusty rushed through the offense untouched. A half second after the running back received the handoff, Rusty tackled him in the end zone. Safety, two points. Stephenville was up five to three.

Standing on the sidelines watching his teammates on offense, Rusty kept his eye on one of Brownwood's linebackers. The kid wasn't particularly big, but he was fast and strong. Rusty marveled at how often the kid was able to disrupt the Stephenville offense. It reminded Rusty of one of those damn mosquitos that fly around the room at night. Makes noise, bites you and flies off time and again, eluding every slap and swat that would be its death. Midway through the third quarter, the kid intercepted a pass and sprinted towards the goal line. None of the offensive players for Stephenville were fast enough to catch him. Brownwood took the lead, ten to five.

As the teams lined up for the kickoff coach Childress yelled, "Rusty!"

Rusty turned to find his coach standing with a clip board near the aluminum bench. "Yes, sir."

"Sit down!" Coach Childress sat next to Rusty and started to draw a play on his clipboard "That little B'wood twerp linebacker is killing us out there. We're taking him out." Rusty was silent, unsure of what was coming. "You're going in as a tight end on the left. We'll fake a hand off to the running back and hand it to the wide receiver who will sweep left to right. You pull and become the lead blocker on the sweep. When the little twerp comes around, I want you to hit him hard. Take his legs out."

"You want me to hurt him?"

"Kick his ass! Make him sit on the sidelines for a while. You got it?"

"Yes, sir."

A few plays later, the Yellowjackets were facing a third down and six. Coach Childress yelled "Rusty. You're in."

Rusty jogged onto the field and joined a weary but determined huddle. The quarterback called the play and Rusty took his tight end position. The play worked exactly as Coach Childress had described. As Rusty ran towards the right in front of the ball carrier, the Brownwood linebacker appeared out of nowhere. Rusty hit him high, taking him off stride and allowing the ball carrier to turn the corner for an eight-yard gain before being run out of bounds. First down.

Rusty jogged off the field and was immediately met on the sidelines by a red-faced Coach Childress. The coach grabbed Rusty's face mask. "What kind of block was that? Didn't I tell you to hit him low? You were supposed to make him feel it! What was that?"

"Well Coach, where I come from, we call it a first down."

"Don't talk back to me boy! Do you hear me!"

Rusty unsnapped his chin strap, removed his helmet and walked away, leaving his coach standing with his fingers still clinching the face mask.

The Stephenville Yellowjackets lost the game eight to thirteen. They had played well, but not well enough to win. Dressing after the game, Rusty could see that his teammates were tired, sore and frustrated. Rusty felt nothing. The loss inconsequential. Meaningless. He spoke to nobody.

Saturday, October 18, 1969

Kathleen had been on dates to the drive-in, mostly with Rusty. She tried to tell herself tonight was no different, just with a new guy. But as the time for Michael to arrive came nearer, her efforts to make the evening feel normal failed. In spite of herself, nervous anticipation fluttered in her stomach. Even her mother's occasional comments about how sweet Rusty had been didn't dampen her spirits. Kathleen sat in front of the bedroom mirror and carefully removed her curlers. She liked the way her hair flowed as she brushed it out. Taking extra time to apply her makeup, she inspected herself in the mirror and liked what she saw. Burgundy polyester slacks and a multi colored long sleeve blouse with ruffles on the sleeves completed the look. Ready for her date, she walked into the kitchen, finding both of her parents at the kitchen table.

"My my, don't you look purdy. Them boys will be coming to you like flies to honey."

"Oh, Daddy," she blushed.

Her mother gave her a look as if she were being inspected. "You do look nice. The shampoo you've been using really makes your hair shine. I may need to try some of that myself."

"Mom, can you at least try to be nice to Michael when he gets here?"

"Aren't I nice to everybody?"

"Yes, but---"

Her mother held up her hand to stop the conversation. "You know the silver necklace of mine with the horseshoe pendant that you like? Why don't you go find it? It will look good with your outfit."

Kathleen smiled. "OK. Thanks, Mom," she said as she turned towards her parents' bedroom. Finding the necklace, she put it on and once again inspected herself in the mirror. She smiled at her reflection.

§§§

Michael took a deep breath to calm his nerves as he stopped in front of the gate to the Wilcox farm, pondering what to do next. Should he park outside the gate and walk to the house, or open the gate and risk letting the cattle escape? He decided he could open the gate, rush through with the VW, then close it quickly. He didn't need to hurry. The cattle barely moved and mostly ignored him as he drove onto the Wilcox farm. Securing the gate behind him, the VW Bug's suspension squealed in protest as he bounced along the short dirt road towards the house.

Stopping the car, Michael picked up the red carnation he had bought and walked towards the front porch. From somewhere in back of the house there was a loud *moo*. As if announcing his arrival, he heard another *moo* as he knocked on the screen door. Michael rubbed his hands on his blue jeans, trying to dry the nervous sweat as he waited. No answer. No sign of life anywhere, other than the cows grazing in front and the one making noise in the back. Now what? He knocked again.

He heard Kathleen's voice from somewhere in the house. "Mom, can you get that?"

The cool autumn breeze rustled some leaves across the yard. Another *moo*. Michael looked back at his car, small and insignificant next to the pasture. The sun was sinking but his spirits were rising in anticipation. Suddenly, the front door opened. Michael couldn't help but stare for a moment at Kathleen. She looked like a dream.

"I am sooo sorry Michael. I thought my parents were in the house to let you in."

"No problem. You look amazing." He handed her the carnation.

"How sweet. Can't remember the last time anyone gave me a flower. Come on in and I'll put this in water."

Michael entered his first farm house, taking in the pleasant but unusual smells. Wooden floors creaked a little beneath his Adidas sneakers as he followed Kathleen into the worn and faded linoleum floored kitchen. Kathleen's hair bounced as she walked. He couldn't take his eyes off of her. Maybe it was the makeup. Or maybe his eyes were playing games with him. He felt like the luckiest guy alive.

"Looks like your parents went out somewhere."

"I don't know. Maybe you can meet them after---"

An older woman, probably Mrs. Wilcox, came rushing through the back door into the kitchen. "Kathleen, you father needs you. Three fifty two's in trouble."

"Damnit, Mom. We were about to go out."

"Watch your mouth young lady. Your daddy needs you."

Kathleen turned to Michael. "Sorry, be right back." She took off her necklace and handed it to her mother before rushing into a bedroom.

Michael turned to Mrs. Wilcox. "Hi. I'm Michael. What's a three fifty-two?"

"Three fifty-two is a cow and I'm Mrs. Wilcox to you. She's trying to deliver her calf and she's having a hard labor." Mrs. Wilcox turned and rushed out the back door, leaving Michael alone in the kitchen.

A moment later, Kathleen appeared. The blue denim bib overalls, flannel shirt and work boots looked strange for a girl in makeup with bright shining hair. "I have to help my daddy, then we can go. Sorry."

"Anything I can do to help."

"Sure, you can hold the flashlight for us."

Michael followed Kathleen out the back door. About forty yards from the house stood a metal barn lit with a dim yellow light. A metal corral adjoined the barn on one side and kept a cow captive. There was another loud *moo*. Michael had never been on a farm, but he sensed the cow's distress. Bud Wilcox came out of the barn carrying a chain. He looked at Michael and gave a quick "Hi there."

Kathleen entered the corral and faced the cow, laying a hand gently on her neck. "Hold on, girl. You're going to be fine."

Kathleen's dad said, "Shine that there light over here, would ya."

Michael turned the light on the cow's rump as Bud requested. To Michael's surprise, Bud reached his bare hand into the cow. "It's a big calf, I can tell by the hooves." He pulled his hand out, grabbed the chain and reinserted his hand. In a second, he had the chain somehow secured inside the cow and pulled, hard. Two hooves with a chain around them appeared. Kathleen moved to the back and she and her father pulled together. Nothing happened.

"She's pushing hard, Daddy."

"I know. Let's try again." They pulled hard on the chain, but the hooves refused to move. Kathleen lost her balance, slipped and landed in the dirt and mud. She stood quickly, mud streaked across her face and hay stuck to her hair. She and her dad were starting to sweat.

Michael felt he should do something more. "Can I help?"

Bud said, "You betcha. We need the come-along."

Michael was bewildered. "OK, where are we going?"

Kathleen continued to pull on the chain with her dad. She gave Michael a smirk as if he had said something stupid. "In the barn, there's a chain hanging from the wall with two hooks and a lever. It's called a come-along. Can you get it for us?"

Michael rushed into the barn, found the come-along and brought it to Bud. One end of the come-along was attached to a metal post, the other to the chain that was still wrapped around the unborn calf's hoofs. Bud cranked the lever while Michael held the light on the cow's backside. The hooves started to move out, then the calf's head. The hoofs and head were covered by a somewhat transparent membrane. Kathleen tore the membrane away with her bare hands, exposing the calf's white face. Bud continued to crank the lever. Suddenly, lying on the ground was a calf. Kathleen knelt down and removed the chain as well as what was left of the membrane blanketing the calf. Michael was speechless as he watched the calf take its first breaths. Kathleen stood up and wiped her forehead. Her hands and clothes were smeared with fluids from the cow, sweat and mud that she tried to wipe off with a rag. "Whew, we did it," she said with an obvious feeling of satisfaction.

Bud smiled. "You done good, darlin."

Michael wasn't sure if Bud was talking to Kathleen or the cow, but it didn't matter. There was something magical about watching the birth. Raw, difficult and natural. As Bud put the come-along away, Kathleen climbed over the corral fence. Michael followed. Standing outside the corral, he shined the flashlight on the calf as the cow inspected the newborn. A billion stars filled the sky, unencumbered by city lights. Kathleen stood beside him as they watched in silence. Michael looked at Kathleen in the dim light. "That was amazing."

She squeezed his arm. "You have to understand. This is our life, our business. It's what we do, what we've always done. Breeding cattle, cutting hay, it's all money in the bank for us." They were quiet for a moment as they watched the newborn. Kathleen shook her head and looked disappointed. "I'm sorry we missed the movie, Michael. Sometimes the timing around here sucks. Why don't you go in the kitchen while I get cleaned up?"

"Can I stay here a minute? I'd like to see what happens."

"I can tell you what happens. Before long, maybe a half hour, maybe an hour or so, the calf will stand and start to nurse."

"OK, but can I watch for a minute?"

"Suit yourself. When you get tired, come on into the kitchen. I need a shower."

"You sure do."

Kathleen gave him a playful punch on the arm before turning towards the house. Michael stayed with his flashlight trained on the cow as she inspected her calf. Witness to a miracle of nature before his eyes.

§§§

Michael walked through the back door, flashlight in hand as Mrs. Wilcox sat at the kitchen table crocheting a sweater. "Have a seat," she offered. "Kathleen will be out in a few minutes."

Michael sat at the kitchen table across from Mrs. Wilcox. "Thanks."

"Was that the first calf you've seen born?"

"First anything I've seen born."

Mrs. Wilcox stopped her crochet for a moment in disbelief. "Didn't you ever have pets? Like a dog or a cat?"

"Yes ma'am, had a pet once. But I never had a dog or cat."

"What was it, a gerbil?"

"Bee."

"Oh, well that's different. Keeping bees is serious business."

"Not bees. Bee."

"Are you trying to tell me you had one bee?"

"Yes ma'am. It was a guard bee. Kept it in the back yard."

Mrs. Wilcox looked as if she were trying not to smile. "I think I'm going to hate myself for asking this, but how in God's green earth did you keep a guard bee?"

"Well, his name was Buzz. I remember one time when I was about six years old a boy a couple of years older was picking on me. It looked like I was going to get beat up, so I ran home. The big boy chased me right into my back yard. Buzz saw what was happening and flew into the boy's left ear. The boy swatted at his ear, but Buzz was too fast. Before long, Buzz was going from one ear to the other and the boy was beating himself silly on the side of his head trying to stop Buzz. The boy ran off, but the next thing I knew his dog ran into the yard."

Mrs. Wilcox tried to look serious, but failed. "That's about the dumbest thing I ever heard."

"Well, Buzz went after the dog same as he had done to the boy. And to this day, you know how you see dogs shaking their heads real fast and their ears are flopping all around? Well, that's the dog thinking about Buzz."

§§§

Kathleen walked into the kitchen wearing blue jeans and a clean flannel shirt, no makeup, her hair clean and damp. She had tried to dress quickly, not wanting to leave Michael alone for too long. The night was clearly ruined. No doubt, delivering calves was not considered a normal date in Oregon. He'd probably run off at first opportunity, never to be seen on the Wilcox farm again. She had been looking forward to tonight. It felt as if she had been teased into feeling good again, only to return to harsh reality.

Michael and her mother were at the kitchen table. To Kathleen's astonishment, her mother was laughing at something Michael had said. "Well, what's this all about?"

Michael grinned. "We were just talking about pets."

Mrs. Wilcox shook her head as she stood up from the table. "Don't even get him started. I'm going to watch TV with your daddy as soon as he gets cleaned up." Unseen by Michael, she winked at Kathleen as she left the kitchen. *What the hell just happened?* she thought.

Kathleen turned to Michael. "What pet? Do you have a dog?"

From the next room, her mother said "Don't go there, Kathleen! Trust me, you don't want to know."

Michael shrugged. "So we missed the movie, let's do something else."

Kathleen couldn't imagine where they would possibly want to go and she was reasonably sure that Michael didn't know either. "Want to pop some popcorn?"

"Sure."

Kathleen got a skillet and some oil from the pantry. Michael took them from her and said "I've got this. You've had a busy night."

Michael poured some oil into the skillet, added popcorn kernels, put the lid on the skillet and started the gas stove. While the oil was heating, Kathleen squeezed lemons for fresh lemonade. The popcorn started popping as Michael moved the skillet back and forth across the stove. The kitchen filled with the sweet smell of fresh popcorn. Kathleen found a large mixing bowl and carefully filled it with the fresh popcorn.

"Let's go check on the calf again," Michael suggested. Carrying the popcorn and two glasses of lemonade, they made their way to the corral. The calf was on unsteady legs, taking its first nourishment from its mother. "That was one of the most amazing things I've ever seen."

Kathleen smiled. "Not exactly your normal first date."

"I don't know how many first dates I'll have, but I know I'll never forget this one. You and your dad were amazing."

"You think so?"

"Hell yes. You worked together like a real team, the two of you."

"Three of us. Don't forget the cow. She was working harder than any of us. Come on, let's go sit on the porch."

They walked around the house and sat on the porch swing, rocking gently. Kathleen wondered if the night might not be the disaster she imagined. The soft glow of the porch light illuminated a world that went no further than the porch, or needed to. She told Michael about the routine her dance team had done during halftime the previous night. She started to tell Michael about how Rusty had made a tackle in the end zone resulting in a safety, but decided against it. Instead, she talked about how the Yellowjackets had lost to Brownwood in a close game. "You should come to a game. It's fun."

"Well, it's not like I know a lot of people around here. It's not much fun sitting by yourself."

Her heart felt broken by the loneliness she detected in his voice. To make matters worse, he wasn't likely to make many friends. He looked different, acted different. The qualities she was attracted to were the same qualities that would make it hard for him to make friends. Plus, he had a fight with Rusty and Jake, two popular boys. "I know it's hard for you, moving here when you did."

"It's a pain in the ass, but I'll be OK."

She looked into his eyes and whispered "Michael Thornhill, you're so much more than OK." He put his arm around her. Not just draped over the back of the chair as Rusty would do, but actually around her shoulders. She leaned into his embrace, closing what little space on the porch swing there had been between them. It felt safe. It felt right. It felt slightly mischievous. They gently rocked for a moment more and stared into space. Kathleen felt that they were on the edge of something, both holding back.

Michael looked into her eyes. "If I only have one friend in Texas, I'm glad it's you." He kissed her gently.

Kathleen put down the bowl of popcorn that had been in her lap and settled back into Michael's arms. He kissed her again, and then again. He opened his mouth and their tongues did a slow dance together. She loved it. Kathleen could feel the desire from his kiss, the passion in his arms around her. The warmth of their embrace was interrupted by the drop in temperature and autumn breeze. "I'll be right back." She got up from the porch swing, leaving him alone with the popcorn in the dark coolness of the evening. Returning with a crocheted blanket, they wrapped themselves in its warmth. He gently kissed her neck and ran his fingers through her hair. They kissed again, then again. Kathleen wished the night could go on forever. Much too soon, the porch light flashed off and on.

Michael frowned. "What's that all about?"

"It's my signal to come in." She gazed into his eyes. "But not yet." She pulled his head closer and their tongues resumed the slow dance. The light turned off and on several more times.

"I hear there's this movie called *Funny Girl* at the drive in. How about we go next weekend?"

Kathleen tried to fake a frown. "Well, I know you asked my mom out first. But since she turned you down, it's a date." She stood up, folded the blanket and picked up the mixing bowl with popcorn, most of which they had neglected to consume. Michael picked up the lemonade glasses to take them into the house. "You'd better let me take those. I don't think my parents want a boy in the house at this time of night. I'll get them later."

Michael put the lemonade glasses down and wrapped his arms around her as they stood near the front door. "Tonight was nothing like I imagined."

Kathleen looked at him quizzically. "Are you disappointed?"

"Nope. It was better than ever. I'll never forget it."

"Me either."

Michael kissed her one last time and turned towards his car. She watched him drive away, wanting nothing more than for him to come back.

Sunday, October 19, 1969

Rusty felt agitated. Church was over at noon and he promised to pick Anna up at 1:00 to work on the fence in Bluff Dale. His mother had been chatting with a couple of church ladies for fifteen minutes with no sign of stopping. They had driven to church together, which was their habit. On this Sunday, he regretted not changing the routine.

Sunday church was important to his mother, though Rusty wasn't always sure if it was religious importance or social. Maybe both. He interrupted. "Mom."

"Oh Rusty, don't interrupt. Where are your manners?"

One of the church ladies looked at Rusty and smiled. "You look nice this morning, Rusty. I can tell your mother raised you right."

"Thanks," he managed, trying to sound friendly. "I have an appointment at 1:00, so I'll need to be going."

Rusty's mom frowned. "Well all right then." Turning to the church ladies, she added, "I guess we'll have to finish this on the phone."

They finally made it home at 12:40. Being a few minutes late to see Kathleen somehow had been acceptable. But Anna was different. It would be difficult to earn her trust, particularly if he arrived late. Outside of her family, she relied on nobody and trusted others even less. Rusty could sense that his football prowess and popularity meant nothing to her. He quickly put on an old pair of blue jeans and a faded flannel shirt. Somewhere hidden in his room were the thick socks he wore with his work boots. No time to look, he put the boots on over the thin dress socks from church and started to rush out the door.

"Stop right there, young man. Where are you going in such a hurry?"

"Mom, I told you. I have to help a friend build a fence in Bluff Dale."

"But you haven't had lunch yet."

"I'll get it later. Should be home by early evening."

"School night."

"I know. Bye, Mom." Rusty hurried out the door and started the truck. By some miracle, he arrived at Anna's precisely at 1:00. Walking onto the front porch, he could hear laughter and talking from inside the house. A part of him regretted not taking Spanish in school. He knocked.

Anna answered the door, wearing bib overalls, an old shirt, John Deere cap and her hair in a pony tail. Rusty couldn't tell if the look in her eyes was pleasure or surprise. Perhaps both. Behind her two boys were playing with toy cars on a cardboard ramp. A little girl, maybe eight years old, was playing with a doll. Anna opened the front screen door to let him in. "Hola!"

Rusty entered the home, which was much smaller than he imagined. The children stopped to inspect the stranger. "How y'all doing?" he tried to sound friendly.

All three children looked at Anna. "Mira. This is Rusty. He's here to help Papa with a fence."

Anna's mother emerged from the kitchen with a paper sack. Her resemblance to Anna was unmistakable. "I made you a treat," she said with a warm smile, handing Rusty the bag.

Anna smiled. "This is mi mam'a. She made fresh tamales for us."

"Umm. They smell great. Thanks! I'm Rusty," he said as he shook her hand.

"De nada," she replied.

Anna looked over her shoulder at her mother as she walked out the door. "Adios."

Their first stop was Anna's father's truck, where they gathered fencing tools. Anna explained that the supplies they would need were already at the job site. With the tools in the back of Rusty's truck, they started towards Bluff Dale.

Anna looked quizzically at Rusty as they drove. "I can't believe you're doing this. I still don't understand."

"Looked to me like y'all could use some help. Isn't that what neighbors do?"

"We're not neighbors."

"OK, friends. We are friends. Right?"

"You want a tamale?"

"Haven't had lunch yet. To tell you the truth, I'm starving."

Anna unwrapped the corn husk from a tamale and handed it to him on a paper napkin. The grease bled through onto Rusty's pants, but he didn't care. Nourishment was what he needed, and the tamales were excellent. Anna gave him another, which he finished and wiped his hands on the napkin and his pants. "Tell your mom these are really good."

Arriving at the farm in Bluff Dale, Rusty was surprised by the size of the project. There was at least a mile of fence needing T posts, then wire. They could not finish it before dark, but they could make some progress.

Anna interrupted his thoughts. "Pappa says the posts should be 8 feet apart. How about I start laying them out and you start driving them in."

"Will do." Rusty put on his gloves, picked up the cylinder t-post driver and started on the first post. Fortunately, it went in fairly easily. The first hour went smoothly, though they were both too busy for much conversation. It occurred to Rusty that he cared a lot more about talking with Anna than he did building a fence. The second hour, his shoulders started to ache and the big toe on his left foot felt hot. The third hour his shoulders started to feel weak and his toe was screaming at him in pain. To make matters worse, he and Anna had hardly spoken.

"We'd better stop," Anna suggested as the sun settled into the far horizon.

Rusty's left big toe felt like it was on fire as they reached the truck and put the tools away. Climbing onto the truck bed, Rusty removed his left shoe and what was left of his sock. Blood dripped on the truck from an angry blister. The thin church socks now mired with blood and dirt were no match for the hard work of the day.

"Dios mio! What happened to you?"

"You ever walk through hot burning coals?"

"No."

"Me either, but I'm pretty sure this is how it feels," he said with a tinge of bitterness. The afternoon was a disappointment. They had made good progress on the fence, but he had hoped to finish more of it. He and Anna had hardly spoken through their labors, his toe was a mess, his shoulders sore and his belly growled in hungry protest. "Think I'll work the clutch barefoot. I need to get you home."

Anna tried to make conversation on the short drive back to Stephenville, but it was mostly one sided. Rusty's pain and soreness made it difficult to concentrate on anything but the road ahead. He managed to nod occasionally, as if he were listening. Mercifully, they arrived at Anna's home as nightfall fully embraced the town. Anna looked at him with concern. "Come into the house. I think I can help fix your toe."

"Naw, it's all right. I'll clean it up when I get home." More than cleaning the toe, he felt malnourished.

"Please. Let me help. It's the least I can do."

"Will it take long?"

Anna opened the passenger door. "Come on in. My brothers will get the tools. Bring your boot with you."

Rusty exited the truck holding his left boot and gingerly limped toward the house. Entering the front door, Anna took his hand and led him to a small bathroom. She pulled a plastic bucket from under the sink and started filling it with warm water. Rusty was dubious. "What are you doing?"

"You'll see." She closed the toilet lid and indicated that he should sit. Her little sister appeared at the bathroom door. "Tell Mam'a I need two tea bags." The girl nodded and rushed away. Anna added Epson Salt to the water and placed the bucket in front of Rusty. Sitting on the floor. She gently rolled up his pant leg a few inches, picked up his foot and tenderly lowered it into the warm water.

"Ouch! That's painful."

"Give it a minute." Using a wash cloth, she gently cleaned his foot, taking care not to touch the blister.

Rusty relaxed as the pain began to subside. He was captivated by the gentle kindness of her care. There was a softness to Anna he had not previously seen. Strangely, he could feel her strength and compassion through her hands on his foot. Her little sister appeared at the door holding two tea bags. "Papa's fixing hamburgers in the back yard. He said he'd fix you one if you want it."

Anna smiled at her sister. "Tell Papa Rusty needs two. Also, be an angel and bring us each a lemonade." As the sister ran off, she turned to Rusty. "I assume you're hungry. I know I am."

"Starving."

Removing Rusty's foot from the bucket, she gently dried it. To Rusty's surprise, she placed two damp tea bags on his toe and propped his foot on the edge of the bathtub. It felt strange, being taken care of. "How did you learn to do this stuff?"

"You mean taking care of feet? In my world, we learn to care for ourselves before we go to a doctor. It's survival. We also take care of our friends." She smiled up at him. "You'll never know how much I appreciate what you did for us today."

He reached down and touched the side of her head, letting his fingers explore the depths of her hair. Suddenly the afternoon didn't seem so bad. He was seeing a new part of Anna, one that his friends at school would never believe. He was privileged to witness a melting of the hard exterior that seemed to define her. And the more he learned, the more he wanted to know. As they gazed into each other's eyes, the little sister appeared at the bathroom door with burgers on paper plates.

"Did you forget the lemonade?" Anna asked as she took the plates from her sister. The sister's eyes got big and she skipped down the hallway. As Rusty was taking his first bite of the hamburger, the sister returned with the drinks. "Thanks, angel."

Rusty savored the hamburgers as Anna sat near him on the side of the bathtub. It occurred to him that eating burgers in a bathroom, tired and dirty with tea bags on his toes must be a humorous sight. "When do you think your dad will able to work again?"

"Quien sabe. Hopefully tomorrow. Mam'a found an extra cleaning job. It's just for three weeks, but we'll get by. If Papa can get the bonus, it should help us through the winter when there's less work. I think we'll be OK."

"You know, most people have no idea how you live."

"We're not looking for sympathy. We work hard for what we have." They finished the hamburgers and Anna carefully removed the tea bags. "Does it hurt?"

"Some. Not bad."

Anna gently put a thin layer of Vaseline on the wound, covered it with a bandage and wrapped it loosely with white medical tape.   "You should wear thick socks to school tomorrow. I'm so sorry this happened to you. It's not what you signed up for, is it?"

Rusty carefully put his sock and work boot on, feeling more comfortable than he had anticipated. Anna's strength, her nurturing way, her refusal to be defeated. It all created an intoxicating desire in him. Rusty laced his fingers in her hair, leaned over and kissed her softly. As they gazed at each other, Rusty was surprised to see Anna's eyes become misty and sad. "What's wrong?"

"You're a sweet boy Rusty, but you don't want me."

"I can't think of a single reason why I wouldn't want to spend more time with you."

Anna offered a sad smile and shook her head. She rolled up his shirt sleeve and put his pale arm next to hers. "You see, we're different and that's a big deal to some of your friends. It sucks, but if you spend time with me, you will lose friends. White people deny it, but there's racism here. They won't talk about it in front of me, and they'll lie and say it isn't true. But I can see it in their eyes. It's the way they are. Plus, I'm going away to school next year. Hopefully, not too far away, but I won't be here for you. And Rusty, you know I have to work a lot, so I can't be---"

"Stop. I don't need you to lecture me."

She frowned. "I wasn't lecturing you. I just---"

Rusty sighed. "I make my own mind up about who I spend time with. If some asshole doesn't like it, then to hell with him. I damn sure don't need the kind of friendship that depends on the color of my skin or the friends I choose to have. And as for next year, I've been giving it a lot of thought myself. I have no idea where I'll be next year." He paused and spoke more softly. "What I do know is that I'm right here, right now, sitting on a toilet in front of someone amazing. You can run away if you want. It's up to you. But I sort of hope you'll stay around."

Anna's eyes misted again, but this time it was not sadness. "OK," she whispered.

He tenderly touched the side of her head, feeling the fullness of her thick black hair. Leaning over, he gently kissed her lips. "You know, this is a first for me."

Anna gave him a dubious look. "I am quite sure that you've kissed lots of girls."

"Never on a toilet!"

She playfully pushed him away before leading him down the short hallway. In the den they found her parents sitting on an old couch with frayed green plaid upholstery. Anna's brothers and sister were on the floor in front of a small black and white TV set watching *The Wonderful World of Disney*. Anna stopped. "Papa, this is my friend Rusty."

Anna's Papa carefully stood up and Rusty shook his hand. "The hamburgers were excellent, sir. Thank you."

"My pleasure, Rusty. My pleasure," he responded.

Anna took Rusty's hand and led him onto the front porch. A cool night air greeted them as the porch boards creaked below their feet. Anna hugged her shoulders in a futile attempt to stay warm. Rusty put his arms around her shoulders and held her close. She sighed. "I have to go study. You take care of your toe," she ordered.

"Yesum." He kissed her softly. "You know, the future may bring changes we never expected."

"Maybe. Think about what you really want. Then go for it. But be sure."

"You have no idea," he replied as he turned towards his truck.

Monday, October 20, 1969

Rusty had known since the visit with Principal Jamison that he would need to find a way to apologize to Ian for kicking his books around the hallway. Apologies made Rusty feel awkward and vulnerable. To make matters worse, he would have to apologize to the strange kid who he had nothing in common with. If not for Mr. Jamison's threat to ban Baked Cotton from school functions if Ian was not in the band, Rusty would have been happy to ignore the effeminate kid.

Rusty caught up with Ian in the hallway between their second and third period classes. Walking beside him, Rusty tried to sound friendly. "Hey, there. What's up?"

Ian hugged his books to his chest, holding them the way girls often do. "Leave me alone!"

"Hey, look Ian, I'm sorry about the other day. You didn't deserve that. We shouldn't have done it."

Ian glanced at Rusty with notable skepticism and poorly disguised fear as he quickened his pace down the hallway. "What do you want?"

"Relax, man. Just wanted to tell you I'm sorry for what happened. It won't happen again."

As Ian walked into his third period Latin classroom, he said "OK" without looking at Rusty.

Shaking his head in frustration, Rusty made his way to his next class as he silently berated himself for assuming Ian would readily accept the apology. The kid was scared, and with good reason. Nobody paid Ian much attention, unless it was to torment him in some way. Rusty needed a plan to earn Ian's trust. As he sat at his third period desk staring at an English textbook, he realized that he was clueless about what to do next.

§§§

Rusty watched Coach Childress shout criticism at his players. Monday after school football practice was not going well. The team lacked energy, and the coach's bug-eyed temper tantrum only made matters worse. To everyone's surprise, an offensive lineman had knocked Rusty off balance during a blocking drill. "What's got into you? You're better than that!" Coach Childress couldn't have been any closer to Rusty's face without crawling into his helmet.

Rusty's blistered toe hadn't bothered him much during the day. But during the drills, it felt as if it were on fire. The pain could not be ignored, nor could Coach Childress. Rusty struggled to react in a measured way as he tried to calm a volcanic anger towards his coach. Unconsciously he made a fist and looked the coach in the eye. "Toe hurts, Coach. I'll be OK."

"Do you want to hit me? Is that it? Or do you want some milk and cookies to make your pinkie toe better? This is football. It's supposed to hurt! You get set for the drill now! We're doing it again."

Rusty didn't move, nor did any of his teammates. In the silence of the next few moments, Rusty could feel the possibility of a mutiny against Coach Childress growing. "Rusty, you get in there for the drill, or the whole team is going to run a mile. All because of your toe!"

Without a word, Jake started jogging towards the track that circled the field. The rest of the team followed, with the exception of Rusty. He went to the sidelines and sat on the bench, feeling some relief as his left foot became free of his cleated shoe. Carefully, he removed his sock and the bandage on his big toe. The blister had been rubbed open and the toe was a bloody mess. Rusty smiled, both because of the freedom his toe felt and the way the bloody wound looked even worse than it felt. The wounded toe got the attention of his teammates as they jogged past.

Coach Childress walked towards the bench. Putting one foot on the bench as he glared down at his star player, the coach asked, "You gonna be ready for Friday night?"

Typical Childress bullshit, Rusty thought. The coach didn't care about his players or anything else, other than winning on Friday night. "I'll be good by Friday, Coach."

"OK then. Here's what you're going to do. You're gonna be here for practice Tuesday and Wednesday, but don't suit up. On Thursday we'll see how the toe is feeling and take it from there. Understood?"

"Yes, sir."

Childress looked at the toe. As he started to walk away, he shook his head and gave a mocking laugh. "Dang, boy. That must hurt."

In another setting Rusty might have broken the bastard's jaw. He said nothing.

§§§

Sitting cross legged on the linoleum bathroom floor, the yellow phone cord stretched under the door and her back to the wall, Kathleen was mildly amused by her friend's reaction. "You went out with who?" Janice's voice was incredulous on the other end of the phone line that evening. Kathleen rolled her eyes. Word of the breakup with Rusty had gotten around school. Janice was the first to know, and the only one who knew about her date with Michael. "So," Janice continued, "don't tell me you had an official date with a hippie." She lowered her voice to a near whisper. "Did he do drugs? What in God's name did y'all do?"

"We delivered a calf."

"Wait, no way," she laughed. "You're telling me that Michael the hippie took you on a date to deliver a calf? When this gets around school, you know everyone's going to be all nosy. I can hear them now, stopping me in the hallway whispering, is she OK?"

"You tell them it was a tough delivery, but three fifty-two is doing just fine."

138

Janice giggled. "Silly, I'm not talking about the damn cow."

"I know you aren't. The calf is fine, too."

"But really, this could change things. Are you going out with him again?"

"Sure plan to. Next weekend."

"Jake thinks Michael's a communist."

"Because Michael tried to defend someone who couldn't defend himself? Janice, you know Jake shouldn't kick Ian's ass like that. Neither should Rusty. It's wrong."

"It's what boys do. You know how they are."

"Are you defending them? How can you do that?"

"Not defending exactly. I just know that boys do crap and it doesn't mean anything."

"I bet it did to Ian."

The phone was silent for a few moments. Kathleen could almost hear Janice's thoughts through the phone line, trying to decide what to say next. Finally, Janice, now sounding very serious said, "Lets don't let the boys mess up our friendship. I was hoping you and Rusty would get back together. Jake and I have a blast with y'all."

"Well maybe y'all can have fun with Michael and me. But don't get the cart before the horse. It was only one date."

"Jake's still pissed at Michael. That hippie better watch his back."

"What in God's name does that mean?"

"I don't know."

"Look, I don't know what's going to happen with Michael and I don't give a damn what Jake thinks about it. If we end up with boyfriends who don't like each other, I'm still not giving up on you and to tell the truth, I'm not giving up on Jake either."

"Thanks." Something in Janice's voice sounded relieved, as if she had feared a different response from Kathleen. "Kathleen, Jake's going through some tough shit. I don't know if I'm supposed to tell you this, but since his brother was drafted, his parents have been really up tight. Sometimes they get real strict with Jake for no reason. Jake's really scared something's going to happen to his brother. So are his parents. You can't tell anyone."

Kathleen sensed that Janice might be starting to shed tears. She tried to reassure her friend. "Jake's brother's a good guy. I know Jake looks up to him. I bet he'll be fine. Are you OK?"

"I've been better," Janice tearfully replied. "I'm worried about Jake. It scares me because I don't want to lose him like you lost Rusty. He's different now, like he's about to explode. His family isn't making things any easier. Like the other night, Jake was five minutes late getting home and his dad yelled at him. Can you believe it? Five minutes!"

"I didn't think Jake's dad ever yelled at anyone. He's pretty quiet."

"I know. A couple of days ago, I dropped my keys and they hit the side of Jake's car. Made a tiny scratch. You couldn't hardly see it. Jake yelled at me!"

Kathleen felt horrible for Janice. "You don't deserve that."

"I'm so scared. I don't know what I'd do without Jake. Sometimes we just don't talk because I don't know what to say to him and I'm scared he'll get pissed off for some little thing," Janice cried. "Breaking up with Rusty must have been the worse feeling ever for you."

"Weird, I thought it would be. I mean, it was hard, but I think I'm doing OK."

Janice was quiet for a moment, then softly said "I have to go." The phone went dead, conversation over.

Kathleen remained on the bathroom floor for a moment, trying to understand what just happened. She and Janice had been friends most of their lives. They could finish each other's sentences and often knew each other's thoughts. Kathleen returned the phone to the kitchen, wishing she could help her friend and not knowing how.

§§§

"What in God's name am I supposed to do? Ian's such a wimpy weirdo!" Rusty almost shouted at Anna as he drove her home that evening from her Dairy Queen job. Ian's rejection of his apology bothered him even more than the confrontation with Coach Childress.   "I mean, I was friendly, I apologized and all he could say was OK, as if I was lying to him. He may as well have told me to go to hell! He didn't believe me at all." Rusty didn't think Anna would understand, but she was the only one that he could talk with.

Anna looked concerned. "Did you mean it?"

"Mean what?"

"The apology. Was it real?"

"What do you mean?"

"Were you really being friendly?"

"Of course!"

"Then why did you just call him a wimpy weirdo?"

"Because he is!"

"Sounds like you're really not friendly towards him. Why bother in the first place?"

"Because I had to! We need him in the band."

"So, you had another motive and Ian doesn't trust you. Sounds like Ian's a smart guy."

Rusty stopped the truck in front of Anna's home. The front porch light left shadows in the truck, as if a dim light had been left on. The conversation with Anna had not gone as he had anticipated. He searched for something profound to say in response to Anna's conclusion. Staring out the front windshield, he remained quiet.

"How many boys are on the football team?"

"I don't know, maybe 30. What's that got to do with anything?"

"How many boys on your team are not white?"

"None."

Anna hesitated. Rusty sensed that his answer was not what she was expecting. "Dios mio. Have you ever played on a team that wasn't all white?"

"Yes."

"And I bet you and the guys on those teams sometimes got together to do whatever you boys do for fun. Right?"

"Sure. What's wrong with it?"

"Nothing. How many times did you invite the boys who were not white to join you?"

"Well, hell, they wouldn't want to do whatever we were doing."

"Did they tell you that?"

"No. But now that you mention it, we didn't ask them. We just knew."

"Did you?" The question hung heavy in the still air between them. "Really? I mean, did you ever try to get to know any of the non-white guys? Other than as teammates?"

"No, but it wasn't like we were jerks towards them." Rusty began feeling defeated and confused.

"I wonder how they felt, being a part of the team but not included. As if everyone knew them, but not really."

Rusty was quiet for a moment. Taking a deep breath, he slumped in his seat feeling defeated. Anna's intense gaze provided no comfort. "OK, I get it. They probably felt like they were left out because of us, the way we were off the field."

Anna put her hand on Rusty's shoulder. As he stared down at his feet, she softly said "Welcome to my world. And welcome to Ian's world, too."

Tuesday, October 21, 1969

The telephone rang after dinner at the Wilcox farm house. Kathleen was putting dishes away as an autumn breeze blew cold against the warm house. Her parents were in the den, looking over the TV guide for the evening's entertainment. "I'll get it," she called from the kitchen.

"I'm sure you will," her mother responded with a touch of sarcasm.

"Hello."

"Um, is Kathleen there?"

"This is Kathleen, silly. Who did you think it was?"

Michael sounded cautious. "Well, in your house a guy has to be careful. No offense, but you and your mother sound a lot alike on the phone."

Kathleen laughed. "Well, I don't think you're her type, so I guess you'll have to settle for me."

"How you doing?"

"Weird day."

"What happened?"

"Well, first off, Janice told me Jake stopped a couple of greaser looking guys from stealing Ian's violin. Even gave one a black eye."

"I think I saw that kid after school. He's one of those guys who always wears a leather jacket and smells like cigarette smoke. Don't know him."

"Well, that's good to know. Anyway, Janice told me these two guys tried to jump on Ian when he was walking home from school. Jake sees it and actually defends Ian. Then he gave Ian a ride home. And that's not all. Janice said that Jake apologized to Ian for all the hell he put him through. A few days ago, he was kicking Ian's books around the hallway and getting you suspended. I mean, I'm glad he helped Ian out, but I don't get it. Jake doesn't even like Ian. I don't know Ian very well, but they seem about as different as you can get."

"What else did Janice say?"

"It was kind of weird. She said Jake was going through some things, but I think there's more going on than she's willing to tell me. We've been friends since second grade. We talk all the time. But tonight, it was like she didn't want to say too much."

"So, the guy I saw trying to look tough with his leather jacket and a black eye, Jake did that to him?"

"Strange as hell, isn't it?"

"Watch your mouth young lady," Kathleen's mom yelled over the TV from the den. Kathleen stretched the phone cord into the bathroom and closed the door.

"Maybe Jake was trying to do the right thing for the first time in his sorry ass life," Michael offered.

"Slow down, now. You don't know Jake like I do. We've been friends since we were little kids. He's really a good guy."

"You think Ian would agree with you?"

"Not sure. What do you think is going on?"

"Sometimes things have a way of working themselves out."

That was not the answer Kathleen was expecting. The phone went quiet. Kathleen sensed that Michael was somehow involved but, like Janice, was not talking. "Why are you calling me tonight? What's up?"

"Checking on how the day went for the new calf and you."

"In that order? Aren't you the romantic one!"

Michael stammered, "No, I um, you know that's not what I meant. Just wanted to say hi."

"Well, since you asked, the calf is doing fine and I had a pretty good day, other than the strange parts with Jake. You OK?"

"I'm fine. Had a good time last weekend. Never thought I could be helpful with delivering a calf."

Kathleen laughed. "OK, wrangler, don't get too proud. It's not like you're the only rooster in the hen house you know."

"You don't think I can handle cattle, do you? At least I know what a come-along is. Anyway, I'm looking forward to the weekend."

"Me, too."
"Bye."

§§§

Michael hung up the phone. Before him was additional information Oregon State had requested to complete his application. To his surprise, he hesitated. For a moment he thought of the friends he missed in Oregon and his one new friend in Stephenville. He wondered if he would have the same feelings leaving Kathleen in Stephenville as he had leaving Diane in Oregon. As he completed the information for Oregon State and sealed the envelope, he realized that saying goodbye to Kathleen might not feel the same as leaving Diane. It could be worse. Or perhaps Kathleen was a momentary distraction, nothing more. Perhaps not.

Wednesday, October 22, 1969

Rusty and Jake walked towards the school parking lot after football practice. Rusty noticed Michael's blue VW Bug still in the lot. "Michael's still in school. Maybe he can help us with Ian."

"Why the hell would he do that?"

"I don't know," Rusty responded with frustration. "You have any better ideas?"

They casually walked towards Michael's car and leaned their backs against the driver's side door. There wasn't much of a plan. The two boys ignored Michael in school and Michael appeared happy to respond with poorly hidden disdain. They kept the peace by avoidance. The informal truce was working for both sides, but it might not work for long.

After about ten minutes, Michael emerged from the school building, violin in one hand and books in the other. To Rusty's surprise, Kathleen walked out with him. She laughed and playfully punched his shoulder, apparently enjoying some sort of private joke. Neither of them noticed Rusty and Jake at first. When they did, the laughter stopped.

Rusty knew Kathleen had no trouble attracting the attention of other guys, but the idea of her spending time with Michael of all people made his blood boil. As Kathleen and Michael approached the car, Rusty couldn't help himself. "What the hell are you doing with a damn hippie?"

Kathleen shot Rusty with a sarcastic smile. "Well it's good to see you too, Rusty."

Even though they were no longer a couple, her snarky response stung. "What the hell, Kathleen? Don't you---"

"Get your fat ass off of my car," Michael interrupted in a measured, but serious tone.

Jake intervened, and looking directly at Michael said "We need to talk."

Michael looked at both boys. "For the second time, get your fat ass off of my car. Are you both deaf?" Rusty and Jake stopped leaning on Michael's car. With what sounded almost like a congratulations, Michael said "You know Jake, you did a good thing for Ian with those greasers who went after him."

Jake looked directly at Michael. "It was the right thing to do."

"Yes, it was, and I'm pretty sure I know why you did it. But either way, you're right on. It was a good thing for you to do."

Kathleen blinked and looked from one guy to the next. "Someone want to tell me what's going on? You'd have to be some damn Einstein to figure you guys out."

Jake rolled his eyes and looked again at Michael. "Got a minute?"

"Sure," Michael responded. Turning to Kathleen, he said "See you tomorrow."

Rusty nodded at her and Jake waved. "See ya."

Kathleen frowned. "Well I never." Turning towards her car she walked away, never looking back.

"We want to play another gig at the school sock hop," Jake explained. It was an odd way to start a conversation, as the information was known to all three boys. "Can't do it without Ian and Ian doesn't trust us, so if we ask him to play, we're pretty sure he'd say no."

"No shit, Sherlock," Michael replied.

Jake shrugged. "If you talk to him, we're thinking maybe he'd say yes."

Michael smiled. "Why in the hell would I want to do that?"

Rusty tried a different approach. "Come on, man, we're just asking for a favor. It's not a big deal."

"Have you guys actually talked with Ian, told him why you want him in your band? I mean, forget Jamison for a minute. Ian's a great musician. Better than any of us will ever be. He knows his stuff, even the technical music theory crap." Michael paused. "Wait a minute. Jamison told me specifically not to talk with Ian. I do so, you guys tell Jamison and I get suspended again. Get screwed, both of you."

Rusty was exasperated. "That's not what this is about!"

"And I'm supposed to believe you why?"

Jake intervened. "OK, wait. You guys pull in your horns for a minute. What if all three of us talk to him together?"

"Maybe," Michael replied. "I'm still not sure he'd go for it, and I sure as hell can't figure out why I'd want to help you in the first place."

"You and Kathleen sweet on each other?" Rusty asked, trying to sound casually interested and not really wanting to hear the answer.

"We're getting to know each other pretty well. Helped her deliver a calf last weekend."

Rusty laughed. "Not exactly the answer I was expecting. Let me tell you, Kathleen, Jake and I have been good friends since elementary school. We go way back. She's not going to give up her friends for anyone, least of all you. Don't believe me, ask her. You want to make Kathleen happy, help us out with this one."

Michael looked Rusty in the eye. "She doesn't know anything about this."

Jake smirked. "That's obvious. She walked away pissed at all three of us. But Rusty's right. I'm pretty sure you help us, you get in good with Kathleen. Look man, you have a lot to gain and nothing to lose. What's your hang-up?"

Michael sighed. "Ian eats lunch most days by the flag pole, usually by himself. You want to talk with him, that's as good a time as any. Out of my way, I need to get home."

Rusty and Jake stepped away from the car. As Michael threw his books on the passenger seat, Rusty asked "Will you meet us at lunch tomorrow?"

Michael smiled. "May change your reputation, hanging with Ian at lunch. You'll be the talk of the school."

Jake and Rusty said simultaneously, "Don't care."

"See you tomorrow," Michael said as he closed the door to the VW and carefully put the violin on the back seat. Without another word he started the car and drove away, leaving Rusty and Jake alone in the parking lot.

Jake shook his head. "Son of a bitch never said he'd meet us at lunch."

"No, he didn't." Then, thinking of Kathleen, Rusty added "But I bet he does."

§§§

That evening after dinner, Michael phoned Kathleen. His first task was to apologize for being rude to her in the school parking lot. Though her feathers were clearly still ruffled, she seemed to accept the apology. "Since I screwed up and was rude, how about you let me make it up to you? I was hoping you'd want to go to the Dairy Queen for an ice cream. I can be there in a few minutes."

Kathleen had finished her homework and chores. "So you think I'm one of those girls who you can be rude to in the afternoon and then make up for it with a sugary dairy product in the evening?" she chided.

Michael stammered. "Yes. Or no. That's not the way I meant it." He took a deep breath to halt the sudden feeling that he needed to defend himself to Kathleen. In a more measured tone, he said "I was hoping you'd want to get an ice cream tonight."

"Sounds good, but you're never going to get here talking on the phone. Come on over."

"I'll be there quick as a duck on a June bug."

Kathleen laughed. "First off, I never thought I'd hear you say that. Second, do you even know what it means?"

"Hell, no. Heard someone say it downtown and it sounded pretty quick. Trying to blend in around here you know."

Kathleen giggled. "Well Oregon, you'd better get your ass over here."

§§§

Michael parked near the entrance to the Dairy Queen. He and Kathleen found the store quiet. Apparently, Wednesday evening was a slow time for business. Anna, behind the counter, gave a friendly smile. Michael ordered two vanilla ice cream cones, the one for Kathleen dipped in chocolate. They found a booth and sat close together on the red vinyl bench. The empty store almost gave him a feeling of privacy.

"Jake and Rusty want Ian to join their band," Michael said, as if he were revealing a national secret.

Kathleen simultaneously licked a spec of chocolate off of her lip, rolled her eyes and managed a smirk. When she turned to look Michael in the eye, he nodded. "Is that what y'all were talking about this afternoon?"

"That's it. But here's the deal. If Jamison knows I told you about it, I'll probably get suspended again. I'd appreciate you keeping it to yourself, at least for a while. And if Rusty or Jake know I've told you, they'd sure as hell tell Jamison."

"First off, you don't know Rusty and Jake. Not like I do. Second, what in God's name does Jamison have to do with Baked Cotton? No, don't tell me. Jamison's joining the band, too."

Kathleen's sarcasm mildly annoyed Michael. "It was Jamison's idea. He won't let the band play on school grounds again without Ian being involved. No Ian, no band at the sock hop. Rusty and Jake have to find a way to get Ian in the band and they want me to help them. We couldn't talk about any of this in front of you this afternoon. Sorry. Anyway, I'm not sure if I want to help them out. They've been a pain in the ass to me since I got here. Stupid rednecks."

"So you think you're better than them?" She shifted in her seat, leaning against the wall and propping her leg on the bench, securing a distance between she and Michael. "Let me tell you. Rusty and Jake are good people. They're my people. It pissed me off when they picked on Ian and I told them so, or at least I told Rusty. But that doesn't mean they're bad people or ignorant country hicks. They work hard. Maybe you don't believe the same things they do, but guess what, they don't agree with you either. You probably don't know that Rusty's father died in the military. Died a hero, but Rusty still misses his dad. And Jake's brother dropped out of college and was drafted. Infantry. Hello, Vietnam. Then you come in here with your anti-military crap as if you're smarter and better than the rest of us. In their eyes you shit on the very uniform their families die for. How would you feel in their shoes?"

"Vietnam is immoral. It's wrong. We're killing thousands of people for what? It's their civil war, not ours. Our people are risking their lives and dying there every day!"

"Correct. But what gives you the right to not show some respect for people who don't agree with you? Rusty and Jake see the anti-war protesters as a threat and insult to everything they believe in."

Michael stared at the front door of the store, not wanting to make eye contact with Kathleen who was searching his face for a response. He only had one friend in Stephenville. After tonight, there might be less. "So are you OK with what our country's doing in Vietnam?"

"Hell, no. We're killing people who never threatened us. A lot of innocent people. It's morally wrong. And by the way, that view isn't well regarded around here. But, and this is a big but, I still respect the people who don't agree with me on it."

Michael was quiet for a moment, trying to collect his thoughts. "Maybe I've been walking around with my head up my ass."

Kathleen softened her tone. "Sometimes you probably rub people wrong. That doesn't mean you're a bad person. Different yes, but not a bad person. I think you're doing the best you can. It sucks moving to a new town in your senior year. But guess what, things have happened to Rusty and Jake, and that also sucks."

"So maybe I should help them with getting Ian in the band. Maybe I can talk Ian into it."

"Hell yes you should help them! What have you got to lose? Bury the hatchet. They're good guys."

"OK. Not sure I like it, but I get it."

"Sorry. I didn't mean to come down on you so hard. Sometimes I get carried away."

"You could be hanging out with most any guy in school." Michael finished the last of his ice cream and squeezed the napkin in his fist. Making eye contact he asked, "Why me?"

"Well, two things. First, my life until now has been like a preprinted story, where you know the ending long before you reach the last chapter. Most everybody I know plans to get married or go to Tarleton State, maybe both. I'm not saying they're wrong for what they want, but it's not me. There's a world beyond Erath County and this bird has to fly. Maybe I'll be back, maybe not. Tell you the truth, leaving this place has me scared half to death. I don't even know if I can make it happen. We're not exactly rich folks around here, at least not on the farm. I can't wait to see other places, learn about how other people live. But I feel kind of trapped. Then you came along. You're different. You're not like most folks around here. With you, I'm still on the first chapter and I have no idea how the story will end. Think about it. What's the chance that a small-town Texas girl like me would meet a boy from Oregon who can play hockey and help deliver a calf?"

Michael chuckled. "OK, you said two things, what's the second?"

She smiled. "Well, mister, you're one hell of a kisser."

Anna called from behind the counter. "Hey y'all, we're closing up."

Michael and Kathleen left the Dairy Queen and got into Michael's VW. Neither spoke. Michael felt Kathleen's hand on his arm as he reached for the ignition. Her touch, her smile, the look in her eyes was simultaneously reassuring and arousing. Neither spoke. He ran his fingers through her hair, leaned over and kissed her softly. The lights in the Dairy Queen went off, leaving them in the shadow of a street light.

§§§

Rusty was surprised to see Michael's car as he pulled into the Dairy Queen to take Anna home. In the dim street lights, he couldn't tell who was in the car, but there were definitely two people. When he saw them kiss, he assumed the other person was Kathleen. "Why in the hell did she have to get involved with that freak?" he said to himself. It probably wouldn't last long. He was sure Kathleen would eventually get bored with Michael. When that happened, she would dump his ass in a heartbeat. Until then, it felt like she was friendly with the enemy. As he thought about it, his anger started to rise.

Rusty's attention turned to Anna as she walked out of the Dairy Queen. Removing her hair net and shaking her head, her dark hair fell upon her shoulders. She carried herself with an impressive look of confident self-reliance. She was beautiful, and he often wondered why she would want to spend time with him. To his surprise, as she passed Michael's VW, she slapped her hand on the top of the car. Michael and Kathleen jumped apart as Kathleen let out a little scream. Anna never broke stride, which was a challenge given how hard she was laughing. Rusty couldn't control his laughter, either. As Anna got into the truck, he fired up the engine. The headlights caught Kathleen and Michael still looking startled. Rusty put the truck in gear, Anna slid over the bench seat next to him and they pulled out of the parking lot.

"That was a deer in the headlights look if I ever saw one," Anna laughed.

"No kidding," Rusty chuckled. "I think they both shit their shorts," he added as his anger subsided.

Rusty turned off the headlights and killed the truck engine in front of Anna's house. The familiar front porch light provided dim illumination on the street as an autumn breeze whispered through the open truck windows. Rusty had been picking up Anna most evenings after work. Normally, they would only have a few precious minutes to talk before she would have to go into the house to finish her homework for the next day. She never seemed to stop working, striving, pushing for a better tomorrow. Watching her determination, Rusty felt inspired, humbled and, in a strange way he could not understand, intimidated. Anna was a force, consistent in her work ethic. Rusty sensed that each day she would take a meal break, a restroom break and a Rusty break, none of which lasted long. But tonight she lingered. After chatting for a few minutes, he asked "No homework tonight?"

"You're my homework tonight." Turning her back to the windshield, she settled into Rusty's arms, being careful not to lean against the truck's horn.

Rusty kissed her gently and ran his fingers through her soft dark hair. Her smile and the feel of her warm skin next to him made his Wrangler jeans feel achingly tight with desire. He kissed her deeply as their tongues caressed each other in ways that surprised him. She tilted her head and he kissed her neck. He felt sure she could feel the bulge in his jeans, but he couldn't hide it and wasn't sure if he cared to. His hand found its way inside the back of her blouse, feeling her skin warm and soft against his fingers. He waited for a rebuke, a rejection as he kissed her again and then again. Anna ran her fingers over his eyebrows and ears, gently exploring the contours of his face. He was terrified of doing something wrong, but too lustful not to try. She kissed him deeply as his hand moved under her shirt and gently cupped her breast. As they continued to kiss, Rusty moved his hand lower. Anna moved her arm across her belly, blocking any further migration downward. The move was subtle, but unmistakable, even to a boy like Rusty with little experience.

"I'm sorry," she whispered, which sounded to Rusty more like an explanation than an apology.

He kissed her softly. "It's OK. We're good." Rusty smiled and ran his fingers through her hair. For the first time, he felt vulnerable, as he realized that if Anna were to break up with him, it would be much more than a disappointment. It was strange, feeling both vulnerable and strong. He wondered if this was what falling in love felt like. "You know, picking you up from work is sometimes the best part of my day."

"Sometimes?"

"OK, most of the time." He gently kissed her eyebrows. "All of the time."

"You know this won't be easy, you and me."

"I've always done the easy way. It's not that great."

Anna looked at his face as if searching for something. "The other day when you held my hand in the hallway and walked me to my class. Did you see the way we were looked at?"

"Didn't see anything. Don't care."

"Well, ever since then, some girls who never knew I existed have tried to be friendly."

Rusty was confused. "What's wrong with that?"

Anna signed. "It's fake. They don't give a damn what happens to me, except when I'm with you. Some guy in class, I'm not sure which one, called me the wet backer with the linebacker. Some of the rednecks in class started laughing."

"I'd have kicked his ass if I would have been there."

"You going to fight the whole school?"

Rusty held her in his arms, trying to understand. "Look, I just want us to be together. I don't give a damn what other people think. I don't know where this is going, you and me. But I'm sure as hell enjoying the ride."

Anna kissed him one last time before she sat up, slowly slid across the bench seat towards the passenger door and softly said "It's the best part of my day, too. I'm just not ready to, you know." Then, exiting the truck and closing the door, she smiled and gave him a reassuring flirtatious wink. Through the open window she added, "Not yet."

Thursday, October 23, 1969

Michael woke in a foul mood. The lecture he had received from Kathleen the night before at the Dairy Queen still had a sting, even though he had to acknowledge that she was probably right. He had been judged unfairly by his peers, almost none of whom had shown any interest in getting to know him. It was unfair, unjust and discouraging. And yet, Kathleen had made him see that he had done the same to them, or the whole town actually. He felt a judgmental fool.

Thinking of meeting Ian, Jake and Rusty at lunch was nauseating. Although he owed Ian nothing, Michael had a nagging feeling he was somehow deceiving the kid. Outside of music, they had nothing in common. And yet, Ian appeared to have developed a trust in Michael. A trust that might feel like a betrayal after today.

Michael went through his morning classes with a sense of foreboding. The school lunch bell rang, sounding to Michael louder and more abrupt than normal. He grabbed a sack lunch from his locker and found Ian, as expected, sitting alone in front of the school by the flag pole. Ian's white socks exposed pant legs that were too short. His plaid shirt in a strange way matched the square metal lunch pail he opened to retrieve a bologna sandwich on white bread, no crust. *Who in the hell uses a lunch pail?* Michael thought. *What is this, third grade?* He sat beside Ian.

Giving Michael a suspicious look, Ian said "What?"

"I think Rusty and Jake are about to join us." Ian put his sandwich back in the lunch pail as if he were planning to leave. "It's OK. Be cool. They just want to talk."

Rusty and Jake came through the front doors of the school carrying lunch sacks. They regarded Ian in a manner that Michael would interpret as friendly had he not known better. Jake, looking at Ian, began "Hey buddy, how you doing?" Jake and Rusty sat on the ground in front of Ian and Michael. Jake added, "Figured we'd join you for lunch. Hope that's OK."

Ian looked uncomfortable. "Free country. Eat wherever you want."

Rusty took a bite of his sandwich, washed it down with some Coca-Cola and casually said, "Ian, we'd like your help. We hear you're the best fiddler in the school. We have this band, Baked Cotton. You heard of us?"

"Yes. Never heard you play though," Ian replied as he dropped a potato chip on the ground with what looked to Michael like nervous energy.

"We're pretty good," Rusty continued. "But we need some help with the fiddle part on a couple of our songs. We're trying to get ready for the next sock hop. Since we heard that you're a talented musician, we'd like you to join us. It would be fun."

There was an uncomfortable silence as the boys ate their sandwiches. Then Ian responded. "No."

Jake sounded exasperated. "Why not?"

Ian took a drink from his plastic cup. "You beat me up in school, kick my books around, make fun of me all the time and now you want me in your band. You must think I'm stupid! I don't trust you guys, not for a minute."

There was an awkward silence as the boys picked at their lunches. Finally, Michael intervened. "Jake, you'd better tell him what this is really about." Something in Michael was starting to enjoy the scene, with Jake and Rusty looking increasingly uncomfortable.

Jake took a deep breath, looked at Ian and said, "OK, here's the deal. Jamison will not allow us to play at the sock hop or at any other school function unless you're part of the band. Two songs, that's all we need. Then you can go do whatever it is you do. Come on. It'll be fun. Hell, I'd pay money to see the look on people's faces when you walk onto the stage with us."

"They'll laugh at me! I'm just a big joke to you and everyone else."

Michael tried another route. "Ian, you've talked to Jamison, right?"

"Sure, lots of times," Ian replied.

Michael continued. "What do you suppose Jamison would do if Baked Cotton turned this into a big joke at your expense? How many more opportunities would the band have to play at school functions? I'm guessing next to none. They'd be screwed. I'm not exactly friends with these guys either. But they're not stupid enough to piss off Jamison. And let's say you get on the stage, actually it's just a platform, and the whole thing feels like a joke. All you have to do is walk away before you even play a note and the band is in trouble with Jamison. Believe it or not, you hold all the cards here. Besides, the band isn't bad and they'd be a hell of a lot better with you in it."

Ian, looking like he would rather be anywhere else, ate his bologna sandwich in silence. Rusty quickly finished his lunch, shook his head and stood up. "Look Ian, we shouldn't have treated you like we did. I don't blame you for not wanting to help us out after everything that's happened to you. No matter what, I promise you Jake and I will never lay a hand on you again. No more treating you like crap. Those days are over. I'm sorry it happened in the first place. We were wrong. For what it's worth, I respect your decision." Turning to Jake he said "Let's go."

Jake stood and started walking back towards the school with Rusty. As they did, Ian said "Wait a minute."

Rusty and Jake turned. Rusty said, "Don't worry about it. It's OK. We're cool."

"Who's in your band?" Ian asked, to Michael's surprise. "The two of you make a duet, not a band."

Jake said "There's four of us. Tommy Wilson plays bass and his sister Judy's on keyboard."

Ian thought for a moment. "Judy Wilson from the school choir?"

"That's her," Jake replied. "She has one of those electric keyboards. She's good. She doesn't sing for us though, just the keyboard."

"Why not? She's a talented vocalist. I've heard her."

Jake looked uncomfortable. "I'm the singer in the band."

"How did your band get the name Baked Cotton? Nobody bakes cotton."

Jake tried to explain. "We were practicing a couple of years ago on April Fool's Day. Rusty's mom suggested we take a break. She offered us a tray of fresh out of the oven biscuits with butter. The bread smelled great, so we ate it. Or tried to. Turns out, she put cotton in the biscuits. April Fools. We got a good laugh from it, so we decided to call our band Baked Cotton."

"When do you practice?" Ian asked.

Jake smiled. "Saturday morning at 10:00. We meet in Rusty's garage."

"OK, I'll do it," Ian said to everyone's surprise. "But under one condition."

"What?" Jake and Rusty said simultaneously.

Ian looked directly at Jake. "Michael has to be there, too."

It was Michael's turn to be surprised. He almost choked on his sandwich as he asked "Why?"

Ian smiled. "You're good, and I may need a second violin. Or as they'd probably say, a second fiddle."

Jake started to object but was cut off by Rusty. "Two good fiddlers beats one. What do you say Michael?"

Michael remembered his conversation with Kathleen the previous night. He thought about how nobody other than Kathleen had reached out to him for anything. He also had a certain pleasure in seeing Jake uncomfortable, almost angry. "I'll do one rehearsal and we'll see how it goes. You screw with me or Ian and we're out of there."

Jake looked frustrated. "One rehearsal isn't enough!"

Michael chuckled. "Then you sure as hell better be sure it's a good one, because it could be the first and last."

Friday, October 24, 1969

Rusty could hear the band playing a lively tune as he and his teammates suited up in the locker room for their Friday night game. The boys from Fort Worth Wyatt High School were in town to challenge the Stephenville boys. Having won three of their first four games, Rusty's teammates prepared themselves with a nervous, confident swagger. Somebody put a water balloon at the top of a partially opened door to the locker room. Jake happened to be next to walk through the door, water balloon exploding in a wet mess at his feet. The players erupted in laughter. Even Jake smiled.

"What in God's name is going on here?" coach Childress glared at the suddenly quiet team. "We've got a game to play! Those boys from Fort Worth think they're better than you." His voice increased in volume and anger as he spoke, his face blushed red with rage. "Stephenville football has been four wins and six losses for two years running. You better get your head in the game and quit strutting around like you're winners. We have a lot of football left in the season. Those boys from Fort Worth saw y'all acting like you're better than them and you know what? I can tell you each and every one of those boys is as angry as a rooster in an empty hen house! If y'all don't get your heads in this game, they're going to kick your ass right here in front of your home crowd. There's hundreds of people out there who expect to see some football! Yellowjacket football! Do I make myself clear?"

"Yes, sir," the team mumbled.

"What?"

"Yes, sir!" the team shouted.

Rusty had grown tired of Coach Childress and his antics. What Childress intended to be motivating appeared to Rusty to be the pathetic ramblings of an old man whose glory days were already behind him. Childress was always angry, never content, relishing only the violence he could bring to the football field. Rusty wondered if only violence and fury lived in the shambles of his coach's mind. As Rusty looked around the now quiet locker room, he found himself wondering which of his teammates would become the next Coach Childress, angry and disappointed with the direction of his life.

Head Coach entered the locker room to give the boys some final motivational words before the game. Rusty tried to look interested, though he lacked the adrenaline he usually felt before games. Head Coach offered a brief prayer and the boys ran onto the field as the band played the Stephenville fight song.

The autumn breeze and the enthusiastic crowd were a relief to Rusty, a needed escape from the suffocatingly stale locker room air. The national anthem played, the kickoff team took the field and Rusty set his mind to the task at hand.

Even the weakest teams have stars, and for Wyatt High School one of their stars was a quick, sure handed wide receiver. Coach Childress had warned his defense about the kid. Though he was of average size, the wide receiver was clearly the fastest runner on the field. His speed, deceptive footwork and ball handling skills had earned him a scholarship to Stephen F. Austin State University. On the first Wyatt possession, he caught three passes, the last for a touchdown. After five minutes of the first quarter, Stephenville had fallen behind seven to zero.

Coach Childress was livid. As the Stephenville offense took the field, he called the defense together and berated them for giving up a touchdown in the very manner he had been warning them about all week. "You've got to pressure the quarterback!" he yelled. "Do not give him time to find his wide receiver. We've been talking about this all week. And look, if you can put a hit on the wide receiver, make sure you hit him with all you've got! Trust me, you do not want to get into a foot race with that kid."

The Stephenville offense managed a quick touchdown to tie the score. The defense was soon back on the field. Wyatt tried a run up the middle on first down for no gain. Coach Childress called for Rusty to blitz on second down, which resulted in a Wyatt loss of three yards. On third and thirteen for Wyatt, attention was on the wide receiver, lined up on the far side from Rusty. Rather than dropping back to pass as Rusty anticipated, the quarterback ran a sweep, away from Rusty and towards the wide receiver. Rusty recognized the developing reverse and held his position. The quarterback handed the ball to the wide receiver who put his speed on full display running towards Rusty's side of the field. Unfortunately for him, one of the offensive linemen was on the ground injured, forcing the wide receiver to stutter step and vault over his teammate. That's all the advantage Rusty needed. Before the wide receiver could turn up field, Rusty hit him at full speed. The receiver never saw him coming. The impact could be heard in the stands. Though it happened in an instant, to Rusty if felt like slow motion. The crack of pads, the opponent going airborne, the terrified scream when he landed, the arm strangely mangled, broken, suddenly a worthless appendage. A talent destroyed with one hit.

Rusty's teammates swarmed him with head slaps and back slaps. The screams of the receiver quickly dulled their enthusiasm. Everyone on the field and in the stands became whisper quiet. Everyone except Coach Childress, who put his fist in the air and shouted "Atta boy, Rusty! Now that's what I'm talking about!"

As the Wyatt coaches and a trainer ran onto the field to tend to their player, ten defensive players ambled towards the sidelines. A few players on both sides knelt in prayer. Rusty walked towards the locker room that was near the end zone. As he did, he saw an ambulance crew quickly getting a stretcher ready to take onto the field. The receiver's cries of agony branded Rusty's soul. Rusty kept his helmet on, as if it would somehow shield him from the memory of the ugly, mangled arm he had damaged. For a moment he thought he might vomit or perhaps his intestines would explode onto the grass as a pain in his gut grew.

Coach Childress noticed Rusty walking away and turned to a trainer, a sophomore who would do whatever was asked. "Is

Rusty hurt? Go see what's wrong with him. We need him back on the field."

The trainer jogged to Rusty's side. "You OK?"

Rusty didn't answer. He kept walking towards the locker room, ignoring the trainer's question.

"Are you hurt? What's going on?" The trainer followed Rusty into the locker room. "Come on, man, we need you out there. What's the deal?"

Rusty took off his helmet, removed his pads and started to change into his street clothes. The trainer, a kid who loved football but was too small to play the game, looked bewildered. "What do I tell Coach Childress?" he worried as Rusty buttoned his shirt.

"Tell him I'm tired of hurting people."

"He won't like that."

Rusty looked at the trainer and suddenly felt his anger boiling to the surface. "I don't give a rat's ass what that son of a bitch likes!"

§§§

Kathleen could hear the crack of shoulder pads as she sat in her designated seat with the Stingerettes. She couldn't see the damage Rusty had done to the wide receiver, but she didn't need to. Rusty standing, unmoving, eyes fixated on the injured player told her it was bad. How bad, she didn't know. She watched Rusty walk towards the locker room with a trainer, a sign that he must have also been hurt. As paramedics loaded the wide receiver into an ambulance, the young man lifted his one good arm in a weak wave. The Stingerettes responded with respectful but subdued applause. Once the ambulance rolled out of sight and the boys took the field, the Stingerettes broke into a cheer with their white cowboy hats moving in synchrony. Kathleen had little enthusiasm for the cheer as she kept her eyes on the locker room, waiting for Rusty to return. It felt strange when the trainer left the locker room without Rusty and jogged over to

Coach Childress. Whatever the trainer said sure upset the coach. He slammed his clip board to the ground, pointed to the locker room and yelled something at the hapless trainer.

A few minutes later, Kathleen saw the red lights of Rusty's pickup glow in the parking lot. "Somethings not right", she whispered to herself.

The game went on as expected. Without their star wide receiver, the boys from Fort Worth struggled to be competitive. Stephenville dominating, the home crowd's mood turned joyful. Kathleen went through the motions of cheering for her school, a fake smile as she waved her white cowboy hat in unison with her dance team. Her body was in the stands with the Stingerettes, but her worry for Rusty grew faster than the Stephenville Yellowjackets could run up the score.

Midway through the second quarter, Kathleen left her seat. She needed to do something, but was unsure of what that something should be.

"Where do you think you're going?" the Stingerettes coach asked as Kathleen passed nearby. The question was stern, but not unfriendly.

"Sorry, coach. Have to go to the restroom. I'll be right back."

"You'd better be, young lady. We'll be lining up for the halftime show. Make it quick."

Kathleen nodded and hurried to the restroom, which was under the stands not far from the concessions. On the way to the restroom, she saw Bobby, a boy from history class, walking with a sophomore girl. In his left hand he held a large paper cup with ice and a dark soft drink. Bobby's right arm was around his girlfriend's shoulders. The couple kissed and giggled as they walked, oblivious to their surroundings. Kathleen suddenly had a plan. She bumped into Bobby as if by accident, the soft drink spilling across her stockings and Stingerettes uniform. The mess was greater than she had anticipated. Cold, sticky soft drink covered most of the left side of her uniform and stockings. An ice cube found its way into her boot.

"Oh my God, I'm so sorry!" Bobby declared. "Are you OK?"

Kathleen tried to brush the cold drink from her uniform, with little success. "This was my fault. I should have been more careful."

The girlfriend offered, "Let me get some paper towels from the girl's room. Maybe we can dry you off some."

"Thanks, but I don't think paper towels will fix this."

"I'm so sorry," Bobby repeated.

Kathleen looked at the couple. "I've got to get back. We have a halftime show."

As Kathleen walked towards the Stingerettes seating area, she felt as if all eyes were on her.

"What happened to you?" the dance coach angrily asked.

Kathleen tried to brush off her uniform as if the sticky mess would come off in her hands. "Kid ran into me with his soda," Kathleen replied as if she was frustrated.

The coach pointed an angry finger at the soiled uniform. "Kathleen, I can't let you do halftime looking like that. I don't have time for this now. This is really disappointing."

Kathleen looked at her coach. "Yes, ma'am. I know."

"Here's what you're going to do. Do you have any Woolite at home?"

"Yes."

"OK, go home and fill a sink with cold water. Put two caps of Woolite in the sink, make some suds and then soak your stockings and uniform overnight. Tomorrow morning, rinse with cold water and then air dry. Understood?"

"Yes, ma'am."

"Go on then. The rest of us have work to do here."

Kathleen tried to look disappointed as she turned away from her teammates, who now hurriedly readied for the halftime show. Walking towards the Oldsmobile, she could hear the band playing a lively song. The smell of popcorn filled the air. Her desire to dance at halftime had been overcome by worry for Rusty. That worry was as raw as the wet stocking inside of her cold boots. A pair of sneakers in the car would take care of her feet. She worried that helping Rusty with whatever had happened to him might prove more difficult. They had been friends long enough for her to know Rusty would never walk off a field unless something was terribly wrong.

Kathleen guessed Rusty had gone home. As she parked the Oldsmobile in front of his house, his truck in the driveway confirmed her assumption. A jacket covered her still damp Stingerettes uniform minus the boots and cowboy hat. Kathleen rang the doorbell.

The front porch light came on as Rusty opened the door. Just out of the shower, he stood behind the screen door, short wet hair neatly combed, shirtless wearing fresh blue jeans and sneakers. A damp towel was draped over his muscular shoulders. A few tuffs of adolescent chest hair provided a hint of the man he was becoming. "What are you doing here?" he asked, clearly surprised to see her.

Kathleen hesitated. Seeing Rusty clean, muscular and shirtless aroused a desire she neither expected nor welcomed, but could not deny. Finally, she asked "I was about to ask you the same question. Are you hurt?"

"Never been better," he replied as he removed the towel and began putting on a shirt. Once dressed, Rusty stepped onto the porch. "Aren't you missing your halftime show?"

Kathleen sat on the step leading to the front porch, hugged her legs and motioned for Rusty to sit with her. As he sat beside her, she said, "Hell of a hit you made on that kid."

"I think I broke his arm. You should have heard him scream. Maybe the worse sound I've heard in my whole sorry ass life."

They were quiet for a moment. "It's not your fault his arm broke."

"Really? Who else hit him besides me? I must have missed that part."

"That's not what I mean and you know it. You were doing your job, trying to win the game."

"Is it my job to hurt people? That kid has a football scholarship to Stephen F. Austin State. He sure as hell won't be playing any more football this season, or maybe ever." Rusty paused as if he were trying to find the right words. "You asked me once if I ever got tired of hurting people. Good question. Well, tonight, I got tired of hurting people. I'm done."

"You can't just walk off the team."

"Why not? What part of 'I'm done' is hard for you to understand?"

"But you love football."

"Who told you that? Have I ever once said I loved football?"

"You always talk about how you have fun with the guys doing God knows what."

"Fun with the guys is not football. Two separate things."

Kathleen took a deep breath. "So you don't enjoy the game?"

"Nope. Never have. I kept at it because it's what everyone wanted, expected."

"You mean like you're playing a character in someone else's play?"

Rusty gave her a smirk. "Weird way to say it, but yes. Starting tonight, I'm done with that crap."

They were both quiet. Somewhere far in the distance, she faintly heard the band playing their halftime show, the sound muffled by wind through the shrubs circling the house. Kathleen thought about how many times while dating they had talked, saying nothing. Now that they were talking as friends, it felt different, relevant. She turned to look at him and softly said, "I think I understand more than you'll ever know."

Rusty picked up a small stick from the front porch and angrily threw it into the front yard. "Doubt it," he replied in a manner both sarcastic and dismissive.

Kathleen was taken aback by his response and felt herself becoming suddenly annoyed. "What about your scholarship?

What's your mother going to say? What will your teammates say?"

"You know, all my life I've been trying to do the right thing, to be what other people want me to be. Son of a military hero, football player, the whole thing. It sucks! Maybe I want to be what I want to be."

Kathleen found herself becoming confused as she tried to understand. "So you're just going to walk away from a full ride scholarship?" She knew she sounded more judgmental than she intended. "What's your mom going to say when you tell her you quit football? You're walking away from your responsibilities to your teammates, your school and especially to your mother."

Kathleen could tell from the pained expression on his face that she had made him uncomfortable. He looked at her with sadness. "Don't you ever get tired of hurting people?"

Kathleen stared at the dull shadows on the ground. She had always seen herself as the one who comforted others. Rusty's words hit a nerve. They sat in silence. Finally, Rusty added "You're going to be in deep shit on Monday for missing the halftime show."

Kathleen laughed. "True. But not near as much trouble as you're going to be in for quitting football during a game. What are you going to do?"

"Guess I'll try to talk with Mr. Jamison on Monday."

"Jamison may help you through this year, but what about next year? Please don't tell me you're planning to get drafted."

"Don't want to talk about next year," he answered with resolve.

Kathleen looked at him with surprise. "You've been thinking about quitting football for a while, haven't you?"

"I always knew you were smart."

"Weird. We never talked much when we were dating. Now that we're back to being friends, it seems easier." She shook her head in bewilderment. "I'll probably never figure that one out, but I'm glad we're still friends."

"I always thought we talked a lot."

"Well, yes, but not about anything important."

"Maybe some people are better off just being friends." He paused. "We're still good, right?"

Kathleen smiled. "Yes, we're good. I heard you're hanging out with Anna."

"Word sure gets around."

"She seems like a sweet girl."

"Different than anybody I've ever met, that's for sure. You happy hanging with that damn hippie?"

"He's sweet. You two would probably get along OK if you weren't so damn stubborn. By the way, what do you want me to say at school on Monday? You know people will be asking."

"Tell them Michael and I don't get along so well."

Kathleen laughed. "Not what I mean and you know it. What do you want me to say about your quitting football?"

"Just tell them it's none of their damn business. Tell them I've made other plans."

Kathleen stood and faced Rusty. "Well, my friend, whatever it is you're planning, I hope it works out for you." She looked down at Rusty still sitting on the step and managed a sad smile.

"Hey, you're not going to believe this. We added two fiddles to Baked Cotton. Ian and Michael."

Kathleen snorted. "And hell will freeze over and they'll strike oil in your back yard."

"I'm serious. We're practicing tomorrow morning."

"I heard about Ian maybe joining the band, but Michael? Jake hates Michael. You and Michael don't exactly get along either."

"Surprised the hell out of me, too."

Kathleen rolled her eyes and shook her head. "You, Michael, Jake and Ian have a good time tomorrow with whatever it is you're doing. See ya."

"See ya," Rusty waved.

Kathleen watched Rusty go back into the house as she started the Oldsmobile. Driving home in her sticky damp uniform, she pondered the future for Rusty, for Michael and, mostly, for herself. The predictability of her world was crumbling, leaving her with confusing feelings of joy and fear.

§§§

Rusty heard his mom walk through the door not long after Kathleen had driven off. Although she often cheered for Rusty at his games, this night had been spent with her Bridge Club friends. Rusty was stretched out on his twin bed reading *Sports Illustrated*. Appearing at his bedroom doorway, a puzzled frown crossed her face.

"What are you doing here? Are you hurt? I thought you had a game tonight," she began.

"Yes, ma'am, I did." Rusty could see the concerned and confused look on his mother's face. He wanted in the deepest possible way to make her happy. It had not been easy, he knew, being a widowed parent. Between her job, keeping up with Rusty's activities and the grind of day-to-day living, she had precious little time for herself. Her love for Rusty was unshakeable. Rusty was sure of it. He was also sure that her understanding of the challenges facing a teen boy was sometimes tenuous. But she tried. She always tried, and for that he was grateful.

"Well, young man, I think you better put the magazine down and tell me what's going on." She removed several clothing items of questionable cleanliness from a chair near his bed and sat down, waiting for his response.

Rusty sat up and faced his mother. It occurred to him that this might be more difficult than he anticipated. "Mom, I quit football."

There was a moment of stunned silence. Finally, she asked "But why? Are you hurt?"

"No. Not hurt at all. But I busted a guy's arm tonight. He had to go to the hospital. I feel sick about it, kind of like the way it felt not long ago when I hit the quarterback in the head so hard, he didn't know where he was and puked his guts out all over the place. I'm tired of it, Mom. Tired of hurting people."

"Well, then, maybe you shouldn't hit them so hard."

Rusty chuckled. "Mom, you don't get it. It's football. You have to go all out. There's no in between, except maybe in practice. Coach Childress loves it when I hurt people. He thinks it's great. I just can't do it anymore."

"Can't or won't?"

"Yes."

There was a moment of awkward silence. Rusty watched his mom's face as she gathered her thoughts. "God, I miss your father. He'd know what to say."

"I miss Dad, too."

"I think he would say you have a responsibility to your team, your school. We don't walk away from responsibilities in this family."

Rusty winced. His father was a hero, not only to Rusty but to the whole town, or so it seemed. How could an 18-year-old ever measure up? Until now, Rusty had been comfortable, even happy with walking away from football. Looking at his mother's worried expression, thinking of how his dad would have responded, left Rusty suddenly feeling morose.

She tenderly took his hands in her own. "Your dad also always said we should have the courage of our convictions."

"I think I screwed up. I'm sorry, Mom."

She somehow managed to look sad and smile simultaneously. "Son, look at you, almost a grown man. I can't tell you what to do like I used to. It's going to be awfully quiet and lonely around here whenever you move out. I'll probably cry a river when that day happens." She paused, as if a new idea had suddenly occurred to her. "What about your scholarship?"

"Probably lost it tonight."

"Have you thought about next year, what you'll do?"

"I have, Mom, at least a little. Come Monday, I'll try to talk with Mr. Jamison."

"I can help you some with college, but I can't foot the whole bill. You'll have to figure a way to work or something to make up the difference. Maybe Harold Jamison will have some suggestions. You are going to college, aren't you?"

His mom's worried expression broke his heart. "I need to figure some things out."

"What things?"

"Like what I'm going to do with my life for starters." Rusty forced himself to make eye contact with his mom, who still looked concerned and perhaps sad. "Love you, Mom."

"Love you too, son. Somehow, we'll figure this out. I just hope next time you make a big decision like this you talk with me first."

"You would have tried to talk me out of it."

"It took a lot of courage to do what you did tonight. You say it's for the best, and I want to believe you. That cake's been baked. If you don't have a plan, then any road will get you there, but you may not be happy with where you end up. I want you to be happy and successful and you will be. I'm sure of it. I'm here for you, you know that. But--"

"There's always a but isn't there?"

"You need a plan."

§§§

Rusty waited as long as possible to pick up Anna from the Dairy Queen. The last thing he wanted was to see his friends and former teammates. Anna would be busy serving burgers, cleaning spilled drinks and counting the minutes waiting for store closing. Rusty, until now, had been part of the weekly post-game revelry. This night he felt removed, detached. It occurred to him that Anna may have had similar feelings of detachment on many Friday nights. On this night, he was in no mood to answer questions or join in the victory celebrations. Fortunately, most of the parking lot was empty as Anna left the

172

restaurant. Rusty thought she had a hop in her step, a look of joy incompatible with the way he was feeling.

Anna opened the passenger door of the truck, slid across the seat and gave Rusty a quick kiss. "Hi, amigo. Take me home." Rusty started the truck. "You'll never guess what happened today. It looks like Papa's going to get his bonus for the Bluff Dale job and I got a letter from the parish!"

Anna's eyes had an excited sparkle that made him smile in spite of himself. "Parish. That's the same as a church, right?"

"Sort of. But guess what? I got a parish scholarship!"

"For what?"

Anna looked at him and frowned. "It's to help me with nursing school. What's wrong with you?"

"Nothing."

They drove in silence towards Anna's home. Stopping in front of her house, Rusty killed the engine and turned to Anna. "Way to go on your scholarship," he said with poorly disguised lack of enthusiasm.

"Dios mio. I heard you won your game. You should be happy. I was surprised that you were not with your friends in the store tonight. What's wrong?"

"They did win. Good for them."

"They? They is you, mi amigo."

"Not any more. I quit."

Silence. The windows were down, but the air was unusually still. Anna brushed the back of her hand softly across his cheek. "Are you hurt?"

"No, I'm fine." Taking a deep breath, he added "I might have screwed up this evening."

"What happened?"

"I hurt a kid. Broke his arm. Anna, I heard him scream. His arm was all disjointed. They had to take him off the field on a stretcher. Ambulance took him to the hospital." Rusty paused, shook his head and continued in a soft voice. "At first, everyone was jumping around thinking I'd done a great thing." Rusty stared at his feet in regret at the damage he had caused. "It's not the first time I've knocked someone out of a game. Weird thing, that asshole Childress likes it when I hurt guys. Son of a bitch is always yelling, trying to act tough. We're supposed to respect our coaches. In my eyes, he's scum. The guy has no morals."

"But you didn't mean to hurt him, did you?"

"Childress? No, I never even touched him."

"No, silly, I mean the other player. Were you trying to hurt him?"

"Hell, no. It was a clean hit. You can't play the game without hurting people."

"So, something was different tonight, no?"

"I just got tired of it. My coach wants me to bust the guys. Wants me to ruin their scholarships like I probably did tonight. One time I hit a guy so hard he didn't know where he was. Poor guy went to the sidelines and puked his guts out. Coach thought it was great. He keeps telling me to get in there and put some hurt on more guys. He wants me to break some bones. If I run a good play without injuring my opponent, coach is pissed. Happens all the time. It's not right and I won't do it. Not any more. Problem is, what kind of guy would walk away from his team? The boys on the team don't do that."

"So tonight you stood up for your principles."

"You could say that."

"You're right, Rusty. Boys don't do that. Men do."

Rusty sat up straighter in his seat. "How did you get so smart?"

"I'm eighteen years old, trying to figure things out, same as you. I've just had to grow up a bit faster than most of your friends. Doesn't mean I like it. But I'm not crying about it either."

"I probably lost my scholarship tonight. No football, no scholarship."

"So what's the plan?"

"Working on it. I need to talk with Jamison on Monday, hopefully."

"What do you want?"

"Huh?"

"It's not a trick question. What do you want?"

"You mean now or later?"

"Both."

"I want to get myself to where someday I can support a family doing something I'm proud of, something that makes a difference. My dad did a lot of good. Maybe I want to be like him in some way."

"OK, that's a good goal for your future. But you're still in high school. We'll graduate in May. What do you want between now and then?"

"I want to play my drums, hopefully get some gigs. Spend time with you and my friends if they're still around." He paused for a moment, then added "Maybe try harder in school."

Anna smiled at Rusty and in a soft, reassuring way, said "You can do all that. I know you can."

Rusty put his arms around Anna's shoulders, leaned over and kissed her lips. She felt right in his arms, as if she belonged there. Her hair smelled of burgers, fries and sweat, but he didn't care. He gently moved her hair behind her ear so he could see her face clearly. "Weird how you got a scholarship on the very day I lost mine."

"I thought you'd be happy for me."

"I am. A decent guy would have been congratulating you."

Anna searched his face, as if looking for answers to questions that had not been asked. "You're uptight because you think if I go to nursing school, we won't be together."

"Maybe a little."

"Rusty, I have to go to school. My family needs me to. I need me to. Haven't you ever wanted something so strong you were determined to go for it? Like nothing or nobody is going to get in your way?"

Rusty mumbled, "I'm working on it." Anna moved slightly away from him on the truck's bench seat. He was startled to see that she looked angry.

Anna sternly said, "You can do whatever you want to do. But I don't think wallowing on your pity pot is the answer. You have to figure this out. It's important for your future."

"Are you mad at me?"

"Frustrated."

"Why? What did I do?"

"You took a stand tonight. I'm proud of you. I don't give a damn what other people think you should do and I wish you didn't care so much either. Do you even realize how I'm invisible to most of your friends? I'm just the counter girl at Dairy Queen. Well guess what? They don't define me! I define me! It's hard sometimes, but I have to keep my head up and keep my eye on my goals. You should do the same."

Rusty managed a smile. "You're proud of me?"

"God help me, but yes sir."

"You're not mad?"

"Mad, no. Frustrated, yes."

"Why?"

"Because I have to go in the house in a few minutes and my plan for a scholarship celebration make out with you isn't happening."

Rusty quickly took her in his arms and kissed her deeply. He kissed her neck, her eyebrows. He ran his fingers through her hair. As he did, he felt the confidence he lacked earlier in the evening return full force. Anna's hand moved lightly across the crotch of his blue jeans, as if by accident. Or was it?

Anna smiled up at Rusty. "It sucks, but I really do have to go." She slid across the bench seat and started to open the door.

"Wait."

She looked at him curiously. "What's wrong?"

Rusty got out of the truck, opened her door and with his arm around her shoulders walked her onto the front porch of her home. Standing near the home's front door, he took her into his arms and sweetly kissed her goodnight.

Saturday, October 25, 1969

Michael faced the morning chill wearing blue jeans and an Oregon State University sweatshirt. As he walked to his car, violin in hand, he wondered how he managed to find himself in a rehearsal with Jake and his band. Michael felt no friendship and little respect for Jake or his friend Rusty. He was sure the feeling was mutual. And yet, here he was, on his way to Rusty's house to play some music.

Michael had asked Ian if he needed a ride to the rehearsal. Ian had seemed relieved to receive the offer. Michael guessed the last thing Ian wanted was to be alone with Jake and Rusty. Although he felt sure Ian understood the boys could not assault him if they wanted their band to play at school functions, Ian still acted wary.   And who could blame him? He had been beat up, harassed and ostracized by his so-called peers for years.

Wearing plaid pants, white socks, black leather shoes and a pressed long sleeve shirt, Ian was waiting in front of his house when Michael arrived. Michael wondered if Ian realized, or even cared, about how different he looked. Ian put his violin and a zippered three ring binder in the back seat of Michael's car.

As they drove away, Michael inquired "What's in the binder?"

"Music. I think we may need it. Can't believe we're doing this."

Michael laughed. "Me either. Damn weirdest thing I've ever done."

"You think they'll cause trouble?" Ian asked, clearly nervous.

"Be cool. They need you more than you need them. If they give us trouble, we'll just leave. But I bet they won't. Jake wants to play at school functions. Without you, they're going nowhere. You hold the cards, not them. Remember that. Besides, I heard these guys play at the school sock hop a while back. They're OK, but not great. You'll be the best musician in the room by a long shot."

"You're good."

"Thanks. But I'm not you. I'm curious, how much do you practice?"

"Couple of hours a day, then another hour or so studying music."

"What do you mean, studying music?"

"You know, music theory, listening to different types of music, trying to figure out how they get different sounds. Stuff like that."

Michael would normally practice thirty minutes to an hour most days. Two hours was incomprehensible. "Damn, Ian, that's a lot of music. Don't you ever get tired of it?"

Ian shook his head. "I love music. Besides, what else do I have to do? Plus, it's the only way I can get out of this stupid town."

"That part I can understand," Michael replied as they stopped in front of the address Rusty had given them.

The boys rang the doorbell and waited. A middle-aged woman in an apron with flowered prints answered the door. Smiling, she said, "Oh, you must be Rusty's new friends. He told me you'd be coming over." Michael and Ian were silent, caught off guard by the notion that Rusty had referred to them as friends. "You boys go on around the house. They're in the garage."

Michael walked towards the garage with Ian close behind. He could hear the band warming up. Entering the garage, he stopped to take in their surroundings. An old tool chest off to one side, numerous paint cans scattered about, garden tools in one corner and oil stains on the cement floor. He shrugged at Ian. It was a new musical environment for both of them Michael guessed, and it took a moment to adjust to the surroundings.

"Hey, guys. Glad you're here," Rusty twirled his drumstick in a friendly manner. "Michael, this is Tommy and Judy. You probably don't know them."

Michael recognized both from the school hallway. "I've seen you around." The atmosphere felt awkward to Michael, as if they didn't quite knew how to start. The tenuous relationship he and Ian had with the band could unravel at any moment.

"Do you have a music stand?" Ian asked.

"We can fix one for you," Jake answered. He and Tommy wheeled a tall tool chest toward the boys. Opening the third drawer of the chest, Jake offered it as an option to hold the music. "We didn't know if you wanted to sit or stand."

"We'll stand," Michael answered for both of them as he and Ian got their violins out of the cases.

"OK," Jake began. "Let's start with *True Love Ways*. A slow one. Everyone likes Buddy Holly. Y'all ready?"

Ian and Michael nodded and Jake started the song. The violin parts were simple, even boring. It sounded to Michael as if the band was dull, playing all the right notes but without harmony. Not wrong, but not right either. It was an amateurish sound, as if the band needed to be better, but lacked the skill to get there. Michael had a sinking feeling that the rehearsal was a mistake. It had not occurred to him that the music itself could prove to be an embarrassment.

As the tune ended, Jake said "Hey, that was pretty good." He seemed pleased with himself.

Ian and Michael looked at each other. One of those looks that made clear without speaking that neither of them was particularly impressed.

Ian took a deep breath. "I think we should try it again."

Jake smiled. "Will do. I like this song."

"But let's do it differently," Ian said as if he were asking permission. Jake gave him a dubious look. "This time I'll play up a third. Judy, you sing harmony. Tommy, a little less bass. And let's watch the crescendos. They're there for a reason."

Judy looked surprised. "Harmony on which part?"

"All of it," Ian replied.

Jake looked annoyed. "Wait a minute. Buddy Holly didn't have anyone singing with him. Why should I?"

Michael challenged Jake. "So you're Buddy Holly now?"

"No," Jake replied. "But I think we should do it like Buddy did."

"I'll sing the harmony," Judy interrupted to everyone's surprise.

"What the hell," Jake said to nobody in particular. "Get the spare microphone and let's try this."

Tommy set up the microphone for his sister and the band played the song a second time. The sounds blended in a more interesting fashion. When it ended, Jake turned to Ian with thinly disguised irritation. "You happy now?"

Ian responded, "It's better. The crescendos are not pronounced enough and Jake you were a quarter beat late on the second verse. Judy, turn your amp down a little. We don't want to overpower Jake. Let's try it again."

Michael marveled at the contrast between the timid Ian that he usually saw and the way Ian became a force in a musical setting.

The band played through the song a third and then a fourth time, making changes as Ian suggested. Michael enjoyed watching Jake's face twist in annoyance at the process. After the fourth time through, Jake said in a challenging manner "There. You happy now?"

"I think so," Ian replied as he reached for his zippered three ring binder.

"Now what?" Jake sneered.

"A song I want us to try," Ian responded, totally ignoring Jake's attitude.

"Bullshit! You can't come in here and tell us what we're going to play. This is my band! Not yours, you little twerp!"

"Jake, shut up!" Rusty shouted to everyone's surprise.

"You shut up! He can't come in here and take over like this! This is my band, not his!" Jake yelled.

Michael and Ian started to pack their instruments as if they were planning to leave.

"Well, it's my garage and I want to hear whatever it is that Ian has for us," Rusty replied with a steely eyed stare at Jake.

"Stay cool, guys," Tommy injected. "You have to admit, it sounds better with Ian's suggestions. I'd like to see what else he has to offer. Maybe we can take this band to another level."

Jake looked at his band mates. "Looks like I'm outnumbered here." Turning to Ian he said "Come on guys. Don't go. Let's do your song. I didn't mean to lose it there. Let's just play."

Michael and Ian looked at each other. Michael said "Let's give them another chance."

Ian shrugged and he and Michael opened their violin cases. Ian handed out music for *I'll Never Find Another You*, a tune made popular by The Seekers.

Jake shook his head. "My God. This isn't even country. Now you want me to sing a girl song?"

Ian smiled. "Nope. Judy will be the lead singer on this one. You sing up a third."

"What the hell is a third?" Jake asked.

Michael chuckled as Ian tried to explain how to sing harmony. As they spoke, he noticed Jake's persona deflating. Ian had clearly taken over leadership of the band and everyone, with the exception of Jake, was impressed with the change. In addition, Judy's shyness evaporated when she embraced her vocalist duties. As the band played *I'll Never Find Another You*, Jake struggled with the harmonies. After another try, Ian turned to Tommy and Rusty. "Can you guys sing?" They both laughed and even Jake couldn't resist a chuckle. "OK, then, Jake, your guitar sounds good. You focus on that. I'll sing the harmony." To everyone's surprise, Ian and Judy's voices blended together perfectly.

Rusty smiled as the song ended. "Wow, we sound amazing! Judy, you never told us you could sing like that."

Judy smiled. "You never asked me."

Tommy added "I have to tell you guys, this band has never sounded so good. You have any more for us?"

"Yes," Ian answered. "But Jake only wants us for two songs."

"Damn right! You got the Buddy Holly and the girl song. This ain't your band. I mean, we appreciate your coming over to practice with us, but we'll take it from here," Jake said in a dismissive tone.

"Hang on," Rusty interrupted. "I want to hear what these boys can do."

"Me, too," said Tommy and Judy in unison.

Michael chuckled when Jake's eyes bulged. "What the hell?"

The room was thick with tension. Tommy tried to calm his bandmates. "Come on y'all. Be cool. Let's see what Ian has to offer. I like the new sound we're getting."

Jake glared at Tommy. "Screw it," he mumbled, quickly putting his guitar in his case and slamming the lid shut with much more effort than needed. He closed each of the four metal latches on the case with hammer like precision, as if the case were the cause of his anger. The sound echoed through the now silent garage.

"Come on, Jake. Why can't we try something new, see what happens?" Rusty pleaded.

Jake glared at his bandmates. "This is bullshit." Then turning to Rusty added, "You want to play, go play with your wetback girlfriend. I'm out of here."

Michael noticed Rusty's face harden as Jake stormed out of the garage. For a moment, the band sat in stunned silence. Jake's exit left a leadership vacuum, but not for long. Rusty looked at Ian. "Any of your music work without a lead guitar?"

Michael saw Ian hesitate and turn to Michael as if looking for direction. Michael shrugged.

Rusty said, "Come on Ian. We're here for the music. What else do you have for us?"

Ian quietly distributed the music for *Whiter Shade of Pale* which had been recorded by Procol Harum. "Judy, if I sing the melody on this one, you think you can handle the harmony?"

"On which part?" Judy asked.

"I'm not sure. At least on the chorus, but probably all of it."

"Hang on" Michael interrupted. "There's supposed to be a lot of organ on this one. We don't have an organ."

Ian said "I think we can make it work with the keyboard and violins. Let's try."

The band spent the next thirty minutes practicing the song. As the band played, the tension in the room evaporated and Michael found to his surprise that he was enjoying the experience. At least for one morning, he felt as if he were a part of something outside of the school orchestra. As the band worked together, with Ian clearly in charge, the animosity between he and Rusty also melted, at least a little. Music had brought them together for one Saturday morning.

About noon, Michael's stomach growled in protest from a lack of nutrition. To his relief, Rusty announced, "OK, I think we're done for today." Turning to Ian and Michael he asked, "Y'all are coming back next Saturday, right?"

Ian said "OK, but everyone needs to practice their parts before then."

Rusty smiled. "You guys are good. I'm glad you're in the band."

Michael was dubious. "Are we in the band? What about Jake?"

There was an awkward moment of silence. To Michael's surprise, the timid girl Judy was the first to speak. "This was one of the most fun rehearsals we've had, minus Jake's hissy fit. A few more practices and I bet we'll be better than ever."

Rusty added, "See y'all next weekend, same time, same place?"

Michael replied, "Works for me."

"Me, too," Ian added. "Maybe Jake will come around."

Rusty shook his head. "Maybe, but I wouldn't count on it.

§§§

Kathleen sat in front of her bedroom dresser mirror and removed pink curlers. Shaking her head, her now wavey hair fell across her shoulders. As she brushed her hair, she could hear Michael's car drive towards the house. She put on her blue jeans and a long sleeved multi colored blouse in anticipation of their date. Pleased with her look in the dresser mirror, she felt a vague sense of nervousness that she could neither deny nor understand. Michael was different, very different, from the other boys she knew. Sometimes when they talked at school or in the evenings on the phone, she feared that her feelings towards Michael were moving too quickly, as if she needed to slow down but had no desire to do so. Nobody had ever kissed her so deeply or held her so tenderly. There was a desire in his eyes she had never seen from Rusty. The passion was wonderful, and frightening.

The prior evening, after going home to soak her Stingerettes uniform in Woolite and put on some clean clothes, she had phoned Michael to see if he wanted to meet her at the Dairy Queen. A lot of her friends would be there after the football game. Kathleen was relieved when Michael had said yes. The store had been crowded with her friends celebrating the football victory. Strangely, Michael looked more relaxed, almost as if he enjoyed being there. Kathleen was amused when he told her about how he and Ian were planning to rehearse with Baked Cotton.

There was a knock on the front door. Her five-year-old niece who was visiting for the weekend yelled "I'll get it."

Leaving her room, Kathleen could see her niece looking at Michael through the screen door. The niece had one hand on her hip in a sassy pose. "Who are you?" she asked in a manner that sounded like a challenge.

"I'm Michael. Who are you?"

"My name is Ellie. What can I do you for?" she replied, not wavering from her sassy attitude.

"Well now," Kathleen interrupted. "You met my little girl." Kathleen could see the surprise and confusion on Michael's face.

"I'm not your girl! I'm Mommy and Daddy's girl," Ellie said as if she had somehow been insulted.

Kathleen laughed. "You'll always be my girl, and Mommy and Daddy's girl, too. Why don't you ask Michael in?"

Ellie frowned. "I guess that's OK. He's kind of cute. Needs a haircut though," she said as she opened the screen door to let Michael into the house.

Kathleen walked up to Michael, put her arms around his neck and kissed him.

"Eww, gross! Granny, there's a boy in the house!" Ellie hollered as she ran towards the kitchen.

"Mom, we're heading to the drive-in," Kathleen said over her shoulder as they walked out the door.

Her mother hollered from the kitchen. "You kids be careful and don't be out too late. You know the rules."

Kathleen and Michael held hands as they walked towards the VW. As Michael started his car, Kathleen asked "What do you think of my niece?"

Michael chuckled. "I thought your mother was tough. I have a feeling Ellie is even more so. I didn't even know you had a niece. Do you see her much?"

"She's my sister's kid." Kathleen wanted to say more, but wasn't sure if she should. "Sometimes she stays with us on the weekends."

"Older sister I assume."

"Definitely." *What the hell*, Kathleen thought. *He'll probably figure it out anyway.* "My sister's really smart. Good grades. Honor Society in high school. College bound. In love with her boyfriend Dave. Senior year of high school she gets pregnant. Next thing we know she's married to Dave and they're living down in De Leon. Instead of college, she's a secretary at the peanut co-op. Dave works at the Dr Pepper plant doing something with the bottling process. My sister and Dave love each other, love Ellie and they're doing the best they can. But it's really hard. They're doing what they need to do, but not living their dream. At least not yet. My sister wanted to be a physical therapist. I'm not sure it's ever going to happen. I love my sister, but there's no way in hell I'm going to get pregnant until I finish school. And I'm not talking about high school. I'm talking college."

Michael smiled. "No offense to your sister, but I'd be disappointed if you felt any other way."

"Why?"

Michael seemed surprised by the question. "You have dreams, goals. I get it. How come your sister decided to get pregnant?"

"I don't think it was a decision exactly."

They entered the drive-in a few minutes before dusk. Off to the side, some boys were playing football. Kathleen was pleased that Michael showed no interest in joining the game. Instead, they walked hand in hand towards the concession stand where Michael purchased two Coca-Colas with peanuts. Back at the car, Michael hung the silver movie speaker on the car window. The car felt cozy to Kathleen. Although they were surrounded by other cars and trucks, it felt as if they were alone. Kathleen snuggled next to Michael as he put his arm around her shoulders. It felt safe. It felt right and yet somehow slightly rebellious. They talked a little, kissed a little and watched the movie, a little.

As the movie credits rolled, multiple headlights came on and cars began to exit the drive-in. Michael replaced the movie speaker, rolled up the window and hesitated.

"What's wrong?" she asked.

"Nothing. Do you want to get something to eat?"

"No." She thought she saw a look of disappointment on Michael's face as he started the car. "Are you taking me home?"

"Yes? I mean--"

"That's too bad," she softly interrupted with a feeling of excitement, desire and a vague sense of fear.

Michael gently touched the side of her face. "How about we find some place more private?"

"OK."

As they drove out of the drive-in, Michael turned away from town, going the opposite direction of most of the traffic. He found a dirt road which they drove down for a couple of miles until they were alone in the darkness, the road barely illuminated by the full moon, the sky salted with millions of stars. Reaching a secluded dark spot, Michael pulled off the road near what looked to be a hillside. The car's headlights caught a No Trespassing sign on a wide metal gate. Michael turned off the motor, reached over and gently kissed Kathleen. "I have no idea where we are," he said, "And to tell you the truth, I don't care."

"I've lived here all my life, and even I'm not sure where we are." As Michael kissed her neck, she added "But I know it's where I want to be."

Michael moved his seat back, giving Kathleen room to turn her back to the windshield, comfortable in his embrace. Their tongues did a lustful dance. She felt excited and vulnerable as Michael slowly put his hand inside her shirt and felt her breast. Feeling his hand tremble, she sensed that he felt the same nervous tension as she. He hesitated, as if unsure of what to do next. Kathleen unhooked her bra in an unmistakable invitation. The car became thick with the smell of unbridled teenage hormones as their blue jeans found their way to the dark floor of the car. Windows fogged with the steam of their lust as she explored his body and he explored hers. Kathleen felt a vague sense of fear that perhaps the night would end in regret. As he touched her in places nobody had ever touched her before, she relaxed in the warmth of his desire. Through the fogged windows, she thought she saw a light. A second later she was sure of it. She pushed Michael away and moved to the passenger seat as she groped in the darkness for her clothes.

"What's wrong?" Michael asked, clearly startled at the sudden change of mood.

"Someone's coming."

Michael looked into the rear-view mirror and could clearly see approaching headlights. "Shit!" was all he could manage to say as he too quickly made himself presentable. Before he could start the VW, they saw the flashing red lights of a sheriff's vehicle, coming to a stop directly behind. One officer with a large flashlight walked towards them while another remained near the patrol car.

As Michael rolled down the window, Kathleen noticed that the steam on the glass was melting as quickly as the romance of a moment before. The sheriff's deputy shined a light at the young couple. In a stern voice, the deputy with the flashlight looked directly at Kathleen and asked "You all right, young lady?"

"Oh yes sir officer, I'm fine," she replied, thankful that she did not recognize the deputy and he did not seem to recognize her.

The deputy looked carefully at the inside of the car, shining his light on the back seat, the floor boards and finally back to she and Michael. "You two doing drugs?"

Kathleen wished Michael could look more calm. He gripped the steering wheel, which forced him to fully extend his arms and lean forward to compensate for the seat having been moved back. Kathleen wanted to laugh, but thought better of it. Michael in an anxious voice said "No, sir, nothing like that."

The deputy responded as if he was unconvinced. "You have drugs in this car?" he asked with a scowl.

"No, sir. You want to search the car?" Michael asked.

The deputy paused, as if recognizing for the first time what he was seeing. His voice became a tad more friendly as he explained "We've already busted several drug deals in this area. The dump isn't a good place for y'all to be. Understood?"

"The dump?" Michael asked.

The deputy shined his light on a large sign for the Erath County Landfill. Kathleen bit her lip, trying not to break out in nervous laughter as the deputy moved the flashlight to Michael. "Driver's license." Michael pulled out his wallet and handed the deputy his new Texas license. "You too, miss." Kathleen found her purse and produced the license. The deputy looked at it carefully, then looked at Kathleen. "Kathleen Wilcox. Name seems real familiar. Can't place it though. Seems like I've met your parents someplace."

If the deputy meant for the comment to be a threat, it worked. Kathleen felt flush with embarrassment, as she wanted the interrogation to end as soon as possible. The last thing she needed was for some deputy to be talking to her parents. She'd be grounded for sure.

The officer standing next to the patrol car yelled at his partner. "You got a problem there, Roy?"

"No sir," Roy answered. "Couple of youngsters built a love nest where they shouldn't be."

"At the county dump?" the partner near the patrol car laughed. "Well I'll be."

Roy handed Kathleen and Michael their driver's licenses. "Now you listen here," he said in a return to his stern voice. "I want you two to get home now. This is not a safe area. If I ever see you here again, we'll be taking a ride to the station. That place smells like old tennis shoes and you won't like it." Then looking directly at Michael, he asked, "Understood?"

"Yes, sir. We're leaving right now." Michael moved the seat into the correct position, started the car and made a U-turn as Roy walked towards the patrol car. Kathleen could see Roy's shoulders shaking a little, as if he was trying to suppress a laugh. He wasn't alone. Kathleen in a release of tension found herself laughing uncontrollably.

Michael, obviously still startled by the incident, yelped, "What?"

Kathleen laughed so hard her chest began to hurt and she had trouble breathing. Finally, she blurted "You took me to the dump! You're so romantic!"

"I didn't know where the hell we were!" Michael answered, sounding defensive.

"That's obvious, Casanova. I'm sure this will be a night I'll never forget." She noticed that Michael relaxed a little and even gave a chuckle.

Michael shrugged. "Sorry I messed up."

Kathleen put her hand on the inside of his thigh as he drove. "I'm not sorry about anything," she assured him.

Michael stopped the car in front of Kathleen's house. Her parents were on the front porch swing as Kathleen exited the VW, trying to look normal.

Her dad frowned as he watched them step onto the porch holding hands. "You young'uns are home a bit earlier than we was expectin. Y'all OK?"

"Everything's fine, Daddy," Kathleen replied.

"Well, your mamma and me was fixin to go in the house," her dad announced. Then added "Y'all don't linger out here too long, ya hear. Catch yourself a cold in this air."

Once her parents had gone inside, Kathleen turned to Michael. She could see uncertainty in his eyes. Putting her arms around his neck, she kissed him gently. As she did, his smile returned. "What are you doing Monday after school?" she asked.

"Orchestra rehearsal."

"I have a Stingerettes rehearsal after school. Mom needs her car and Daddy has something going on. Can you give me a ride home?" she asked, hoping Michael could see the invitation as more than a ride home without her having to spell it out for him. It seemed to work.

"Definitely."

Monday, October 27, 1969

Rusty's alarm clock startled him awake. He lay still for a moment in the hazy predawn shadows of his room, trying to envision what the day might bring. Since walking off the football field on Friday night, he had felt liberated from the shackles of other people's expectations. For perhaps the first time in his life he had given his own dreams, his own desires, a degree of freedom. No longer thinking first of what other people expected of him was exhilarating, the possibilities endless, and terrifying.

The smell of bacon and fresh baked biscuits were enough to draw him out of bed and into his clothes. Walking into the kitchen, he found his mother had prepared an omelet with egg, cheese and bacon, his favorite. Nesting with the omelet were two fresh out of the oven biscuits.

She smiled as she placed the hot breakfast on the small kitchen table with a yellow linoleum top. "Morning, son."

Rusty was pleased but bewildered. "Omelet on a Monday? With biscuits? You know it's not my birthday, right?" he chided.

His mom poured some grease from her frying pan into an empty coffee can and put the pan to soak in the kitchen sink. Pouring a cup of coffee for herself, she sat with Rusty at the kitchen table. "You have a big day ahead of you. I figured a good breakfast would get it started on the right foot."

Rusty cleared his throat with a swallow of milk. "Maybe I messed up. You know, walking off the football team."

"You took a stand. You did what you thought was the right thing."

"But was it the right thing?"

"I was trying to think last night about what your father would have said about what you did. That man never took the easy road. He took the right road. He would have been so proud of you." Her eyes misted as she asked, "Has it been hard?"

"Quitting football?"

"No, I mean, has it been hard growing up in the shadow of a hero?"

"Sometimes, I worry I'll let people down, let you down."

She squeezed his hand. "You haven't let me down. I worry about you sometimes, but that's what moms do. I love you and I'm proud of you. Find your dreams. Not what other people want, but the dream you want. Then go for it. I'll be here cheering for you, worrying about you, praying for you."

"Thanks, Mom. I'll figure this out, I promise."

"I know."

Rusty finished his breakfast, kissed his mother on the top of her head and walked to the truck with a new feeling of confidence.

Finding a parking spot in the student lot, he noticed Jake in the rear-view mirror pulling into a nearby space. He gathered his books, got out of the truck and waited for Jake to exit his car. During their long friendship they had seldom argued. Rusty tried to calm himself from the anger towards Jake that was lurking inside him. While he hoped to salvage the friendship, Jake's racist comment about Anna and the way he had lashed out at the band on Saturday left him feeling agitated.

"What the hell's wrong with you?" Rusty growled as Jake walked past his truck kicking dirt and gravel with each step.

"Nothing! Not a damn thing."

"Nothing? Not a damn thing?" Rusty mockingly replied.

"Get screwed," Jake replied.

Rusty stared at his friend in disbelief.

Jake turned and hatefully said, "Those losers have no right to screw with our band the way they did. They were going to do two songs, now it seems like they're taking over. It sucks!"

"So what do you want?" Rusty asked.

"What do you mean?"

"It's not a trick question. What the hell do you want?"

"I want our band back. It's Baked Cotton, not Jake and the Wierdos."

"Look, man, if we don't let them play we get banned from ever playing at school again. We're screwed. Besides, we sounded pretty good. Hell, Judy's been in the band all this time, I didn't even know she could sing. She's good."

"You've changed," Jake replied with a look of disappointment. "We used to stick together, you know. Now you've quit football, helped screw up the band and you're spending time with a damn Mexican!"

Rusty hit his palm hard on the hood of his truck, put a finger on Jake's chest and glared at his friend. "Jake, if you don't start treating Anna with respect, I swear to God I'll kick your ass."

Jake turned and walked towards the school without responding. Watching his friend walk away, Rusty considered a future that was increasingly uncertain.

Entering the school, Rusty found his locker amidst the normal busy hallways and high school banter. But this morning felt different. Most students would not look at him. From down the hall some guy, he couldn't tell who, yelled "Quitter!" and several students laughed. He took a textbook from his locker and felt a tap on his shoulder. Closing his locker and turning, he was greeted with Anna's smile.

"Walk me to class?" she asked.

"Can't. I have to try to see Mr. Jamison."

"OK, mister. Then I'll see you later." She squeezed his arm and added "You've got this."

Rusty watched Anna quickly disappear into the crowd of students. Something in her smile, her wanting to talk with him when the other students couldn't look his way, was strangely reassuring.

Rusty walked into the school's administrative office and found Mr. Jamison reviewing a file with one of the secretaries. He felt awkward as he waited for them to finish their conversation. Students hurried in and out of the office, leaving the student office helper with doctor's excuses for missed classes, picking up transcripts and sometimes just saying hello.

Finally, Mr. Jamison finished talking with the secretary and noticed Rusty for the first time.

"Morning, Rusty," Jamison offered, sounding more authoritative than friendly.

"Um, Mr. Jamison, if you're not too busy I'd appreciate your advice on a couple of things. I can come back later if you want." Rusty wished he could sound more confident. Even though he had known Mr. Jamison for years, his confidence was slipping in front of the principal.

Jamison smiled. "I have a few minutes now. Come on in. I thought I might see you today."

"Thanks." Rusty entered Mr. Jamison's office and sat in the hard wooden guest chair as the principal took his seat behind the desk. "I suppose you heard about what happened Friday night at the game."

"Heard about it? I was there. Lots of talk about it in the stands."

"Talk about what?"

"Well, mostly people wondering what happened to get you hurt. Then Coach Childress threw his clipboard down so hard, I thought he might hit the feet of someone in China. I've never seen your coach get so worked up over a player getting hurt."

"Coach Childress loves to see people hurt. You should see the grin on his face, especially when one of our opponents has to leave the game with an injury. Broken bones and stuff, that's his thing."

"Football's a tough sport. You know that. But we don't try to injure others. That's not what we're about."

Rusty looked directly at Mr. Jamison. "That's exactly what Coach Childress is about. He's always yelling at me to not only hit the opponents, but to injure them until they're out of the game. He doesn't care how bad the injury is as long as it's on the other team. I have no respect for him and I won't play for him, not any more."

Mr. Jamison frowned and looked as if he was trying to control his anger. "I love football and I'm well aware that guys get hurt. But in this school, it's part of the game, not something we do deliberately. Understood?"

"I understand. I agree. But Coach Childress, he doesn't agree with you."

Mr. Jamison took a deep breath. "So what you're trying to say is that you're not hurt? You quit because you refused to do what you thought your coach wanted. Am I right?"

"Not what I thought he wanted, what I know. I'm not playing football any more, unless you fire Coach Childress."

"That's out of the question. He has a contract for the rest of the academic year. If you'd like, I can talk with the coaches about letting you be a trainer for the rest of the semester. You're still signed up for sixth period athletics."

Rusty hadn't considered his school schedule. The idea of taking care of laundry and carrying equipment for his former teammates was humiliating. "Can't I switch to a study hall or something? I don't need the credit on my transcript and I doubt if Coach Childress wants me around the team."

"You're probably right. I'll speak to the coach. You can have early dismissal this week until we work something out. Rusty, that's actually the least of your problems. If you lose your scholarship, what happens next year?"

"I want to be in law enforcement. On the police force. I'm just not sure how to get there. My guess is they're not likely to hire a teenager fresh out of high school."

Mr. Jamison leaned forward and looked intently at Rusty. "You know, Rusty, I am sure that you would be excellent at police work. I like it. You're physically gifted, smart, and have a strong moral compass."

"Thanks." The tension in his neck and shoulders started to relax. "Should I work part time and take some college classes?"

"You could, but there's another way. You could volunteer in the military. One of my buddies from the war used his military experience to secure a position in the police academy. If you volunteer, the military will have you take some tests to determine what you're good at. Maybe you could get a position in the military police."

Rusty gave this some thought. "Do they have military police in the Air Force?"

"Sure do. Air Force has the Combat Security Police Squadron. They train in San Antonio at Lackland Air Force Base."

"So I could join the Air Force and stay in Texas? Maybe come home on weekends to help my mom if she needs me?" As Rusty asked the question, he felt guilty. The one he most wanted to see was Anna, who would likely be going to school in Fort Worth.

"Rusty, let's be real here. If you join the Air Force, assuming you get assigned to the Police Squadron, you'll train for about three months in San Antonio. After that, you don't get to choose where you go. You could be assigned to Carswell Air Force Base in Fort Worth. More likely, you'd find yourself in Vietnam, Germany or maybe even Alaska. You would be serving your country and getting excellent experience that would help you get into police work. It's an honorable thing to do. But it's not always easy or safe. Before you talk with a recruiter, you need to be sure you're OK with all that. Don't get me wrong, I think you'd be great at it. But this isn't a football team. You can't just walk away if you don't like where you're assigned or what you're being asked to do. I met some of the finest men God ever put on this earth when I served in the Army. I also learned that, even in the military, there's a few Coach Childress types. This is a big decision for you. Talk with your mom and give it some thought before you make any commitments."

"Thanks. I will." Rusty started to stand but then sat back in the hard wood chair. "There's one other thing I want to ask you about. We have Ian in the band like you suggested. He's actually really good, a lot better than I was expecting. Ian insisted that Michael join us, so he's in the band now, too. We still need to practice some, but I think we'll be ready if the school wants us. There's one catch though. Jake got mad and quit."

Mr. Jamison pointed an intimidating finger at Rusty. "If you or Jake lay a hand on Ian, you'll never play a note at this school again. Understood?"

"Yes, sir."

Mr. Jamison sat back in his chair. "OK then, we'll plan on y'all playing at the Thanksgiving sock hop. It's up to you to figure out what to do if Jake isn't there."

Rusty smiled. "Thanks!"

Mr. Jamison rose from his chair and extended a handshake to Rusty. "No problem. I always try to cooperate with law enforcement."

§§§

Michael felt as if the school day would never end. Something about the way Kathleen had asked him for a ride home from school left him with lustful anticipation. Was it the way she smiled or the look in her eyes? Maybe both. Or was his imagination, his desire, leaving him with a murky view of reality? The way she looked happy to see him boosted his confidence in a way he had never experienced. And yet, he felt as if he were running while holding scissors. One trip, and it could all come to an end with a deep cut. Losing his only friend in town would leave him once again feeling as if he were alone on an island.

The violin section of the orchestra droned through their never-ending afternoon practice. The wall clock seemed frozen in time. To make matters worse, the orchestra conductor was agitated. Nothing the students did was good enough. Finally, the rehearsal reached a merciful end. Michael packed his violin, grabbed his books and walked to the front of the school where he was to meet Kathleen. He didn't have to wait long.

"Hey, cowboy. Let's ride," she flirted.

Michael laughed. "I've never been called a cowboy. Ever."

"That I can believe," Kathleen giggled.

Driving towards Kathleen's home, she provided a recap of her day. Michael enjoyed listening to her. She was in good spirits, a welcome contrast to the disgruntled orchestra conductor he had just left. He tried to hold her hand as they drove, but that became impossible as he frequently had to change the car's gears. Kathleen leaned closer and put her left hand on his thigh. "Tell me when you want to shift gears," she offered.

"Third," he said, and with her right hand she smoothly put the shifter in the third gear position. He put his arm around her shoulders as they drove towards her house.

"I'll get the gate," Kathleen offered when they reached the Wilcox farm. Unlatching the gate, she paused to take in her surroundings. Suddenly appearing agitated, she motioned to Michael to quickly drive through the now open gate. Once he had done so, she hurriedly latched the gate shut and jumped into the car. "Go!"

As Michael accelerated up the dirt road towards the Wilcox house, he asked "What's wrong?"

"You don't notice anything strange here?"

"No."

"There are no cattle! Either Daddy moved them to one of the back pastures, which I doubt, or there's maybe a break in the fence." Michael brought the VW to a stop and followed Kathleen as she ran into the house. "Mom, Dad," she called, but there was no answer. She turned to Michael, "Let's go!" she hollered as she hurried out the back door. Kathleen ran into the barn and put on a tool belt.

"Where do you think the cattle went?" Michael asked.

"We're about to find out," Kathleen replied as she pulled a motorcycle from a corner of the barn. "Get on!"

Michael sat behind Kathleen on the motorcycle, wanting to be more than a rider but not knowing what else he could say or do. He put his arms around her waist.

"Don't hold me. Grab the strap on the seat and hold on. It's going to be a bumpy ride."

Michael did as he was told. Kathleen kick started the motorcycle and headed for the fence on the right side of the farm. Turning left, Michael could see that they would circumvent the portion of the farm behind the house. He had always had the impression that the house was near the center of the farm. He now realized that the back pasture went much further than he had imagined. Kathleen took them along the right side to the far corner and turned left to inspect the back fence. Finding no breaks in the fence, she made a left turn at the back left corner and headed towards the house. There was a tension about her. Michael felt helpless to relieve her worry. They rode past the house and into the front pasture where Kathleen braked the motorcycle, bringing them to a stop.

Kathleen looked over the pasture. "There's no break in the fence and I only saw about 20 heifers." Surveying the pasture, she pointed "Oh God. Look!"

Michael could see tracks through the dirt and straw-colored grass, obviously left by a very large truck. The implications of what he was seeing failed him. "Maybe somebody moved the cattle."

"Or they've been stolen," Kathleen replied as she opened the throttle of the motorcycle and turned towards the house. Once there, she killed the engine and ran into the house with Michael following. Picking up the telephone, she dialed several numbers, each time asking if one of her parents were available. No luck. "That's it, I'm calling the sheriff," she announced in frustration.

Michael sat at the kitchen table, listening to half of the phone conversation. "This is Kathleen Wilcox. I think our cattle may have been stolen." There was a pause, then "Yes sir, that was me." Another pause, then she said in exasperation "Well I don't know, he's sitting right here. You want to ask him?" Another pause, followed by Kathleen giving directions to the farm. "Fine, we'll see you in a few minutes. Goodbye." She hung up the phone and turned to Michael as she rolled her eyes. "You'll never guess who that was at the Sherriff's."

"Beats me," Michael replied. "I don't know a soul at the Sheriff's Department."

"Yes, you do. Remember officer Roy? He's on his way over here now."

Michael looked at her with a blank expression. Suddenly his eyes widened. "Wait, was he the guy from the county dump? The one who thought we were doing drugs?"

"Bingo."

Michael laughed. "This could be awkward."

"No kidding."

§§§

Kathleen paced the floor waiting for the phone to ring, waiting for her parents to come home, waiting for Officer Roy. Thoughts of a romantic late afternoon with Michael were long forgotten. Her family's livelihood was at stake. So much that they had worked for had disappeared. Officer Roy finally opened the gate and drove his squad car towards the house.

She and Michael stood on the front porch when officer Roy approached. He wore a white well maintained cowboy hat, Sheriff's uniform and holstered pistol. Kathleen noted that he was muscular and carried himself in a no-nonsense manner. He tipped his hat and said "Didn't expect to see you two again so soon. What do we have here?"

At that moment, Kathleen's mother drove through the gate in the Oldsmobile with her father behind in the pickup. Kathleen turned to Roy. "I think someone stole our cattle. Thank God my parents are finally here."

Roy turned to watch the parents drive toward the house and stop near the front porch. Her dad exited his truck in a hurry. "What's wrong?"

"Daddy, somebody took most of the cattle! All we have left are some heifers. I checked all the fences, no breaks, nothing. So I called the Sheriff's office."

Her daddy shook hands with Roy. "Bud Wilcox. Don't I know you from somewheres? Ya sure look familiar." Then he read Roy's last name from a metal plate on his chest. "Roy Waddell. Hang on now, you're Jimmy Waddell's boy ain't ya?

"Yes, sir."

"Well, I'll be. Jimmy's little brother and me, we been friends since junior high. I remember when you was born. Now look at ya. All growed up and a Deputy Sheriff. You're lookin good, son."

Kathleen grew exasperated by the small talk. "Daddy, the cattle are gone!"

Her father shook his head. "Breathe easy, darlin. Nobody stole no cattle. We done sold em, except we kept them heifers out back. Sold a bunch of hay, too." Bud turned back towards Roy. "I'm sorry, Roy, I've been rude. This here is my wife, my youngest daughter, Kathleen and her friend, Michael."

"Yes sir, we've met," Roy responded as Kathleen blushed in spite of herself.

There was an awkward silence, broken by Kathleen's mother saying "There's no need for us to stand out here and catch a chill. Roy, why don't you come on into the house and have some coffee?"

Roy tipped his hat and said "Thank you, Mrs. Wilcox, but I'd best get back to the station. It's about to get dark and you never know what the young people around here will be doing in the evenings. If y'all ever need anything from our office, you be sure to call, you hear. We'll be here for you. Good evening."

Kathleen watched Roy walk to his patrol car, start it and drive away. She turned to Michael. "I appreciate the ride. See you at school tomorrow?"

Michael seemed to understand that this was his invitation to leave. "Sure. See you tomorrow." Michael drove away in the dust of Roy's cruiser.

Kathleen followed her parents into the house and sat at the kitchen table with her father as her mother began preparing dinner. "What happened, Daddy?"

"Well darlin, your mother and me, we been watchin cattle prices get higher and higher. Seemed like a good time to sell a bunch of the herd. We won't be needin as much hay this winter so we sold that, too. Got some good money for it. Guess you could say we're in high cotton, cept of course we got no cotton."

"Darlin, that's only part of the story," Kathleen's mother added.

Kathleen felt nervous. "What?"

Her dad smiled. "Your mom and me, we's sure mighty proud of you. We think you're gonna make a fine nurse one day. The way we figure, you get a couple of them scholarships, go down to UT Austin, get a part time job, get a loan and you still won't have enough. But now you do. The profits on them cattle gonna carry you through."

Kathleen was worried. "You can't do that. You have to live, too. I can't let you do that, it's not right."

Kathleen's mother said "Don't you worry about us. We'll be just fine."

"But, Mom, I haven't even been accepted yet."

"Not yet," her mother responded as she put apple cobbler into the oven. "But if them people at the University of Texas have a lick of sense, they'll let you in. You keep workin hard on your studies and things will take care of themselves."

Kathleen sat quietly, trying to understand. "You sold the cattle and a bunch of the hay to help me get to school next year." Tears came to her eyes. "Y'all have no idea how much that means. I hope I don't let you down."

"You won't," both of her parents said simultaneously.

Tuesday, October 28, 1969

Kathleen didn't need an alarm clock to wake her up. She hadn't slept, not much anyway. The night before she had spent an hour on the telephone with Janice trying to explain why her parents had sold most of the cattle and a lot of the hay. Something didn't feel quite right, but she wasn't sure what it was. Janice was a good listener, but no help, so she phoned Michael. He was no more helpful than Janice. As she dressed for school, the discomfort she felt gained some clarity. How would her parents live until the herd was built back up? What if they made this investment in her and she failed? What if she didn't get into the University of Texas? And if she did get into the university, what was to become of Michael? She realized that losing Michael might be the sacrifice she would have to make to become a nurse. Besides, he had made it clear that he was determined to get back to Oregon. She dreaded the possibility.

Kathleen walked into the wonderful aroma of fresh baked biscuits that her mother was taking out of the oven. "Morning, Mom. Your biscuits are the best. Daddy's favorite breakfast. I can't believe he's not at the table already."

On the breakfast table was a note in her mother's handwriting that said "Dr. Hessell, 8:30."

Kathleen frowned. "Where's Daddy? Is he sick?"

Her mother placed a plate of biscuits in front of Kathleen and sat down at the table with a cup of coffee. "Kathleen, he went to work. Got a new job. Actually, an old job. Mr. Richter called and wanted him back."

"Mr. Richter from the trucking company? I thought he didn't like trucking. In fact, he told me those three years when he was a trucker were miserable. He said it was boring and mostly he hated being away from his family all those nights when I was a toddler. That's why he quit. Why is he going back now?"

"Well, Mr. Richter has a problem. The fool drivers he's been hiring have been getting too many tickets. Last week, one of the drivers laid a truck on its side down in San Angelo. Went around a curve too fast. Anyway, Mr. Richter said that if his insurance keeps going up, he'll be out of business. When your dad drove, he had a clean record. No tickets, no accidents in the three years. Richter made him a good offer, pay with benefits including health insurance, four days per week and it's all day runs out of Fort Worth. He'll be home every night. And with the cattle mostly sold, he can still keep up with the work around our place. Not sure if he'll keep driving when the herd gets built back up, but we'll cross that bridge when we get to it."

"I still don't get why Daddy went back to doing something he doesn't much care for. There's a lot of other things he could do."

"Kathleen, you're not listening. The money's good and it's not permanent. It's what he wants to do. You know he'll do whatever needs doing for his family."

Kathleen buttered a biscuit in silence, trying to understand. Suddenly, the situation became clear, as if the sun was suddenly shining on the dark side of her understanding. "Mom, it's not fair. Daddy sold the cattle so I can go to school. Now he's having to drive a truck so y'all have money to live on. Maybe I should come up with another plan. You know, something less expensive for school."

"Sweet girl, he loves you more than the air he breathes. Doesn't always understand you. But he loves you all the same. He knows how bad you want to go down there to Austin for school. He'd be mighty disappointed if you gave up on your dreams. We think you'll be a fine nurse one day."

They were both unusually quiet, the clicking of the kitchen clock slowly marking the passing of time as Kathleen stared at the note about the doctor's appointment. Health insurance. Why had that been mentioned as an important part of her daddy's job? Worry suddenly flashed across Kathleen's face. Reaching across the table she tenderly squeezed her mother's hand. "Mom, are you sick?"

"Lord no. Fit as a fiddle as they'd say. Why would you say that?"

"Well, looks to me like you have an appointment this morning with Dr. Hessell."

Her mother suddenly looked serious. "It's not my appointment, it's yours. I made it for you."

"I'm not sick."

"Yes you are."

"What are you talking about? I'm fine."

"You're love sick, or at least getting close to it. Your daddy and me, we can see it in your eyes. And for what it's worth, we see it in Michael's eyes, too. The way you looked at each other when you came home Saturday night. It's the same look Dave and your sister had."

"Somehow I don't like where this is going."

"Kathleen, I love being grandmother to Ellie and I think your sister found her a good man in Dave. When your sister was in high school, we lectured her about not having sex. We thought it was the most sensible thing to do at the time. We both know how that worked out."

"Mom! I'm not my sister. We're different." Kathleen was uncomfortable, wanting to be anyplace but sitting at the breakfast table talking about sex with her mother. "I can't believe we're talking about this!"

"Don't you raise your voice to me, young lady! I won't have it. Maybe you and Michael are having sex, maybe you're not. Maybe you aren't doing anything now, but maybe you will later. I don't know and I don't imagine you're going to tell me. What I do know is this. Sometimes things get out of hand. A moment of pleasure can bring a lifetime of responsibility. So I made an appointment for you to see Dr. Hessell. Can't make you go, but I sure think you should. A lot of girls are on the pill these days, probably a lot of girls in your school."

Kathleen responded with sarcasm. "What am I supposed to do, walk into the office and say 'Hi Dr. Hessell, I may want to screw someday, so you have any protection for me?'   It's embarrassing!"

"You don't need to talk like that. Dr. Hessel's a good man. He already knows why you're there."

Kathleen was incredulous. "You told him?"

"Yes. And you know what he said? He said he's seeing more and more high school and college girls for the same thing. It may bother you, but it sure doesn't bother him. Kathleen, it's his job. He's not there to judge."

"I can't believe my mother wants me to have sex with my boyfriend."

"I didn't say that."

"Well, it sure sounds like it!"

"Your father and I are doing everything we can to give you all the tools you need to be successful. We've been around the block a few times ourselves. We can open doors for you, and we will. But we can't make you walk through them. If I were you, I'd keep that doctor's appointment this morning."

Kathleen threw her paper napkin onto her breakfast plate. Her chair made an angry scream on the linoleum floor as she abruptly pushed it back from the table. "Fine!"

"Kathleen."

"I can't talk now! I have a doctor's appointment."

§§§

Michael hadn't seen Kathleen in school. Strange. They had gotten into the habit of meeting up for a couple of minutes before first period class. This morning she wasn't there. Walking to his third period class, Michael saw Janice putting a book in her locker. Although Janice and Kathleen were friends, Janice had seemed uninterested in getting to know Michael. Perhaps it had something to do with Michael's conflicts with her boyfriend Jake. Perhaps she just didn't like him. When Michael gave it some thought, he realized that the feeling was mutual.

206

"Hey, Janice. You seen Kathleen today?" Michael inquired, trying to sound friendly.

Janice closed her locker. "No. I'm not sure where she is. Hope she's not sick. Maybe she got stuck doing something on the farm."

As if on que, Kathleen appeared. She no doubt was surprised to see her best friend and boyfriend talking. "OK, fess up Michael. Are you flirting with Janice or is she flirting with you?" she teased.

Janice rolled her eyes. "We were wondering where you were this morning."

"Doctor's appointment."

Janice looked concerned. "Are you sick?"

"No, I'm fine," Kathleen replied.

Michael had an uneasy feeling. Something didn't seem quite right. "Are you OK?"

"You wouldn't understand. Female issues. I'm fine."

There was an understanding look between Janice and Kathleen, as if they were communicating without using words. Michael started to say something but was cut off by Janice, who held up her hand to stop him. "Don't ask, Michael. You don't want to know."

"I have to go. Bell's about to ring for third period," Kathleen announced as she and Janice turned to walk down the hallway.

Michael found his third period class in a daze. Sometimes if felt as if Kathleen and Janice were communicating in code. He would never figure out the code, and the girls seemed to like it that way.

§§§

Rusty saw Jake sitting alone at lunch, shoulders slumped, using more energy staring at his food than eating it. He hurried to take a seat across the table before Janice joined him. "Hey, man," he started, "I spoke with Jamison. We got a gig!"

"What gig?"

"Next month. Jamison wants us to do the Thanksgiving sock hop."

"I'm sure it pays well," Jake responded sarcastically.

"What's up with you?"

"That little smartass came in and tried to take over our band," Jake declared with quiet intensity.

"He may have put a burr under your saddle, my man, but he sure as hell didn't take over the band. Come on, be cool. Ian was just trying some things out on us."

"You and Ian have a good time with your gig. Hell, the music he wants to play isn't even country."

"Hang on. You're the one who talked me into doing *Born to be Wild*. Not exactly a country tune either. But you know what, you were right. It was fun."

Jake shook his head. "Ian wants to play music by The Seekers!"

"I know. I thought it was weird, too. But you have to admit, it sounded pretty good. Especially with Judy singing. That girl hardly ever talks, much less sing. Who knew?"

Jake looked directly at Rusty. "Then you, Judy and Ian have fun with your sock hop gig. When y'all get done screwing around with my band, our band, let me know. You got a damn queer and a hippie."

"You don't know Ian's queer."

"You don't know he isn't."

Rusty found himself becoming frustrated with his friend. "Look, I want to play the damn music. Come on, we need you."

"Jamison said we have to let Ian play two songs. That's it. Two."

"We're going to do more."

"What the hell! You and your freak friends do as many as you want. Then I'll tell them to get the hell off the stage and we'll be right back in business like we used to be."

Janice sat next to Jake. "Hey, guys!" Her friendly greeting provided a jolting contrast to the tension of the conversation she had interrupted. "Uh-oh. Are y'all having boy troubles today?" she chided. When neither of the boys responded, she added "Come on, you two. Don't get your panties all in a wad. Y'all work it out. You always do."

"Maybe," Rusty said.

Jake looked directly at his friend. "Maybe not."

§§§

There was a knock on the door as Rusty's fifth period class neared its end. His teacher answered the door, took a note from a student helper and gave it to Rusty. The note read "Please report to Mr. Jamison's office after fifth period." Rusty guessed that Jamison had spoken with Coach Childress. As the bell rang, he gathered his books and made his way down the hall to the principal's office. A student helper stood behind the counter of the office. "Is Mr. Jamison available?" Rusty inquired.

"Yes, he's expecting you. Go on in," the student helper responded in a somewhat unfriendly manner.

"Mr. Jamison, you wanted to see me?" Rusty asked as he entered the office.

"Come on in and shut the door," Jamison said. Rusty did as he was told, once again settling into the hard wooden guest chair across from the principal's desk. "I had a talk with Coach Childress. He doesn't want you around the team. Says it would be a distraction. His recommendation is to give you a failing grade for the semester and be done." Rusty started to object, but Mr. Jamison held up his hand. "Here's the deal. Coach Childress cannot fail you if he doesn't give you an opportunity to be with the team, even as a trainer. He doesn't want you near the team, so we reached a compromise. You will be suspended from football, effective immediately. Your transcript will not reflect athletics this semester and you will be required to attend sixth period study hall."

Rusty felt relief that he would not have to do laundry for his former teammates, anger towards Coach Childress for wanting to fail him, and frustration about being asked to attend study hall. "How about I just leave after fifth period? It's all the same. Study hall is a waste of time."

Mr. Jamison looked at Rusty sternly. "First off, you have options. You can refuse to do the study hall and take an F in athletics. Your grades are good, but not stellar. Here's a novel idea. Why don't you go to study hall and actually study. See if you can get your grades from good to exceptional?"

Rusty laughed nervously. "Well, if you put it that way, OK, I understand. But it's only for this semester, right?"

"Next semester you have more options. You can leave school after fifth period or you can add a course to your schedule. Last spring you were on the track team. Coach Childress is coaching track this year, so your prospects for track are, shall we say, a bit limited."

"Maybe I'll get an after-school job."

"That would be fine." Mr. Jamison sat back in his chair and carefully regarded Rusty. "Being an adult means learning to live with the consequences of your decisions. It also means being serious about your future. If you have a shorter school schedule next semester, I suggest you use the extra time to better yourself. Work, take an extra class, whatever. Do not waste your time doing nothing."

Rusty sensed that he was being challenged by Mr. Jamison. "I won't let you down."

Mr. Jamison leaned forward in his chair and looked piercingly at his student. "Do not let yourself down. That's what's important. Nobody in this world owes you anything. Set your goals, don't look back. You have a good head on your shoulders. Quit doubting yourself! Put in the work and you'll be fine."

Saturday, November 1, 1969

Michael wasn't sure he wanted to rehearse again with Baked Cotton. Jake's hissy fit during the first rehearsal was like a storm cloud over the band. However, the music itself was borderline enjoyable, particularly with Ian leading the action and Judy singing.

Entering the garage, Michael found everyone with the exception of Jake. Two electric space heaters provided some comfort from the outside cold. Ian had chosen to drive himself, apparently more secure in his surroundings. Each band member was practicing their parts, none of them playing the same song. During a momentary lull in the cascade of incompatible sounds, Michael asked "Where's Jake?"

Rusty hit his cymbal hard in apparent frustration. "You know what, the hell with him. Sometimes you got to roll with what you got. Let's play."

Ian took over the rehearsal as if it were his band. Somehow, he managed to come up with violin parts for several of the band's songs. Without Jake on lead vocals, Tommy's sister Judy volunteered to sing and did it well. Tommy tried to sing a couple of songs, but it didn't go as well. His voice was painfully off key. To Michael's surprise, the atmosphere began to feel more relaxed. Shy girl comes alive, effeminate guy takes charge and a kid like Michael from Oregon has fun playing in a country band. Even Rusty acted more animated. They were all having fun. A lot of fun. Two hours went by in what felt like minutes to Michael.

At about noon, Tommy announced, "Hey guys, Judy and I are supposed to have lunch with Aunt Clara, so we gotta go."

Rusty twirled a drum stick in his fingers and said "I think we're ready for the sock hop!"

Ian frowned. "We can do this, but it would sure sound better with a lead guitar."

"You guys figure it out," Tommy replied as he and Judy left the garage.

"You know," Ian offered with a broad grin, "I think this is the most fun Saturday I've had in high school."

Michael and Rusty looked at each other in stunned silence. It had been fun, but the most fun Saturday in high school? Hardly. "Hey, man, you did good," Rusty said to Ian.

To Michael's surprise Ian starting talking, a lot. He spoke about the music first, then talked about his high school experiences. Many of those experiences had to do with being bullied, ridiculed and made to feel horrible. Michael had the impression that this was as close as Ian had come to developing any friendships. Rusty sat in silence, shoulders slumped, as Ian reported tale after tale of being the recipient of cruel intentions.

§§§

The sting from a cold autumn afternoon wind was like a warm summer breeze next to the pain Rusty felt listening to Ian describe the abuse he had endured in school. Rusty had always considered himself a good person. And yet, through years of watching Ian being victimized at school, he had never once stepped in to help, never did the right thing. In fact, he had laughed at some of the verbal abuse Ian had endured. Guilt by inaction left a bitter feeling in his gut. To make matters worse, one of Ian's chief tormentors was his friend Jake. It was time to correct the wrongs of the past. To do so, he'd have to give Jake a visit.

Jake's dad came to the door in response to Rusty's knock. "Hey, buddy, how you been? Get in here. It's cold as a penguin's butt out there."

Rusty entered the modest frame house. "Jake home?"

"In his room. Go on back there. You know the way."

Rusty walked down the short hallway and found Jake, guitar in hand, sitting on the floor with his back to the twin bed practicing. "Hey," Rusty interrupted.

Jake looked up surprised. "What are you doing here?"

"Brought by some music from band practice. What happened to you? Figured you'd be there this morning."

"I don't need your damn music. Let your squirrely friend practice however many songs you plan on doing, then get him and his hippie weirdo out of my way. If he's taking over our band, then I'm done."

Rusty sat with his back to the wall. "You wouldn't believe what I've been through. Had to listen to Ian talk for an hour. Michael was there, too. Hell, Ian talked so much, my mom made us sandwiches."

"Should I give a damn?"

Rusty took a deep breath, trying to control the anger stirring within him. "Ian said last year someone replaced the book marker in his English book with a rubber. Thank God it was unused. Anyway, Ian went to open his book in class and a rubber was stretched out on the page like a book mark."

Jake laughed. "I remember. That was hilarious! Everybody was laughing. It was great."

Jake's reaction made it clear to Rusty who placed the condom in Ian's book. "Why did you do that?"

"Cause it was funny! What's wrong with you?"

"It cost Ian's mother two hundred dollars." Jake looked confused, so Rusty tried to explain. "Ian was upset. It didn't help that the next period, some girls tried to talk him into letting them put makeup on him."

"What the hell does that have to do with two hundred dollars?" Jake asked. "That's a lot of money."

"It was for counseling. Apparently, it took several counseling sessions for Ian to calm down."

"We were just having fun. Didn't mean anything by it."

"You remember the day you and me, we were kicking Ian's book down the hallway between classes?"

Jake gave a smirk. "Sure do. That's the day Michael tried to defend the little queer. Son of a bitch jumped me and got us both suspended. You wouldn't believe how pissed my mom was."

"Turns out, he wasn't defending Ian at all. He was defending you. We didn't know it but Ian brought a knife to school. Switchblade. He was ready to use it, definitely on you, maybe on me, too. Michael knew what was happening. As Ian was reaching in his sock for the knife, Michael went after you so Ian wouldn't. Ian got scared and ran away. Later, Michael took the knife from Ian. Could have been a bloody mess in the school hallway. So basically, that hippie saved your ass."

Jake was quiet for an uncomfortable amount of time. "Michael was there when Ian told you all of this?"

"Eating ham sandwiches in my kitchen."

"Well hell, what do you want me to do about it now?"

"Sock hop is next Saturday. We'll be a lot better if you're up there with us."

Jake glared at his friend. "Bullshit! You come in here, try to make me feel guilty about Ian. Maybe he got what he deserved. I'll set up for the sock hop, and when you guys get done with however many songs you're planning to do, Ian and Michael can get the hell off my stage and we'll have some real fun. Until then, I'll be on the dance floor with Janice. There's no way on God's green earth I'm letting Ian take over our band. Can't believe you bought his sob story about how we screwed around with him. We were only having fun. It wasn't that bad. I remember lots of times you were laughing with the rest of us. So don't try to sell your high and holy shit with me. I'm not buying."

Rusty felt disappointed and annoyed with his friend. "If someone had told me that I'd have a good time hanging out with two weird guys like Ian and Michael, I'd have thought they were crazy. They're different, but not bad guys. Fun to be around."

"I can't believe you're saying that," Jake mumbled.

Rusty laughed. "Me neither. Weird things happen sometimes."

"No kidding."

"They haven't taken over the band, just made it better. Surprised the hell out of all of us. Come on man, give them a chance."

Jake looked at his friend and said "I'll think about it. Still can't believe that you like hanging out with those freaks."

Rusty stood up and dropped several pages of music on the floor next to Jake. "Practice your music," he said and turned towards the door, leaving his friend speechless on the floor, guitar in hand.

Saturday, November 8, 1969

Michael arrived as Mr. Jamison was letting the band into the empty gym to set up their instruments for the Thanksgiving sock hop. The hallway outside of the gym was crowded with classmates waiting for the dance to begin. Since the rehearsal the previous Saturday, Michael had been looking forward to the event until he saw Jake walk into the gym with a scowl on his face. Avoiding eye contact with the band, Jake jerked his guitar out of the case and plugged it into the amp Tommy and Michael had set up. Jake played a few loud chords, propped the guitar against the wall and walked towards the exit without speaking to anyone. Michael yelled at his back in a mockingly friendly manner "Hey, buddy, good to see you too!" Jake never turned, but he gave Michael his middle finger as he hit the gym's exit door.

"What's wrong with him?" Ian asked to nobody in particular.

Rusty, seated at his drum set, replied "Don't worry about it. He's got a burr in his saddle that he don't know what to do with."

Michael shrugged. "Let's just do our thing. If he comes around, fine. If not, we sound pretty good without him."

"Amen to that," added Tommy.

As Mr. Jamison opened the doors, Jake, wearing a white tee shirt and a denim jacket, held hands with Janice as he led their peers towards the platform stage. Mr. Jamison reminded the students to remove their shoes. Everyone did, with the exception of Jake who took a position leaning against the wall to the side of the stage. As the students gathered in front of the stage, they noticed first that Jake was not with the band. Seeing Michael and Ian, someone loudly said, "You've got to be kidding me." Someone else yelled "Freak show!"

Michael noticed Ian looking in all directions, as if he expected to be attacked. In a low voice Michael said to Ian, "See the guy that was yelling at us? He can't help it; he has a carrot up his ass." Ian laughed a little. "Worse part is, he shared the carrot with Jake."

Ian smiled, but not for long. Someone yelled "Queer!" Someone else hollered "Commie Hippie!" and most everyone laughed. From somewhere among the students, a tomato was launched towards the band. It narrowly missed both Ian and Rusty. It did not miss Jake. There was more laughter as red tomato juice dripped from what had been Jake's white shirt. Jake looked startled as he brushed tomato seeds off of his shirt. Someone else yelled "Quitter!" at Rusty.

Michael saw Kathleen glaring at someone. He next saw Mr. Jamison walking quickly from the back of the gym towards the band. Michael had seen Jamison angry, but the look on his face was at a different level. When he glanced at Ian, the kid looked like he might start to cry. Michael whispered, "We're done. Let's get out of here."

"Sounds good," Ian replied.

The boys turned and ran into Jake, his face as red as the tomato stain on his white shirt. Classmates were talking loudly and laughing. Someone yelled, "Hey, Jake, looks like your shirt has a sunburn!" More laughter.

Jake hesitated. Michael wondered how the popular, well-liked kid would respond to ridicule. "This is bullshit!" Jake declared to Ian and Michael. "Let's play our music, all of us, including both of you."

Michael stepped off the platform stage and firmly responded "I am not getting back on that platform for two lousy songs."

"Well, hell, play as many as you want. You too, Ian. Come on. Let's do this!" Jake declared as if he were giving a pep talk to the football team. Without waiting for a response, Jake jumped onto the platform, grabbed his guitar and started playing *I Take a Lot of Pride in What I Am*. Rusty had a stunned look on his face, but started playing his drums after a couple of measures. Judy and Tommy joined in a few beats later.

Michael saw a couple of boys with boots in their hands being escorted out of the gym by Mr. Jamison. The boys looked guilty. Jamison still looked angry and Ian had a confused, uncertain appearance. Michael knew that Jamison would cancel the sock hop if Ian was not part of the band. He took a deep breath and asked Ian "Maybe we should give it another shot?"

There were a few snickers as Ian approached the microphone to sing with Jake. Michael sensed the crowd was becoming more relaxed. Kathleen had found a boy to dance with, one of many she would find during the sock hop. She may dance with the guys, but he would be the one taking her home. Kathleen winked at Michael over the shoulder of her dance partner.

There was subdued applause as the song ended. Jake put his arm around Ian's shoulders and announced to the crowd "I'd like y'all to meet the newest members of our band, my good friends Ian and Michael." There was more polite applause. The band played *Born to be Wild* followed by Judy and Ian's duet *I'll Never Find Another You*. The mixing of musical styles, the harmonies and the fiddles in the background built a crescendo of appreciation from the crowd. As the sock hop ended two hours later, the same students who had laughed and ridiculed the band earlier now seemed reluctant to leave. Mr. Jamison, standing near the exit, smiled. The applause was enthusiastic.

Rusty sat with a goofy grin on his face as the students put their shoes on and left the gym. "Told you," Rusty said to Jake.

Jake turned to the band "You done good, boys. You too, Judy."

"I say we go to Dairy Queen and celebrate," Rusty suggested. "Besides, I'm hungry."

"Sounds good to me," Jake said. "I'll find a clean shirt and meet you there." Then turning to Michael and Ian added "Y'all are coming too, right?"

Ian looked uncertain. "Why?"

Jake walked over to where Ian was putting his violin away. Placing his hand on Ian's shoulder he said "Look man. Up until this evening I didn't understand. Didn't know what it was like to be in your shoes. When the tomato hit me and I heard all the shit they were yelling, well, it was an education for me. Nobody treats my band like that, and you're as much a part of the band as anyone else. So come to Dairy Queen." Then, looking at Michael, he added "And you, too. Both of you."

"OK," Ian answered with a tentative smile.

Kathleen walked up from behind Michael and wrapped her arms around his neck. "How about we split a strawberry shake?"

Michael felt a surge of satisfaction. In a small way, this little town in the middle of nowhere didn't feel so foreign. He no longer felt as if he were alone on an island surrounded by strangers. It felt as if he had somehow arrived at a place he never imagined. Stephenville, of all places, no longer felt like a hellhole.

August, 1970

Kathleen sat between Janice and Michael in the small Catholic chapel. They had arrived a few minutes early, giving her time to take in the unusual surroundings. She had been to church thousands of times, but never to a Catholic place of worship. Jesus hung from a cross that in protestant churches was empty. There were kneelers and incense, both new to her. But what got her attention most was the strikingly handsome groom standing proudly in front of the chapel in his blue Air Force dress uniform. The newly converted Catholic groom had three days leave, just enough time for a wedding before heading back to base. Next to him stood his best man Jake, looking uncomfortable in his new suit.

As Ian played a beautiful classical violin tune, Kathleen thought about how their lives had changed over the past few months. Janice, her baby bump starting to show, had married Jake two weeks prior. Kathleen had been the Maid of Honor. Janice had a job as a checker at Gibson Department Store, though she hoped to attend cosmetology school after the baby was born. Jake had been lucky to draw a low draft lottery number. Michael's father of all people had helped him land a job in landscaping at Tarleton College. Jake's face was deeply tanned from a summer of mowing grass for the college. Somehow, Jake had in his mind that he would attend classes part time to become an accountant. Nobody knew where that idea came from. Kathleen hoped he would follow through with the plan, but doubted that he would.

It felt to Kathleen as if her world and Janice's were going in very different directions. Janice, in her small two-bedroom rental home not far from where Anna grew up, was preparing to be a mother. She and Jake would stay in Stephenville, likely for the rest of their lives. Kathleen, on the other hand, was going to the University of Texas at Austin to study nursing. When she and Janice discussed the future, it was clear their journeys were taking them down divergent paths. She hoped they would remain friends, but their life experiences were already very different.

Then there was Michael, sitting close, holding her hand, his hair now almost as long as when they had first met. They had spent many evenings talking, discussing their future, their dreams, their hopes for a better tomorrow. Slowly, over the weeks and months, their feelings grew. Kathleen was in love, and she knew it. She tried to be excited when Michael was accepted into Oregon State, but the effort fell flat.

In July, Kathleen invited Michael to come with her for a campus visit in Austin. They heard music at The Broken Spoke, walked down Guadalupe Street, swam the cold waters of Barton Springs and listened to an anti-war speech. The atmosphere had a feeling of youthful rebellion mixed with a hunger for knowledge and an energy that made the place alive in ways Kathleen had never felt before. She loved it, and so did Michael. So much so that Michael applied for admission. Too late for the fall semester, he would go to Oregon State for one semester, then transfer to the University of Texas in the spring.

Baked Cotton played their last gig at a graduation party in May. Kathleen found it strangely entertaining that the band with Ian and Michael had become good friends. What started as a Saturday morning practice routine evolved into frequent socializing. They still had very different views of the world. Over time, they learned to accept their differences. Music brought them together. Friendship kept them together.

The small crowd in the chapel stood as Anna, holding her father's arm, walked down the aisle wearing a beautiful white dress she had purchased in Mexico. Kathleen had never seen Rusty so happy as he stood at the front of the chapel watching his bride walk toward him. When Anna reached the alter, her father kissed her cheek and gave Rusty an affirming handshake. The bride's father took his seat. Janice, Kathleen and Michael were finally able to sit as well.

As the priest went through the marriage rituals, Kathleen couldn't help but wonder what life would be like for the newlyweds. Anna planned to attend nursing school in Fort Worth on a full scholarship. Rusty, having completed basic training, would begin instruction in the Security Police after the wedding. He hoped to be stationed in Texas, though deployment to guard an Air Force base in Vietnam was likely. There would be many long months of separation, probably loneliness and a fear for Rusty's safety. Jake's brother Clay had spent time in Vietnam and seemed to have survived the ordeal reasonably well. Perhaps Rusty would have a similar experience. None of that mattered in this moment. Kathleen only felt joy as the handsome airman kissed his bride.

§§§

For the second time in his life, Michael felt like he was driving through the gates of paradise, going the wrong way. The hot sun baked his spirits as he crossed the Llano Estacado from Texas into New Mexico in his VW Beetle with no air conditioning. Somewhere up ahead, the verdant forests of Oregon were calling him to a place that was always his, and would never be again. Each mile took him further from his parents, his friends and, mostly, Kathleen. He fervently hoped she would be waiting when he transferred to the University of Texas for the spring semester. It was only four months, and yet it felt much longer.

Michael marveled at how much had changed in just one year. The friends he had made, the love he had found in the most unlikely of places. Texas no longer felt like a hellhole. It felt like hope. Belonging. Home.

Acknowledgements

First, thank you to all of the readers who have read and (hopefully) enjoyed *The Fall of 69*. I hope that you have found it to be entertaining and thought provoking.

Thank you to Chris Angell Sallis and Rebecca Pahlka for their careful and thoughtful feedback from an early version of the manuscript.

Amelia Clark (ameliadesigned.com), gave life to the cover. Her patience in working with an author who has no visual arts experience will always be appreciated.

Thank you to Robyn Conley (robynconley.com), "The Book Doctor." The value of her thorough manuscript review cannot be overstated.

Finally, a special thanks to my wife, Patricia Gaupp. She tolerated many days when I would isolate in our study for hours on end writing and revising the manuscript. She also read the manuscript numerous times, providing encouragement and useful suggestions for each iteration. To her, this book is dedicated.

About the Author

William Gaupp for many years harbored a desire to write. The demands of a career in healthcare administration and raising a family afforded little time for creativity. Now retired, he has found a new freedom to create literature, poetry and some music. When not writing or traveling, he enjoys spending time with family and friends at the family farm in central Texas.

Several of William's creations can be viewed at www.williamgaupp.com

Book Club Discussion Topics

Michael described the population of Stephenville as full of "backwards cowboys." Rusty described Michael as a "damn hippie." Convinced that they knew all they needed to know about each other, the boys made little effort to learn more. When have people failed to get to know you because of a label that they ascribed to you (liberal, conservative, religious, rich, poor, etc.)? When have you missed an opportunity to get to know someone because of the label that you attributed to him/her? Do labels tell us all we need to know about a person? How can we get beyond those labels in our social interactions?

Who was your favorite character? Why?

Who was you least favorite character? Why?

What parts, if any, of the book did you find humorous?

Although she was born and raised in Stephenville, Anna felt socially isolated. Given her family's financial limitations, what, if anything, could she have done as a minority student to become less isolated?

Would you recommend this book to a friend? Why or why not?

The book was written within the context of the Vietnam War, which was a very divisive issue in the United States and beyond. Do you see any parallels with our society today?

The author tried to convey the principal, Mr. Jamison, as a firm but fair mentor to his students. Outside of your family, who were your mentors? What made them effective?

Rusty didn't enjoy playing football and was ridiculed by his peers when he quit. How does one decide when it's worth the cost to stand up for your principles? Have you ever been in a similar situation? If so, what did you do?

The author tried to present a balanced view of each character's perspective based on their personal experiences. Was the effort successful? Were there characters that you became more fond of as you learned more about them?